W9-AVD-035

MURDER IN THE KITCHEN

Lucy got out of her car and immediately noticed the scent of burned sugar.

That explained it, she thought, walking up the drive. Poor Mimi had burned her cookies and was probably frantically mixing up a new batch.

Her eyes were already stinging, and she could hear the smoke alarm ringing when she got to the kitchen door. She opened it cautiously and was forced back by a noxious cloud of smoke. She was beginning to think she should go back to the car and call the fire department, when the smoke began to thin, thanks to the open door, and she noticed Mimi slumped over the faux-granite island.

Taking a closer look, she noticed Mimi's eyes, half-open and sightless. Then, she saw something else. It was the wooden hilt of a large chef's knife that was protruding from Mimi's back . . .

Books by Leslie Meier

Mistletoe Murder

Tippy Toe Murder

Trick or Treat Murder

Back to School Murder

Valentine Murder

Christmas Cookie Murder

Turkey Day Murder

Wedding Day Murder

Birthday Party Murder

Father's Day Murder

Star Spangled Murder

New Year's Eve Murder

Bake Sale Murder

St. Patrick's Day Murder

Published by Kensington Publishing Corporation

Bake Sale Murder

LESLIE MEIER

PLAINFIELD PUBLIC LIBRARY
15025 S. Illinois Street
Plainfield, IL 60544

KENSINGTON BOOKS
KENSINGTON PUBLISHING CORP.
http://www.kensingtonbooks.com

KENSINGTON BOOKS are published by

Kensington Publishing Corp.
850 Third Avenue
New York, NY 10022

Copyright © 2006 by Leslie Meier

All rights reserved. No part of this book may be repro-
duced in any form or by any means without the prior
written consent of the Publisher, excepting brief quotes
used in reviews.

All Kensington titles, imprints and distributed lines are
available at special quantity discounts for bulk pur-
chases for sales promotion, premiums, fund-raising, educational or institutional use.

Special book excerpts or customized printings can also
be created to fit specific needs. For details, write or phone
the office of the Kensington Special Sales Manager: Kensington Publishing Corp., 850 Third Avenue, New York,
NY 10022. Attn. Special Sales Department. Phone: 1-800-
221-2647.

If you purchased this book without a cover you should
be aware that this book is stolen property. It was reported
as "unsold and destroyed" to the Publisher and neither
the Author nor the Publisher has received any payment
for this "stripped book."

Kensington and the K logo Reg. U.S. Pat. & TM Off.

ISBN-13: 978-0-7582-0702
ISBN-10: 0-7582-0702-6

3 1907 00214 5489

First Hardcover Printing: December 2006
First Mass Market Paperback Printing: December 2007
10 9 8 7 6 5 4 3 2 1

Printed in the United States of America

For Ben

Chapter 1

"I'd like to kill that kid."

Something in her husband's tone of voice caught Lucy Stone's attention. He sounded like he really meant it, and in more than twenty years of marriage Bill had never, until now, expressed homicidal tendencies. It was true, however, that the roar of Preston Stanton's Harley could drive even the most mild-mannered soul over the edge.

"What's the matter with his parents?" yelled Bill. "We never let our kids drive around like that, making a racket."

Lucy waited before answering, easily following Preston's noisy progress down Red Top Road, where he paused to rev the motor several times at the stop sign before roaring on off towards town. Only then could she make herself heard without raising her voice. "We could complain to the police. There are noise limits for motorcycles, you know. I checked."

"That's not likely to get very far. His mother works at town hall and you know how those town employees stick together."

"At least we'd get it on record." She paused, reaching up to pat her husband's beard, lightly touched with gray. "It might come in handy as a defense when they put you on trial for murder."

Bill wrapped his arms around her waist and pulled her close. "Very funny." He was bending to kiss her when they were interrupted by their youngest daughter, Zoe.

"Mom! I'm going to be late!"

Lucy checked the clock and sighed, pushing Bill away. It was almost eight, time to get Zoe to Friends of Animals day camp. Zoe, almost nine, was the caboose on the family choo-choo, five years younger than her next oldest sibling, her sister Sara. Sara, 14, would be a freshman in high school when school reopened in just a few weeks. This summer, Sara had her first job; she was working as a chambermaid at the Queen Victoria Inn where she was following in her older sister Elizabeth's footsteps. Elizabeth had spent her summer abroad, backpacking around Italy and France with a couple of girlfriends. Home for barely a week, she'd returned early to Chamberlain College in Boston, where she was going into her junior year, to help with freshman orientation. Lucy often wondered where the years had gone; her oldest, Toby, was engaged to his long-time girlfriend Molly and they were saving for a house.

Zoe broke into her reverie. "Mom! We've got to get going!"

"Right." Lucy grabbed her purse, automatically fishing for her car keys as she checked to make sure the coffee pot was off and the dog's water dish was full. "Let's go."

Stepping off the porch, Lucy's eyes were drawn to the new houses Fred Stanton, Preston's father, had built on the old Pratt property. "He didn't actually build those houses," scoffed Bill, a restoration carpenter known for his meticulous work, "he assembled them."

It was true, in a way. The houses were modular homes; they'd been built in a factory and delivered in sections. Fred and his crew had bolted them together and done the finish work, a process that had gone remarkably quickly. It seemed to Lucy that the houses had sprouted, like mushrooms on a rainy night. One day the old Pratt house was standing there, looming over them, and the next it was gone. Before they knew what had happened, their country road had turned into suburbia.

Designed to have high curb appeal to the potential buyer, each little house had an oversized Palladian window front and center, and a double-door entry overlooking a landscaped front yard boasting two small yew bushes and a couple hundred square feet of sod. It had been a particularly dry summer but now, in August, the sod was still the same bright emerald green it had been in April when it was installed, thanks to the sprinklers the new neighbors ran day and night. The sprinklers clicked and sputtered, lawnmowers roared, barbecue smoke filled the evening air. It was enough to make you miss the Pratts, thought Lucy, starting the car.

She didn't actually miss the Pratts, she admitted to herself as she carefully backed the car around, but she did miss seeing their house at the very top of Red Top Hill where it once seemed to symbolize the simple, rugged way of life that was becoming increasingly rare, even in Maine. It was the kind of house a child might draw, a too-narrow rectangle topped with a triangular roof. The windows were rectangles, too, without shutters. The siding was weatherbeaten gray clapboard, and the white paint on the trim boards had peeled off long ago. There was no landscaping to speak of, no bushes softening the stark lines of the house, and no lawn at all. Just a dirt yard with a chicken pen and a rotting old car or two, kept for spare parts. It wasn't a friendly house; it might as well have had a big "Keep Out" sign nailed to it. Which was just about right because the Pratts hadn't been friendly people. They'd been horrible neighbors, mean and quarrelsome. They were gone now. Prudence had died, been murdered, actually, and her husband Calvin and son Wesley were in the county jail for stealing lobsters out of other people's traps. All that remained of the Pratt family was the name of the street that now bisected their land. The developer, Fred Stanton, had named it Prudence Path.

She was starting down the driveway when she saw Fred's wife, Mimi, marching along the road, headed their way. Only Zoe's presence in the seat beside her kept her from saying a very bad word.

"Lucy, could I just have a quick word with you?" asked Mimi, bending to look into the car window. She was talking in that false, bright tone a lot of women use when they're broaching an uncomfortable topic.

"Sure, Mimi. What's up?"

"Well, Lucy, it's really the same old thing," sighed Mimi, adding a fleeting, tight little smile. "I'm afraid those bushes of yours are really a safety hazard. They block the sight lines on Prudence Path, you know. Why, just yesterday I was almost hit by a speeding truck when I was pulling out, on my way to work."

"I don't see how you can blame my lilacs for

somebody going too fast on Red Top Road," said Lucy.

"Well, of course, you are right. The truck was going way too fast. But the fact is that I couldn't see the truck because of your bushes." She smiled again and Lucy wondered if she'd had her teeth whitened or something. Maybe it was just a reflex, a nervous twitch. A tic. "I've spoken to you about this before, numerous times in fact, and I'm afraid I'm going to have to file a formal complaint."

"So go ahead and file," said Lucy, impatiently checking her watch. She knew Zoe hated to miss the opening circle at day camp when commendations and prizes from the previous day were handed out.

"I'm not sure you understand exactly what that means," said Mimi, looking concerned. "A traffic officer will conduct an investigation and, if he determines the bushes are a hazard, the town highway department will cut them."

"They can't do that! The town can't touch my bushes. And they're not just bushes, anyway. They're lilacs and they're absolutely gorgeous in the spring."

"I'm afraid they can, Lucy, even if they are lilacs." Mimi was positively grimacing, attempting to illustrate how terribly painful this was for her. "You see, I work at town hall—in the assessor's office—and I know they do it all the time. Why, just last week they cut Miss Tilley's privet hedge. Of course, she's in her nineties and nobody expects her to clip her hedge herself. . . ."

"The town cut Miss Tilley's hedge?"

"That's right."

"Oh, Mimi, that's terrible. That hedge gives her relief from the traffic noise."

"Not anymore," said Mimi, with a mincing little shrug.

Lucy didn't run her over as she sped down the driveway, she just wished she could. The woman was infuriating, coming on all mealy-mouthed and nicey-nice when she was planning to destroy bushes that had been growing for at least a hundred years, probably planted by the original builders of the Stones' antique farmhouse. But, shrugged Lucy, her encounter with Mimi had cleared up one thing. She now knew where Preston got his annoying tendencies—he'd inherited them from his parents.

"It's about time," sang out Rachel Goodman, when Lucy finally pulled open the screen door at Jake's Donut Shop. She was fifteen minutes late for the weekly Thursday morning breakfast get-together that was a ritual for the Gang of Four, as they called themselves. In addition to Lucy and Rachel, the group gathered at the booth in the back included Sue Finch and Pam Stillings. Pam was married to Lucy's boss at the *Pennysaver*, Ted Stillings, whose many hats included those of publisher, editor-in-chief, and primary newshound. Lucy worked part-time, writing features and helping Phyllis, the other staff member, with listings of local events.

"Sorry," said Lucy, taking her usual place. "I had another confrontation with Mimi Stanton about my lilacs. She says they're a traffic hazard."

"That's what they told Miss Tilley," said Rachel, who provided home care for the town's oldest resident. "The town sent a bunch of highway workers to cut down her privet hedge. She pulled a Barbara Frietchie, you know, declaring that they might as well cut off her "old gray head" before she'd let them clip her hedge, so the foreman relented and they just gave it a little trim."

"Tinker's Cove is really changing," mused Sue. "Remember when it used to be a quiet little fishing village, with a handful of summer people? Now there's summer traffic all year 'round. You can't even get a parking spot on Main Street anymore."

"What happened?" asked Rachel.

"Growth," said Pam. "It's supposed to be a good thing."

"Well," said Lucy, as the waitress set a cup of coffee in front of her, "I wouldn't mind all these new folks if they'd know their place. Take Mimi, for example. She doesn't have the good sense to know she's new in town and maybe she ought to keep a low profile and learn how to blend in before she goes around ripping up people's prized lilac bushes."

"She's not really new," said Sue, sipping her coffee. "She's worked at town hall for years. The family's been around forever; they lived in Gilead until Fred built that new subdivision. He's got another project going out by the yacht club. Luxury condos. Sid's been putting in a lot of custom closet shelving for him. California style, you know. The closets are as big as my bedroom."

"Who has that many clothes?" wondered Rachel, who was still wearing the sandals, jeans, and ponchos she wore in college.

"I do," said Sue, a noted shopaholic. "In fact Sid's promised to do one for me. In Sidra's old room."

"Don't you want it for her? When she comes home with the grandchildren?" asked Pam.

"No sign of that yet," said Sue, pouting. "So I might as well have the closet."

They all laughed.

"What about you, Lucy? Any sign that Toby and Molly are going to start a family?"

"Heavens, no," exclaimed Lucy, raising her eyebrows. "They're not even married."

"That doesn't stop anybody these days," observed Pam.

"Besides," finished Lucy, "I'm too young to be a grandmother."

They were still laughing when Lucy's standing order of two eggs sunny-side up with a side of corned beef hash, no toast, arrived.

"Before you got here, Lucy," began Pam, "we were trying to think of a way to raise some money for the Hat and Mitten Fund."

"More money?" Lucy broke one of the yolks, letting it run into the hash. "I thought you were all fixed now that the children's shop at the outlet mall gives you all their leftovers at the end of the season."

"That's worked out great," admitted Pam. "But now I think we really ought to help out with school supplies."

"School supplies?" Sue was skeptical. "What do they need for school besides a pen and a pencil?"

"That was the old days," said Pam. "Now all the teachers give out lists of supplies that they expect each child to have, things like floppy disks and calculators and separate notebooks for each subject. Even tissues and spray cleaner for their desks. It adds up, especially if you have three or four kids."

"We never had to supply all that stuff," said Rachel.

"That's because the school provided it, but

those days are gone. The school budget has been cut every year and there's no room for extras."

"It's true," agreed Lucy. "We have to pay a hundred dollars so Sara can be a cheerleader."

"You're letting Sara be a cheerleader?" Rachel, a fervent women's libber, was horrified.

"It's a sport," said Lucy, defending her daughter. "You should see the flips and stuff they do."

Pam rolled her eyes. "It's simply another example of female submission to male dominance. Why can't she play football?"

"Football's so violent," objected Rachel.

"She doesn't want to play football, she wants to be a cheerleader," said Lucy.

"This is getting us off the track," said Sue. "We all know how difficult it is for many working parents to pay for these required school supplies. The question is, how can we help?"

"I'd like to set up a revolving fund that I could dispense to families as the need arises," said Pam. "I'm pretty sure that once we get it going we'll get donations from local clubs and businesses. What we need is some seed money."

"How much do you need?" asked Rachel.

"Maybe two or three hundred dollars," said Pam. They all sat silently, staring at their plates.

"A magazine drive? That way the kids could help themselves," suggested Lucy.

"The PTA's got that locked up. We can't compete with them."

"How about a giant yard sale," suggested Rachel. "Why, my cellar alone . . ."

"No way. What do we do with all the leftover junk?"

"I know," said Sue. "Let's have a bake sale."

"But we haven't had one in years," objected Pam.

"I know. That's why I'm sure it will be a huge hit. People will line up to buy all the goodies they've been missing."

"Like Franny Small's Congo bars," sighed Pam. "Remember them?"

"Do I ever," said Lucy, patting her little tummy bulge. "I think I'm still carrying them around."

"They were worth it," said Pam.

"No, no. If I'm going to put an inch on my hips it's going to be from Marge Culpepper's coconut cake," declared Sue.

"How did she get the frosting so light?" asked Lucy.

"It was a real boiled frosting, made with a candy thermometer and everything. So amazing. Nobody cooks like that anymore," said Pam, with a sigh.

"It's a good thing," said Rachel, who was a health nut. "We'd be big as houses and our arteries would be clogged with trans fat."

"If I'm going to die from eating I want it to be from Cathy Crowley's rocky road fudge," declared Lucy. "I'd die happy."

"Oh, yeah," sighed Pam. "That's the way to go."

"I think it is," said Sue. "A bake sale is definitely the way to go. I mean, if we're this excited about fudge and cake I bet a lot of other people will be, too. And we can charge a lot because everything will be top-quality and homemade."

"Affordable luxuries," agreed Rachel. "Very hot right now."

"So we're agreed?"

"Agreed. All we have to do is call for donations."

"I can't," said Pam. "I've got to help my mother move into assisted living next week."

"And I'm visiting Sidra in New York," said Sue.

"I'm filling in for Bob's secretary, she's on vacation," said Rachel.

"I guess that leaves me," said Lucy. "No problem. I've done it a million times, I'm pretty sure I've still got a list of volunteers from our last bake sale in the back of my cookbook." She picked up the check and put on her reading glasses. "Okay. How much is fourteen dollars and thirty-eight cents divided by four?"

Chapter 2

Lucy loved everything about the *Pennysaver* office from the jangle of the little bell on the door to the dusty wood venetian blinds that covered the plate glass windows to the tiny morgue where the scent of ink and hot lead from the linotype machine still lingered. Originally known as the *Courier & Advertiser*, the paper had been covering all the happenings in Tinker's Cove for more than one hundred and fifty years.

Phyllis, who served as receptionist and listings editor, also seemed to harken back to an earlier era, the sixties, with her dyed bouffant hairdo and bright blue eyeshadow. She was given to wearing bright colors, generally accessorized with oversized pieces of costume jewelry. Today she'd encased her ample frame in aqua pedal pushers and a bold floral print shirt topped with a string of beads that could have inspired a mother hen to sit a while.

"What's new with the gang?" asked Phyllis, by way of greeting.

A stack of the latest edition of the *Pennysaver* stood on the counter in front of her desk, practically hot off the press. Lucy picked one up and flipped through, making sure her byline was in all the right places. She grimaced, spotting a misspelled headline: APPEALS BORED DEBATES NEW ZONING REGS.

"They want to have a bake sale so the Hat and Mitten Fund can help families buy school supplies."

"That's a good idea. My cousin Elfrida was complaining about how much it costs to get the kids ready for school. Of course," sniffed Phyllis, "she didn't have to go and have five kids."

"Then I guess I can count on you to bake something for the sale. How about those whoopie pies everybody loves so much?"

"No way, José," said Phyllis, touching up her Frosted Apricot manicure. "I'm on the Atkins diet and if I so much as look at a carbohydrate I gain five pounds."

"It isn't the looking . . ." began Lucy.

Phyllis rolled her eyes. "Listen, do you know what it's like to give up bread and pasta and cookies and eat nothing but steak, steak, steak? Do you realize I can't even eat a baby carrot?"

"It must be tough."

"It's agony. And if I make whoopie pies I won't be able to stand the temptation. I'll eat at least half of them."

"I understand," said Lucy. "You have lost a lot of weight."

"And I plan to keep it off, no matter how much bacon and whipped cream I have to eat."

"Why does there seem to be something wrong with this picture?" mused Lucy, pulling her mail out of the box and flipping through it.

"I know. It's crazy, but it works. It really does." She sighed. "Pizza is the worst. You can't eat the crust."

"Good lord."

"I know. And hamburgers. No bun."

"No, that's not what I meant," said Lucy, as the bell on the door jangled announcing Ted's arrival. "It's this letter."

"What about it?" asked Ted. His hair was still wet from his morning shower and, in contrast to his usual preoccupied scowl, he was grinning, relaxed, and practically exuding geniality. He was always like this on Thursdays, before the irate readers' phone calls began.

"It says the varsity football players have been hazing the JV boys at their training camp."

"Who sent it?" Ted was studying the editorial page; he hadn't found the typo yet.

Lucy studied the sheet of typewritten paper and the envelope it came in. There was no signature, no return address. "It's anonymous."

"Throw it in the trash," advised Ted, picking up one of the papers and admiring the front page.

"But maybe there's something to it."

"You know our policy, Lucy," he said, turning to page two. "We don't print anonymous letters, we don't follow up anonymous tips. We've got to know who our sources are . . . DAMN!"

"I don't know how we could have missed it," said Lucy, carefully choosing a plural pronoun.

"APPEALS B-O-R-E-D!" Ted's eyes were blazing. "I'll never live this down."

"Probably one of them Freudian slips," said Phyllis. "Those Appeals Board meetings are deadly dull." She shrugged. "It's not like anybody reads those stories."

"Somehow that doesn't make me feel better," said Ted, who was slumped in his chair, staring at the scarred surface of the oak rolltop desk he'd inherited from his grandfather, a legendary small town newspaper editor. His sepia-toned portrait hung on the wall above Ted's desk and today his expression seemed somewhat reproachful.

"Listen, Ted," said Lucy. "I'm doing that story on the new staff members at the school for next week's paper. Maybe I could ask around a little bit." She bit her lip. "That new coach, Buck Burkhart, is actually my neighbor. He lives over there on Prudence Path."

"It's probably just some overprotective mother," said Phyllis. "You know the type. Rushes to the doctor the minute the kid sneezes."

Lucy reread the letter. "Anyone who values the traditions of sportsmanship and fair play can't help but be dismayed by these degrading activities . . ." It was written by someone trying to set out a rational, convincing argument. But then the tone abruptly changed: "It breaks my heart to see the harm done to a sensitive, idealistic young man." The writer, whoever he or she was, clearly believed something destructive and dangerous had happened to a loved one. Lucy couldn't ignore it.

"Sara might have heard something," she speculated, thinking out loud. "She knows some of the kids on the team."

"Okay, Lucy," agreed Ted. "Go ahead and ask around. But be careful. This is the sort of thing that can damage people's reputations, even ruin their lives. We can't print even a whisper of this unless we're absolutely certain of our facts."

"I'll be careful," promised Lucy, glancing at the portrait. She thought the old man's expression had changed. He seemed interested.

But when she drove over to the high school to pick Sara up after cheerleading practice, Lucy couldn't think of a way to broach the subject. She was parked by the field, watching the girls go through their routines. They looked so cute and young and thoroughly wholesome with their bouncy pony tails and pink cheeks and white teeth that she didn't want to spoil the mood by bringing up an uncomfortable topic like hazing. She was so totally absorbed by their acrobatics, holding her breath as one of the girls was tossed high into the air, that she didn't notice when a woman approached her car and stuck her face through the open window.

"Hi! I'm Willie Westwood and you're Lucy Stone, right? You live in that adorable farmhouse up the road."

"That's me," said Lucy. Willie's smiling, freckled face was inches from hers. "You must live in one of the new houses on Prudence Path."

"That's right," said Willie, straightening up to her nearly six-foot height. She was dressed in skin-tight beige riding pants, knee-high black boots and a grubby T-shirt that proclaimed she'd rather be riding. "My daughter Sassie, she's the redhead. She mentioned that your daughter is on the squad, too."

"Really?" Lucy couldn't imagine what this was leading to.

"Well, what I was hoping was that we could work out some sort of carpool thing. I don't know about you but I'm always coming and going with a million things to do and it would be a big help if I didn't have to get over here every afternoon. Especially since you never know how long the practice is going to take. I mean, yesterday I was supposed to help out at my husband's office, he's a vet, you know, but I got stuck sitting here for almost an hour, waiting for them to finish." She lowered her voice. "That's Frankie LaChance, over there." She cocked her head towards a cute little Volkswagen convertible. "She lives next door and her daughter Renee is on the squad, too, but just between you and me you can't count on Frankie to be dependable."

"Oh," was all Lucy could think to say.

"So it's a deal? We'll take turns picking them up. I'll do tomorrow, but I can't do Monday."

"Deal," said Lucy, giving Willie's hand a shake. "Monday. You can count on me."

Then the girls broke formation and began picking up their things. Lucy watched as Sara walked across the field, accompanied by Sassie and another girl whose curvy figure and assured walk made her seem much older.

"That's Renee LaChance," hissed Willie, raising her eyebrows.

"How old is she?" asked Lucy.

"A freshman. Can you believe it?"

"Well, girls nowadays . . ."

"Believe me, that girl is trouble," warned Willie.

That evening, after the supper dishes had been cleared, Lucy took her cordless phone and her battered Fannie Farmer cookbook out onto the porch and sat down in her favorite wicker chair, the one with the comfortably worn cushions. The book bristled with sticky notes and recipes torn from magazines and newspapers and she took her time leafing through it. There was that orange loaf cake she used to make, and the low-cal Caesar salad she'd never gotten around to making. And shish kebab, that would be good on the grill. Finally, in the very back, she found the list she was looking for, now yellow and brittle with age.

The women's names were all familiar, but she hadn't spoken to many of them in years. Once they had all been connected by a network of shared interests: school, scouts, youth soccer, and Little League. They were constantly calling upon each other for rides for the kids, for refreshments, for a volunteer to chaperone a school field trip. What had happened? wondered Lucy. Why hadn't she spoken to Marge Culpepper or Franny Small in such a long time? Once they'd been among her dearest friends but now she hardly ever saw them, and then only in passing, when they exchanged jaunty waves as they drove off in opposite directions.

"Marge? It's Lucy Stone."

"Land sakes, if you aren't a blast from the past, Lucy Stone."

It was a bit awkward. Lucy didn't feel as if she could impose after such a long silence. "So how have you been?"

"Fine, just fine."

"Great. How's Eddie?" inquired Lucy, asking about Marge's only child, who was Toby's age.

"He's in Iraq, you know. In the Marines."

Lucy was stunned. "I didn't know. I'm glad you told me, I'll keep him in my thoughts."

"And your family?"

"Elizabeth spent the summer backpacking in Europe and now she's back at Chamberlain. Sara's got her first job, she's at the Queen Vic. Toby's engaged. . . ."

"Engaged. My word. Time sure flies."

"It sure does. That's one reason I'm calling.

We're having an old-fashioned bake sale for the Hat and Mitten Fund, next weekend at the IGA, and I was hoping you'd make that famous coconut cake of yours."

"Oh, my word. I haven't made that in years."

"That's the idea. We thought we'd bring back some of those goodies everybody loved so much."

"I wish I could help out, but I don't have time. I'm training for the Think Pink Triathlon, for breast cancer, you know."

Marge, who had always seemed slightly older than her years thanks to twenty extra pounds and a tight perm, had never struck Lucy as the athletic type. "Triathlon?"

"Yeah. I've been doing it for years now, ever since I was declared cancer free. It's great, this year it's in California. I can't wait to go. Last year I made the top half of finishers and I'm hoping to make the top ten percent this year. I've really been working on my swimming, that's where I'm weakest. The cycling's a breeze and my running's okay. It's the swimming that slows me down."

"Well, good for you," said Lucy, absolutely floored.

"By the way, Lucy, I don't think I ever asked you for a pledge. How about it?"

"Oh, sure, put me down for twenty-five dollars."

"Do you think you could make it fifty? Or a hundred? I'm supposed to raise five thousand."

"Okay. Fifty. And good luck with the triathlon," said Lucy, clicking off the phone. At this rate, she'd be broke before she got any donations for the bake sale. She decided to call Franny Small next. She wouldn't be asking for money, she had plenty of her own since she founded a madly successful jewelry business. Originally made from bits and pieces of hardware, the line had evolved into a perennial favorite with fashion editors and department store buyers.

"Franny? Hi! It's Lucy Stone."

"Lucy! I was thinking about you just the other day, wondering what you're up to these days."

"Not much, just the same old work for the newspaper."

"And the kids?"

"Everybody's great. Listen, Franny, I'm calling because the Hat and Mitten Fund is having a bake sale next Saturday and I was hoping you could make some of those fabulous Congo bars you used to make."

"I'd love to," she answered, and Lucy's hopes rose, only to be dashed when she added, "but I'm leaving for China in the morning."

"China?"

"Right. That's where I get a lot of my jewelry made."

"Really?"

"Yeah. It's a nuisance in a way, because it's so far away and I have to go over at least four times a year."

Lucy was astonished; the only foreign country she'd ever visited was Canada. "Four times a year? How many times have you been?"

"Oh, I've lost count. Too many. These days it seems I'm always flying somewhere. Milan for ribbons, Paris to see the couture shows, Africa for beads. I really couldn't manage except now I travel first class and it does make a difference."

Enough, already, thought Lucy. This was getting annoying. "In that case, do you think you could make a cash donation?"

"Sure. I'll tell my assistant to take care of it first thing in the morning."

"Thanks," said Lucy. "And have a nice trip."

She'd struck out twice, but she still wasn't out. Lucy had high hopes from the next name on the list, Cathy Crowley. She was a devoted homebody who made sure her husband, Police Chief Oswald Crowley, came home to a hot supper after a hard day spent maintaining the peace in Tinker's Cove.

"Rocky Road Fudge? I haven't made that in years. In fact, I'd be surprised if I still had the recipe."

"The recipe's probably on the Internet," suggested Lucy.

"Oh, I'm sure it is. Everything else is," chuckled Cathy. "But I don't have time. I'm busy getting the RV ready. Ozzie's retiring, you know. The banquet is Saturday night and we're leaving Sunday morning for a cross-country trip to the Grand Canyon."

Come to think of it, Lucy did remember Ted saying something about the banquet. "Be sure to give him my congratulations," she said. "And have a great trip."

"We will! You know what they say: 'Don't come a'knockin' if the trailer's a'rockin'!'"

Lucy wished Cathy hadn't left her with that particular image. She really didn't want to think about Chief Crowley in anything but his neatly pressed navy blue uniform and spit-polished black shoes. She turned back to the list but, looking down the list of names, she came to the conclusion that any more calls would be pointless. Of the ten or so that remained, several had moved away, one had died, and one was in rehab.

It was time to admit she'd struck out. She dialed Pam's number.

"We have to come up with another plan," she said. "I didn't get a single donation. Nobody bakes anymore. They're all too busy running off to China and the Grand Canyon."

"I'm not surprised," said Pam. "I started thinking after the meeting and I realized most of the old gang have gone on to develop new interests. Face it, when was the last time you made your Double Dutch Chocolate Brownies?"

"I can't remember. We have fruit for dessert these days. Or frozen yogurt."

"Us, too." Over the line, Lucy could practically hear the wheels turning in Pam's head. "We need new blood. Younger people. People with higher metabolic rates, who can eat cookies without gaining weight."

"All the kids have summer jobs, school sports have already started . . ."

"I mean young people like your neighbors, the folks in that new development."

"Prudence Path? I hardly know them," protested Lucy.

"Why don't you invite them all over for dessert and coffee one evening? Don't you think it's about time you got to know your neighbors?"

Lucy had her doubts, but she didn't want to disappoint Pam. "Okay," she said.

Chapter 3

Pam was the first to arrive on Monday evening, bearing a foil-covered pan of blueberry cake.

"I figured it was the least I could do since I wrangled you into this," she said.

Lucy agreed but kept that thought to herself. She'd whipped around the house when she got home from work, tossing all extraneous items into a laundry basket, which she hid in the pantry, and hitting the mantel and table tops with a squirt of spray cleaner and a quick wipe. Bill was out at his weekly poker game, Sara was babysitting, and Zoe was happily ensconced in her room with the new Harry Potter book. The coffee pot was hissing and sputtering on the kitchen counter and she figured she was as ready as she'd ever be to meet the neighbors.

"Are the new neighbors all coming?"

"Four out of five," said Lucy. "Mimi had to work."

"So tell me what they're like," said Pam, uncovering the cake and cutting into it with a knife.

"I don't really know them very well," said Lucy, producing a plate.

"Didn't you stop by with cookies when they moved in?"

"No, I didn't," grumbled Lucy. "I wish Prudence Path had never been built."

"But now that it's there you might as well get on good terms with your new neighbors." Pam shrugged. "You might need them someday."

"I got along fine without them before," said Lucy, filling the cream pitcher and setting it on a tray along with the sugar bowl. "Willie Westwood is okay. Her daughter is a cheerleader, like Sara, and she suggested carpooling."

"Westwood, Westwood. The name's familiar . . ."

"Her husband is that new vet, over by Mac-Donald's Farm. She's very horsey herself. She's almost always in riding togs."

"Who's the lady with those adorable twins? I've seen her around town."

"Bonnie Burkhart. Her husband is the new guidance counselor at the middle school and he also coaches football. Sara babysits for the twins, Belle and Belinda. She says they're really sweet."

"They sure look cute in those matching outfits."

"Who wears matching outfits?" Rachel had let herself in the kitchen door, along with Libby, the Stone family's Lab. Libby was wiggling ecstatically, which Rachel took as a compliment, but Lucy suspected her enthusiasm was directed at the tray of cookies Rachel was carrying. Lucy grabbed the dog and hauled her outside to the kennel. When she came back, Rachel and Pam were arguing.

"You shouldn't dress twins alike," said Rachel. "It stifles their individuality."

"Lots of twins like dressing alike," said Pam. "Some even do it as grown-ups."

"They even go to special twin weekends," added Lucy. "I saw it on TV. Weird."

"I agree," said Rachel. "I don't think it's healthy."

"I was just filling Rachel in on the neighbors," said Pam. "Who's the hot lady with the VW convertible?"

Rachel's eyebrows shot up. "She's your neighbor? The one who always wears high heels and spandex?"

"I haven't made her acquaintance," said Lucy, raising an eyebrow, "but Bill has. He says her name is Frankie LaChance and she's very friendly."

"Ooh," chorused Pam and Rachel.

Lucy shrugged. "Just because she has a fabulous figure and she's divorced . . ."

This time the oohs were louder and longer.

"She has a daughter Sara's age. Renee. She's 14 and thinks she's terribly sophisticated."

"Sounds like a handful," said Rachel.

"Who's sophisticated?" Sue had arrived, along with a tray of miniature cream puffs.

"You are," said Lucy. "These look delicious. Did you make them yourself?"

"I did. I wanted to impress the new neighbors."

"These certainly ought to," said Lucy. "Even Pear and Apple's mom."

Sue's eyebrows shot up. "Pear and Apple?"

Lucy nodded. "Sara babysits for them, too. One is three and the other is almost a year old. She says they're very serious children."

"No wonder, with names like that," said Sue.

"Poor things will get teased when they go to school," said Rachel.

"Don't worry about them. They'll be at the head of the class. Chris is one of those supermoms.

There's absolutely no TV in their house, they only have classical music and Sara has to play educational games with them."

"What kind of educational game can you play with a one-year-old?" asked Pam.

"Beats me," said Lucy, as the front door bell chimed. "Well, girls, it's showtime!"

Willie was at the door, dressed tonight in a linen shift with a silver brooch in the shape of a horse's head pinned to one shoulder, along with Chris, Pear and Apple's mom. Chris was dressed in a sleeveless top and a pair of tailored slacks; it looked like a business outfit without the jacket.

"Lucy, I don't know if you've met Chris Cashman," said Willie.

"We haven't met but I have heard about your babies from my daughter Sara," said Lucy. "She says they're remarkably intelligent children."

"I hope they are," said Chris. "We're certainly doing our best to give them every advantage. Of course you have to, these days, with the global economy and all. They're not going to be competing for jobs with American kids who majored in binge drinking, oh no. They'll be up against those Indian children who learn computer programming in preschool and Chinese kids who can do calculus and play the violin while figure skating."

Lucy chuckled appreciatively, hoping Christine was joking, but doubting that she was.

"I know what you mean," said Sue, proffering her hand and introducing herself. "It's a different world now and we have to prepare them for it. Are you a full-time mom?"

"I sure am. It's a full-time job, isn't it? I mean, I used to think I was busy when I was working but that was nothing compared to motherhood. I'm on call twenty-four/seven now."

The women smiled and nodded knowingly.

"What did you do before you had the kids?" asked Rachel.

"Investment banking."

"Wow. That's a big change. Do you miss working?" asked Pam.

"Oh, no!" exclaimed Chris, a bit too quickly. "Motherhood is my job now, and nothing is more fulfilling, right?"

"I've never found it so," said Willie. "But maybe that's just me. I prefer horses to people. You always know exactly where you stand with a horse."

Nobody quite knew how to respond and Lucy was relieved when the doorbell rang announcing a new arrival. Bonnie Burkhart was standing on the stoop with her hands together, wearing a flowered dress with a prim little collar. Her white pumps were spotless.

"Everybody, meet Bonnie Burkhart," said Lucy. "She's the mother of those adorable twins we've all seen around town."

While the women clustered around Bonnie, peppering her with questions about what it was like to have twins, Lucy slipped into the kitchen to get the coffee. She was returning with the tray when the doorbell rang once more and Frankie LaChance breezed in. She hadn't waited for Lucy to open the door; she'd opened it herself.

"Hi! I'm Françoise LaChance but everybody calls me Frankie!" she said, introducing herself.

Conversation stopped as everyone turned to greet Frankie, who was wearing a figure-hugging striped top and a pair of equally tight short-shorts.

Her shapely tan legs ended in a pair of espadrilles with long laces that wrapped around her ankles.

"Coffee?" said Lucy, breaking the awkward silence.

As the women took coffee and helped themselves to baked goods they fell into two distinct groups. Lucy's friends were clustered at one end of the living room sofa while the Prudence Path women had formed a loose circle at the refreshment table. Frankie was out in the cold until Sue noticed and drew her into the conversation. Lucy, taking her role as hostess seriously, joined the Prudence Path group.

"It's too bad Mimi couldn't make it," said Bonnie, biting into a piece of blueberry cake.

"I can't say I miss her much," said Willie, who was working her way through four of Sue's tiny cream puffs. "Gosh, these are good."

"I heard she complained about your pig," said Chris.

Lucy saw her opportunity to enter the conversation. "You've got a pig?"

"Just a tiny little pot-bellied one. Her name is Lily. She's awfully cute but Mimi doesn't seem to appreciate her. She thinks she's a farm animal instead of a pet and she reported us to the zoning board."

"She's after me to cut my lilacs," confessed Lucy. "I think she's got a lot of nerve to complain about my bushes, considering what a nuisance her son is with that noisy motorcycle of his. Now that's what I call annoying."

"I think he's just trying to get away from his father," said Chris, who was sticking to black coffee.

"I hear him yelling all the time, and not just at the boys. Mimi gets her share of abuse, too."

"He's a piece of work," said Willie, polishing off her last cream puff and moving on to the blueberry cake. "I can't believe the problems we're having with our house. Half the doors don't close because they're hung crooked."

"My bathroom looked great when we first looked at the house but now I realize I was fooled by the mirror," said Bonnie, patting her lips with a napkin. "It's really tiny. You can't turn around in it unless the door's closed."

"I know," said Chris. "In fact, I've got a list a mile long that I'm sending to the state consumer affairs department. The final straw was when I discovered the garbage grinder in the sink was installed backwards."

"No!" They were all shocked.

"I had the plumber fix it and sent Fred the bill, but so far I haven't gotten a check."

"Don't hold your breath," advised Willie, who had refreshed her plate and was starting on a new batch of cream puffs.

Lucy was so absorbed in getting all the details on Fred's shoddy construction so she could give Bill a full report that she was disappointed when Pam tapped her cup with a spoon and invited everyone to sit down.

"I'm so glad you all came," she began, smiling warmly. "I know Lucy has been eager to meet her new neighbors and we're always happy to welcome newcomers to Tinker's Cove, which a lot of us think is a little bit of heaven right here on earth. We have abundant natural beauty with the ocean right at our door, and our Main Street has been named one of the ten most beautiful in New England. We're blessed to live in such a gorgeous area, but, unfortunately, for a number of residents, beauty doesn't pay the bills."

A few of the women nodded knowingly.

"That's why a group of us started the Hat and Mitten Fund a number of years ago," she continued. "The purpose of the fund is to provide warm clothing for the town's less fortunate children, and it's here that I'm going to give you a shocking statistic. Fully fifty percent of the children in the Tinker's Cove public schools are eligible for the government lunch program."

"I had no idea," said Frankie. "I thought everybody in Tinker's Cove was well off. I mean, the price of an average house is well over three hundred thousand now."

"It's a common misconception," said Pam. "People see all these big second homes lining the shore but, believe me, if you follow some of the back roads into the woods you'll find families living in extreme poverty. And that's why, in addition to providing coats and mittens and hats, this year we'd like to be able to help our families buy school supplies for their kids."

"How do you operate?" asked Chris. "Do you collect cast-off clothes?"

"That's how we started, but the fund has grown through the years. Now the children's store at the outlet mall gives us all their unsold coats at the end of the year. The women's groups at local churches supply the hats and mittens and we also get cash donations from local businesses to fill in any gaps. But I estimate we'll need to raise about two hun-

dred fifty dollars in seed money for the Pencil Box
project. Once I have that I can ask our sponsors
for matching donations."

"I know," exclaimed Frankie, giving a little
bounce. "Let's do one of those nude calendars,
like in that movie."

Bonnie gasped. "You mean, pose nude for photos?"

"Well, yeah, but they screen off the naughty bits
with a plant or something."

"We were thinking of something different," said
Pam, to relieved sighs from the group. "We're
planning on holding a bake sale on Saturday. Sue,
would you like to take it from here?"

"Thanks," said Sue, getting to her feet. "We decided on a bake sale because it's a proven method
of raising money fast. In the past, we've been able
to raise at least two, sometimes three hundred dollars. So we've scheduled the sale for Saturday morning at the IGA downtown. I hope you'll all bake
your favorite recipes, ask your friends for donations, and volunteer to work at the table for an
hour or two." She was just sitting down when Chris
began peppering her with questions.

"Why not hold the sale Labor Day weekend?
The holiday will bring a lot of people to town, no?
And why at the IGA? I'm sure there's a lot more
traffic at the outlet mall."

"But we always . . ." protested Sue.

"Well, maybe it's time to change. Time to think
big. Maybe you can raise five hundred, or even a
thousand dollars."

"That would take an awful lot of baked goods,"
said Sue. "We just don't have that many bakers."

"We could concentrate on stuff that's easy to

make," suggested Pam. "Like Rice Krispie bars. I can turn out an awful lot of them, and people like them. They're sort of retro and remind them of their childhoods."

"With all due respect, Pam, I think we ought to offer something more wholesome than Rice Krispie bars," protested Rachel. "Now I have a recipe for Carob Oaties that's very fast and simple . . ."

"I agree that we need to choose items that are easily made," said Chris, producing a pad and pencil and jotting down a few notes. "And I think we can take our cue from Henry Ford."

"Henry Ford?" Lucy was puzzled.

"Right. He introduced standardization, and that's what we should do, too. We'll pick a limited number of items with high customer appeal and everybody will follow the same recipes. That way we can increase production significantly with just a few volunteer bakers."

"That makes sense," said Pam, getting a dark look from Sue.

"But everybody's on diets these days," said Bonnie. "Who's going to buy baked goods?"

"We need items like low-carb snacks, maybe home-baked dog treats, even bottled beverages. Stuff that appeals to men, too. Remember, they'll be at loose ends while their wives shop."

"I think Chris is onto something here," said Lucy, remembering her futile phone calls. "I think we have to admit times have changed and we have to adapt if the sale is going to be successful."

"I heartily agree," said Rachel.

"But we've always. . . ." protested Sue.

"I agree with Sue," said Pam. "I think we're taking a big risk. Why fix something that's not broken?"

"But it is broken," said Lucy. "I had absolutely no luck getting our old volunteers to participate. And a lot of people are on those low-carbohydrate diets these days."

Rachel clucked her tongue in disapproval.

"Okay, to summarize," said Chris, consulting her notes. "I propose we hold the sale Labor Day weekend, at the outlet mall. Is everyone agreed?"

Sue sat stony-faced, but the others all nodded.

"Next, we have to decide what to sell. Any suggestions?"

"Low-carb seems to be a good idea," said Bonnie.

"I definitely think we should have cold bottled beverages. The men will snap them up," said Frankie. "And people are always looking for coffee."

"I have a great recipe for home-made dog biscuits," said Willie. "My husband gives them out at his office and he says people have started asking if they can buy them."

Chris looked up from her notes. "You know, all the best craft shows are juried—that is, a panel of judges selects the very best crafts. Maybe we should try something like that with our baked goods, especially since low-carb can be tricky."

"I think that's a great idea," said Bonnie. "We'll bake up a bunch of recipes and have a taste-testing to choose the best ones. Then we can all use those recipes that we know really work. And we can wholeheartedly recommend them to the customers."

In her corner, Sue seemed to be choking. Lucy got a glass of water for her and patted her back while she drank it, but Sue didn't say thank you.

"Okay, all in favor of a taste-testing?" asked Chris.

Receiving a chorus of ayes she continued, "Let's say a week from tonight. Same time, same place, if that's okay with you, Lucy."

"It's okay," said Lucy, uncomfortably aware of the daggers Sue was shooting her way.

"Let's say everybody brings at least two different recipes, that will give us sixteen choices," said Chris.

"I just remembered," said Willie. "I won't have time to make the dog biscuits. I've got a horse show coming up. But I'll make a couple of the heart-healthy cookies my mom makes for my father."

"Anybody for the dog biscuits?" asked Chris.

Nobody volunteered.

"I'm telling you, they're not hard to do and they'll be a big seller," said Willie.

"Okay," said Lucy. "I'll do the dog biscuits."

"Great." Chris closed her notebook. "I think this was a very successful meeting."

"She would," hissed Sue, following Lucy into the kitchen, where she had gone to get a fresh pot of coffee. "Little Miss Bossy. She's taken over the whole thing."

"Well, that's what we wanted, wasn't it?" said Lucy, grabbing the pot and heading back to the living room.

"I don't like it one bit," said Sue.

"You mean you don't like Chris," said Lucy, pausing at the kitchen door.

"No, I don't." Sue furrowed her perfectly shaped brows and stuck out her Bobbi Brown lips in a pout. "And I'm going to show her. I'm going to come up with a killer recipe that everybody loves, just you wait and see."

Chapter 4

As soon as the dinner dishes were done on Tuesday night, Lucy decided to dig out the food processor so she could experiment with the dog treat recipe. She'd wasted no time in getting the recipe from Willie; with the next meeting scheduled in less than a week she had no time to lose. She knew it was ridiculous to feel pressured about making dog biscuits for a bake sale but somehow she did. Chris had that effect. Maybe it was her corporate attitude, so different from the relaxed approach of Lucy's friends. Until now she'd thought Sue was high-powered, but she was a slacker compared to Chris.

Lucy also had a nagging feeling that Sue was angry with her. She'd tried calling several times but all she'd gotten was Sue's answering machine. Sue was usually very good about returning calls but she hadn't called back yet. Maybe she was out of town or something, but Lucy didn't think so. She certainly hadn't mentioned any plans for a trip. She was pretty sure Sue was giving her the cold shoulder as punishment for supporting Chris's ideas in the meeting and she couldn't help feeling that was unfair. She thought a strong friendship like theirs that had endured for twenty years or more ought to have room for differences of opinion, but apparently Sue felt differently. *Too bad*, thought Lucy, experiencing a touch of anger herself. Sue wasn't her boss and she was entitled to her own thoughts and feelings. She only hoped this rift wasn't going to continue for too much longer; she missed her phone chats with Sue. In fact, looking over the recipe for "gourmet" dog biscuits, she could just imagine what Sue would say.

"Raw liver? Yuck."

Sue hadn't suddenly materialized in her kitchen to voice her disgust, it was Zoe, who had been eager to help with the project—until she saw the glistening red lump of raw meat sitting on the kitchen counter.

"It's for dog biscuits. Gourmet dog biscuits."

"Mom," said Zoe, her expression very serious, "I don't think people understand what dogs really like to eat. They don't like dog food at all. Not really. They only eat it because they have to. They would really rather have people food. Do you know what Libby's favorite food is? Apple pie. With ice cream."

Lucy smiled. "I think you're probably right. Libby loves people food, but it's not actually very good for her. Dog food has all the nutrients she needs to grow and stay healthy. That's why we're going to put this nutritious lump of liver in the biscuits." She dropped the liver into the food processor. "It's full of iron . . ." she said, pressing the button and producing a brownish red sludge. "And protein," she continued, but she was talking to an empty room. Zoe had fled the carnage in the kitchen.

* * *

Zoe's disdain for the gourmet dog treats continued the next morning, when Lucy suggested she take some along to Friends of Animals day camp to taste-test on the dogs there. "I don't think so, Mom," she said, with a sniff. "They're my friends and I don't want to insult them."

"Libby liked them."

"No, Mom, she didn't. She buried them."

"That means she likes them, right? She's saving them for later."

"If she liked them, she'd eat them right up."

"Maybe she was full." Even as she spoke, Lucy knew this was wishful thinking. Libby was a Lab and she would eat until she burst, that's just the way Labs were. She'd eat sticks and rocks, she'd eat dead animals, she'd eat horse apples, she'd eat just about anything except the gourmet dog biscuits. The truth was unavoidable: the dog biscuits were a failure. "I guess I'll have to find another recipe."

"Try the Internet, Mom," said Zoe, jumping out of the car. "I bet they have some good ones." Then she was gone, running off to join her friends.

Lucy was a bit jealous as she drove on to work. If only there were day camp for grown-ups. She'd love to spend the day singing songs and practicing her backstroke and making something pretty in arts and crafts instead of slaving away over a computer trying to write an interesting story about the finance committee's last meeting in time for the noon deadline.

"This came for you," said Phyllis, handing her a business-size envelope.

Lucy took it, noticing there was no stamp and no return address. "Who brought it?" she asked.

Phyllis shook her head. The Aqua-Net was working; not a single tangerine curl budged. "Dunno. Somebody must have pushed it through the mail slot. It was on the floor when I got here this morning."

That wasn't unusual. Lots of people hand-delivered letters to the paper. There was no sense wasting a stamp if you were going to be downtown anyway, plus your letter would get there faster. Lucy put it with the stack of unopened mail, mostly announcements of local events, that was waiting on her desk and poured herself a cup of coffee.

"So how are things?" she asked Phyllis, taking advantage of the fact that Ted hadn't arrived yet.

"I had some friends over for dinner last night. We had steak and whipped cream."

"Yummy," said Lucy, thinking Libby didn't have it so bad after all.

"Don't knock it. I've lost another five pounds."

Lucy looked at Phyllis, resplendent in lilac slacks and a flowered blouse instead of the muumuus that used to be her summer uniform. "You look fabulous."

Phyllis's cheeks grew pink. "Thanks."

The bell on the door jangled, announcing Ted's arrival. Lucy gave him a big smile by way of greeting and headed for her desk, where she started opening the mail. Ted was all business on deadline day.

"How's that story on the new teachers going?" he asked, setting a cup of coffee on his desk and opening his briefcase.

"It's almost finished. I still have to talk to Buck Burkhart; I have an appointment with him at nine."

Ted pulled out a notebook, flipping it open. "Okay. You've got new teachers, the finance committee meeting, the selectmen's meeting, what else?"

Lucy had opened the letter on the top of her pile, the one with no return address. "Maybe there's more to this hazing than we think. Listen to this: 'players were subjected to a number of indignities including being forced to drink copious amounts of alcohol and having their heads shaved.' That last part is true enough. Sara told me they'd shaved their heads but she thought it was voluntary." Lucy returned to the letter, her eyes bulging at the next sentence: "'They were then forced to undress and required to play the game of Twister in the nude.'"

You could have heard a pin drop. Ted and Phyllis were speechless.

"It's another one of those anonymous letters," she said, by way of filling the silence. "And I think it's got the ring of truth, if you know what I mean. It's weirder than fiction."

"Naked Twister?" Phyllis's ample bosom was heaving. "Kids today sure know how to have fun. We thought spin the bottle was hot stuff. What did we know?"

"I don't think it's funny," said Lucy. "What do you think, Ted?"

Ted was examining the letter. "I wish the sender had signed it. Then I'd have a better idea what to think. This could be the work of a loony. Or somebody who has a grudge against the school. It could even be somebody who didn't make the team."

"I don't think so, Ted. It sounds real to me. So did the first letter, for that matter."

The bell on the door jangled just then, announcing Sue's arrival. "Why so serious? Did somebody die?"

Lucy was relieved to see that Sue didn't seem to be holding a grudge. Indeed, she looked inordinately pleased with herself as she set down a foil-covered plate on the counter.

"Hardly," said Phyllis, fanning herself with a press release. "Somebody wrote a letter saying the football team plays naked Twister."

"Naked Twister? I never thought of that. It sounds like fun." Sue was smiling, just thinking about it. "With the right person, of course. I don't know if Sid would be up for it. He's not really all that flexible, anyway. It would have to be somebody younger, somebody like Johnny Damon. Or maybe that football player, Tom Brady. Now there's a cutie."

"Sue!"

"Just teasing," she said, removing the foil and revealing a pyramid of frosted chocolate squares. "Voila! You must try these."

They all took a step forward, drawn by the aroma of chocolate.

"Those look delicious."

"Are they brownies?"

"Do they have carbs?"

"Yes, to all three. Now taste them."

"I can't," said Phyllis, rushing out of the office.

"Atkins," said Lucy. She picked up one of the luscious-looking squares of chocolate.

"MMMph," said Ted, practically inhaling one and reaching for a second. "Mmmm."

"Ted tends to overreact," said Lucy. "He never met a food he didn't like." She took a bite and found herself swooning and moaning with pleasure. "These are better than sex," she said, when she'd recovered her senses.

"That's inspired, Lucy! That's what I'm going to

call them. Better-Than-Sex Brownies. I think they're going to be a sensation at the bake sale."

"What's in them?"

"Trade secret."

"They're not low-carb, are they?" She cocked an eyebrow. "Chris won't like that."

"Chris will love them. They're going to sell like hotcakes. And we can charge a small fortune for them. Trust me. Once the word goes out people will be flocking to buy them. They'll be coming in droves. In busloads. Screaming for Better-Than-Sex Brownies."

"Some people might find the name offensive," said Ted, reaching for a third.

"You don't want to spoil your appetite," said Sue, snatching the plate away.

"Please," said Ted, a hint of a whimper in his voice.

"Take it back about the name."

"It's not offensive at all," he said. "I was wrong. Very wrong. Now can I have another? Please?"

Sue was magnanimous in triumph. "Of course you can. In fact, I'm going to leave you the whole plate."

Ted seemed to go a bit weak at the knees and grabbed the counter for support.

"I must go now," said Sue, striking a Superman pose. "I have a few more recipes to try."

"You're not happy with these?"

"A true artist is never satisfied," she said. "To paraphrase Picasso, or perhaps it was Cezanne, I believe I am only beginning to know chocolate."

"It's certainly a noble quest," said Lucy, as Sue departed. The bell on the door was still jangling when Lucy took another brownie. Ted had apparently entered a chocolate coma and was reclining in his chair, his feet on the desk and a smile on his face. A definite first for deadline day, thought Lucy, as she prepared to leave the office for her interview with Coach Buck.

Tinker's Cove Middle School was ready for the school year to begin. The empty halls had been painted and the floors polished, the one-armed desks in the classrooms were arranged in orderly rows and a bright "WELCOME" banner hung over the front door. Even the air smelled of floor polish; there was none of the adolescent stink she always associated with the school—a mix of sweat, cheap cologne, and old sneakers.

The staff in the main office were all present and accounted for, however. Unlike the teachers, administrators worked through the summer, preparing for the new school year. Angela Dobbins, the school secretary, was busy enrolling a new student when Lucy arrived but waved her down the hall. "Mr. Burkhart's in his office," she said. "Three doors down."

The door was ajar but Lucy gave a little knock before sticking her head in. Buck Burkhart was sitting at his desk, leafing through a file. Until now, Lucy had only seen him from a distance as he came and went from his house on Prudence Path. Up close, she realized he was older than she expected, considering the ages of his wife and children. Bonnie seemed to be in her early thirties and the twins were six, but Buck was at least fifty, judging from his gray hair and the deep lines that ran from his nose to his mouth. He was quite fit, however, and jumped to his feet to greet Lucy.

"It's great to meet you," he said. "I've heard such nice things about you from Bonnie. And, of course, we love Sara. She's great with the twins."

"It's nice to meet you, too," said Lucy. "Sara really enjoys babysitting for the girls. She says they're adorable and polite, too."

"I can't take much credit for that, I'm afraid," he said, grinning. "Bonnie's in charge of the kids."

"Oh, you can never underestimate the importance of a strong father," said Lucy, wondering how she'd become part of a mutual admiration society. She sat down and opened her notebook, determined to cut to the chase. "So tell me, what brought you to Tinker's Cove?"

Buck leaned back in his chair and propped his elbows on the desk, tenting his hands. "I saw the ad in a professional magazine and, well, it caught my interest. We'd been living in Lawrence, Massachusetts and we were beginning to think it wasn't the best place to raise the girls. There's a lot of drugs, a lot of crime. I found the work there very challenging, very interesting, don't get me wrong, I felt I was doing a lot of good. But it was time to think of the family, of the girls, and what would be best for them." He paused. "And when I came for the interview, well, I just fell in love with this town. It's real small-town America, the kind of place where there's a real community. You know what they say, 'It takes a village to raise a child,' and I felt that was what we'd find here in Tinker's Cove."

Lucy didn't want to burst his bubble; she figured he'd learn the truth soon enough. Tinker's

Cove was picture-perfect on the outside, but life was hardly idyllic. There was domestic violence and drug abuse and poverty and all the other problems that were part of modern life.

"I understand that in addition to your job as a guidance counselor you're also coaching the high school football team?"

"That's right. I love a challenge and I understand the Warriors haven't had a winning season in fifteen years."

"Something like that." She chuckled, then grew serious. "How do you plan to change that?"

He leaned forward and fixed his eyes on hers. "Drills, drills, drills. I believe conditioning and preparation are the keys to winning. In sports and in life. That's why I'm hoping to introduce an ambitious new career exploration program that will give students an opportunity to explore the world of work and the opportunities it affords. I'm going to set up mini-internships, job-shadowing, get the kids out of the classroom and into the workplace. And we're going to bring the workplace into the school, too, with career days and speakers. Let them hear from a veterinarian or a newspaper reporter or a realtor what their job is all about. Let them ask questions."

"Those all sound like terrific ideas," said Lucy, softening him up for the big question. "To get back to the football team, I've heard some rumors about hazing during training. Is that part of conditioning?"

The question didn't faze Buck in the least. "Absolutely not. That's the sort of thing I simply will not tolerate. Who's making these allegations?"

"We don't know. They're anonymous letters."

Buck gave her a condescending smile. "I know you reporters are always after a juicy story, but don't you think you should be ashamed of yourself? I mean, anonymous letters?"

"The sender might have been afraid of repercussions."

"Now, that's just ridiculous. If one of my players has a problem, I expect him to come to me and we'll solve it together. That's how my team operates. Teamwork. And that's what we're going to be doing in the guidance department, too. We're going to develop teams that give the kids an opportunity to discuss issues like bullying, peer pressure, even drugs and alcohol. Open forums where the kids can discuss these things in a supportive atmosphere and learn how they can get help if they need it."

Lucy was scribbling busily, trying to get it all down. "Are these programs that you're importing from Lawrence? Were they successful there?"

"I think you could say that. Very successful, but I don't want to blow my own horn."

"And where did you work before Lawrence? And where did you go to college?"

"Boston University. A great sports school. I mean, I always loved football but when I got to BU I learned to *love* football."

"Did you play?"

"Sadly, no. Just pick-up games with guys from the dorm."

"I'm not clear on this. Don't coaches need some sort of certification?"

"Not really. It's the kind of thing you learn to do by doing. I started out helping out . . . oh, that was years ago. I've been coaching football for twenty years or more." He looked at his watch. "Oops, sorry, but I've got a meeting with the principal and I'm late."

Lucy got to her feet. "I don't want you to get in trouble, not when you're just starting a new job." She extended her hand. "Thanks for your time."

"No problem," he said. "It was a pleasure. Let me see you out."

Lucy still had a million questions to ask, but there was no opportunity in the short walk from the guidance office to the front hall. All she really had time for was a quick request that he remember her to Bonnie before they parted at the main office. She hurried back to the *Pennysaver* office, wondering if Ted was still mellow from the brownies.

He wasn't. "Lucy, I've got a hole on page one and I need that story."

"I'm right on it," said Lucy, tapping her head. "It's all up here. I just have to type it up."

Lucy sat at her desk and booted up her computer, taking a moment to organize her thoughts. Then she was off and running, flipping through her notes and writing up Coach Buck's ambitious plans. But when she looked for information about his previous experience all she was able to find was the fact that he'd attended Boston University. She was trying to make a follow-up phone call when Ted spoke up.

"Are you done yet?"

"It's coming, it's coming," said Lucy, who was getting a busy signal. She put the phone down and dashed off the final paragraph of the story.

"Great. Now I just need the Fin Com story."

"Nothing much happened. They just went

through the Highway Department budget and didn't change a thing."

"Make it short and sweet then."

Lucy smiled. "Aye, aye, sir."

Deadline was noon, which meant that Lucy got out of work earlier than usual on Wednesdays. She ran some errands and picked up some groceries, but she was still a half hour early when she drove over to the high school. She was surprised to discover practice was already over and Sara and Sassie were sitting on the ground, passing a water bottle between them, waiting for her.

"So, girls, what do the players think about Coach Burkhart?" she asked, once they were buckled in and on the road. "I just interviewed him for the paper."

"He's okay," said Sassie.

"Is he tough on the boys?"

"What do you mean?" asked Sara.

"Well, he seems to put a lot of emphasis on conditioning. That means drills and stuff, doesn't it?"

"I guess."

"They haven't complained?"

"Nah."

This was going nowhere, thought Lucy, and she knew from experience that it wasn't going to get better. When teenagers didn't want to talk, they didn't. You could ask questions until you were red in the face but it didn't do any good. They'd only open up when they were ready. She snorted. Good luck to Coach Buck with his open forums. She'd be amazed if he got anywhere with them. And even if they did seem to open up, chances were they'd just be putting him on, telling him what he wanted to hear.

"So, what do you think of Brad and Angelina?" she asked. "Will their relationship last?"

"I bet he really misses Jen," said Sara.

"Yeah. Angelina drags him all around Africa and makes him visit all those slums and refugee camps." Sassie sighed. "That couldn't be much fun."

Now this was a subject they had opinions about, thought Lucy, listening to the girls hash over the latest Hollywood gossip. They were still at it when she turned onto Prudence Path and into the West-woods' driveway. Willie must have been keeping an eye out for her because she popped out of the house as soon as Lucy braked.

"Got a minute?" she asked.

"Sure," said Lucy, wondering what was up.

"Girls, go on inside. There's some Fuji water in the fridge."

The girls looked at each other, shrugged, and disappeared inside.

"I didn't want to talk about this in front of them," said Willie, whispering.

"Right," said Lucy.

"But I just wanted to let you know that Renee LaChance is spending an awful lot of unsupervised time with that kid with the motorcycle."

"Preston."

Willie nodded. "I see him coming out of her house all the time when Frankie isn't home."

"Have you told Frankie about this?"

"No, and I'm not going to. I mind my own business," said Willie. "Besides, that's not the point. The point is that once this sort of thing starts it spreads like wildfire. I'm worried about Sassie and Sara."

Lucy was beginning to think Willie was out of her mind. "It's hardly catching, like measles."

"Trust me on this, it's worse. Once one starts they all want to do it. Frankly, I'm worried about those bus rides with the football team. Things could get out of hand."

"I really don't think you have to worry," said Lucy, patting her hand. "I just interviewed Coach Burkhart and he seems to have things well in hand. I'm sure he won't let things get out of control."

"I hope so. You have to watch them every minute, you know. They're sly. I just saw a Doctor Phil show about it."

Lucy was relieved to see Sara coming out of the house, water bottle in hand. "Well, thanks for the warning. I've got to get my meatloaf in the oven."

"Oh, I almost forgot. How did the doggie biscuits come out?"

"Great," said Lucy, lying through her teeth. "Fabulous. Thanks for the recipe." Sara hopped in the car and Lucy backed out of the driveway. "Are Sassie and her mom close?" she asked as she accelerated down the street.

"I dunno."

Why did she even try? wondered Lucy, braking and turning into her own driveway.

Chapter 5

With the beginning of the school year looming on the horizon, the last weeks of summer seemed to speed up. It was something Lucy noticed every year. July crawled by, filled with long, lazy days. Then you turned the calendar page to August, the back-to-school ads began to appear in the paper and before you knew where it went the summer was almost gone. This year, with the bake sale scheduled for Labor Day weekend, it seemed worse than usual and all too soon she found herself readying the house for the taste-testing meeting. She kept telling herself that nobody was going to examine her housekeeping, and since her assignment was dog treats it was unlikely anybody would actually taste them. She had a free pass, so to speak, so why was she practically trembling when she opened the door and saw Chris standing there?

"Everything ready, Lucy?" asked Chris, lugging in a case of bottled water.

"The coffee pot is ready to go," said Lucy, annoyed to find herself practically standing at attention.

"No coffee, tonight, I think. We don't want to confuse our taste buds. That's why I brought water."

"Oh, good idea," said Lucy, with a noticeable lack of enthusiasm. Sure, it was decaf, but she could sometimes fool herself into thinking it was real coffee with an actual caffeine boost.

"What, no coffee?" It was Sue, practically stepping on Chris's heels and carrying an attractively arranged plate of Better-than-Sex Brownies as well as a pan of Rocky Road Fudge.

"We don't want to confuse our taste buds," said Lucy, echoing Chris. "We're having water instead."

"My taste buds never get confused," said Sue, checking to make sure the coffee pot was ready to go and then switching it on. "Now where do you want these babies?"

Lucy resisted the urge to check with Chris and told Sue to put them on the coffee table. "The dog's outside so it should be okay."

"Lucy, if you don't mind a teensy little suggestion," said Chris. She didn't wait for Lucy's reply but continued, "let's use your dining room. We'll need to take notes and I think it would be more comfortable if everyone is sitting at a table."

Lucy's and Sue's eyes met. "Sure," said Lucy. "I'm not sure if I have enough pens and paper."

"No problem," said Chris, opening her briefcase and producing a pile of small notepads and a handful of new pencils. "I thought of everything."

"Now if she could only cure cancer," muttered Sue, under her breath.

"There's the doorbell," said Chris. "Lucy, why don't you get the door and, Sue, you can help me carry these things into the dining room."

"Yes, sir," said Sue, adding a salute for emphasis but Chris didn't seem to notice.

Mimi was at the door, full of apologies for missing the earlier meeting. "I had to work, you know, but I'm so glad I could make it tonight. I think the Hat and Mitten Fund is a wonderful idea. In fact, the town employees make a donation every year."

"And we're very grateful for it," said Pam, who had followed her up the walk, carefully balancing a tray of oatmeal raisin and peanut butter cookies. "No yolks," she whispered to Lucy, with a wink. "And I used applesauce and canola oil instead of butter."

"Ooh, yummy," cooed Sue, receiving a warning glance from Lucy. "Sorry, Pam. I'm just a little tired of Miss Bossy Pants." She cocked her head towards Chris, who was setting out the pads, pencils, and water bottles on the dining room table.

"Oh, Lucy," she called, "I think we need a few more chairs."

"No problem," replied Lucy, as the doorbell chimed again. "Will you girls grab a couple of chairs from the kitchen?"

"Sure, Lucy," said Sue. "We'll set out the cream and sugar, too."

Lucy was beginning to get a headache, but she smiled brightly as she opened the door to admit Willie and Bonnie. "Thanks for coming, go right on in to the dining room," she told them, keeping the door open for Rachel and Frankie. She pointed them in the right direction and then dashed into the kitchen for the doggie treats, which she added to the array of baked goods on the dining table. "All present and accounted for," she announced, taking the last empty chair, next to Mimi.

"Then I'll call the meeting to order," said Chris, producing a gavel and tapping the table.

"Hey, who made you chairperson?" demanded Sue. "Pam's in charge of the Hat and Mitten Fund."

Pam shrugged. "It's fine with me. Chris can be President Pro Tempore."

"And what's that supposed to mean?" demanded Mimi. Her tone was a tad too aggressive and put off the other women, who seemed to avoid acknowledging her question.

"Temporarily," said Rachel, always a champion of the underdog. "For this matter only. The bake sale."

"Well why didn't she say that?" grumbled Mimi, glancing resentfully around the table.

"Moving right along," said Chris, briskly tapping the table again, "I propose we each introduce our products. Don't forget to include a brief synopsis of the recipe including expense and level of difficulty. By way of example, I'll begin." Chris produced a square tin from her briefcase, which Lucy was beginning to think must have the same magic properties as Mary Poppins's carpet bag, and pried it open. "These are my Kitchen Sink Cookies. They're a version of a peanut butter cookie with the addition of raisins, a few chocolate chips and nuts."

Across the table, Pam grimaced at Lucy as if she knew her healthy peanut butter cookies were doomed.

"The main virtue of this recipe," continued Chris, "is that it's easy to make and the recipe makes a lot of cookies. They do contain butter and white sugar, but those ingredients are offset by the peanut butter, raisins, and nuts, which make them a relatively healthy treat. As I mentioned, the amount of chocolate chips is really quite small but they have a big impact."

She passed the plate and everyone took a cookie, bit into it, and chewed.

"Mmm," said Lucy. "How do we score them?"

"One to five," said Chris. "Rachel, would you collect the papers and add up the scores?" When Rachel agreed she pulled a calculator out of her briefcase and slid it across the table to her.

Time passed quickly as the women nibbled on cookies and sipped water and jotted down their scores. Willie was the only one who tried the dog biscuits, but she pronounced them quite good. Chris was willing to take her word for it, but suggested Lucy give the dog treats an egg wash to give them more eye appeal. Her second entry, lemon-poppy seed muffins which she'd whipped up from a mix at the last minute, didn't score well, which was fine with her. Pam's oatmeal cookies got the okay, but her peanut butter cookies were judged inferior to Chris's Kitchen Sink Cookies. Though Frankie's chocolate genoise was voted delicious but not practical for the bake sale, her madeleines passed muster. Bonnie's homemade arrowroot cookies got an enthusiastic nod but Rachel's carob oaties and granola goodies were deemed to have too much fiber. Mimi's pumpkin-raisin cookies got a cool approval—they were awfully good but nobody wanted to admit it—and Willie's angel food slices were judged too difficult and expensive to make.

"Difficult for whom?" demanded Willie. "Anybody can whip up egg whites."

"Too wasteful," said Frankie. "What are we supposed to do with all the yolks?"

"Feed them to the dogs, that's what I do," said Willie. "Especially if I've got a pregnant bitch."

"Well, I don't have a bitch," snapped Frankie.

"That's what you think," countered Willie.

"Let's taste Sue's brownies," said Lucy, interrupting Frankie before she could utter a rejoinder. "They really are better than sex."

"Nothing's better than sex," chuckled Frankie.

"You ought to know," said Willie.

"At least I haven't forgotten, like some people," said Frankie.

"Time out," called Rachel. "We're considering the brownies. I give them a five."

Sue beamed at her.

"I think the name is adorable," said Pam. "Can you make little labels?"

"You can do anything with a computer, right?" said Sue.

"These are amazing," agreed Frankie. "I love how the butter taste is there but it's not overpowering, and the sweetness of the sugar is balanced by the slight bitterness of the chocolate. I would love the recipe. I also give them a five."

"I'm sorry, I like the brownies but I find the name objectionable. I don't think the labels are a good idea at all," said Bonnie.

"Neither do I," said Mimi, eager to form an alliance after the chilly reception she'd received so far. "There's plenty of sex on TV and movies, I don't think we need to bring it into our bake sale."

"That's not exactly what I meant," said Bonnie, quickly distancing herself from Mimi. "I just think that if we're going to have labels they ought to be informative and list the ingredients."

"For Pete's sake," said Sue, "it's just a name. It's not like they've got obscene decorations or anything."

"I love the humorous name, and the taste," said

Lucy, staunchly defending her friend. "I give them a five." She passed her scorecard to Chris, who was busy adding up the numbers.

"The brownies come up short," said Chris. "It's just as well, I think. They must be loaded with trans fat."

"Maybe you should have called them 'Cardiac Arrest Brownies,'" said Mimi. If it was meant to be a joke it flopped, earning disapproving stares from everyone.

Sue was about to utter a rejoinder when Rachel covered her hand with her own and said quickly, "Let's not forget we're all working for the same goal here."

"Right," added Bonnie. "We're all on the same team."

"If we're going to meet our goal we need to talk about quantities," said Chris, flourishing her calculator. "And pricing."

"I'm going to get some more coffee," said Sue, getting to her feet. "Anyone else want some before we get down to facts and figures?"

Lucy doubted Sue really wanted more coffee; she figured she was simply trying to provoke Chris. It seemed a worthy goal, so she got up, too. "I'll just make sure the pot's still hot," she said.

Once they were in the kitchen, with the door closed, Sue exploded. "Do you believe it? Too much trans fat! Too sexy! 'Maybe we should call them Cardiac Arrest Brownies!' Who are these people? Where'd they come from?"

"They're my neighbors," moaned Lucy, pouring the coffee.

* * *

"How'd the meeting go?" asked Phyllis, when Lucy arrived at work the next morning. She was taking apart an Egg McMuffin, saving the egg and sausage and discarding the muffin, and the air was redolent with the scent of fast food.

"They rejected Sue's brownies," said Lucy.

Phyllis widened her eyes, which were already highlighted with bright blue eye shadow. "How'd she take it?"

"Not well. She's supposed to make nutty meringue bars—Chris says nuts are the new broccoli—but I'm afraid she may fill them with explosives or something."

"You could call them Atomic Bomb Bars. Catchy, no?"

"Just remember," said Lucy, pulling her mail out of the box, "you heard it from me first. World War III begins on Labor Day weekend, at the outlet mall." She was flipping through the envelopes. "All it will take is for somebody to say something negative about her baking."

"I just hope the meringue gets done in the middle."

"Me, too," said Lucy, flipping one envelope back and forth, looking for a return address. "I think I've got another anonymous letter."

"Open it," demanded Phyllis. "Maybe there's more about Naked Twister."

"Not Twister," said Lucy, scanning the letter. "Something called 'Butts Up.' The coach makes the freshmen all line up holding their ankles and the upper classmen pelt their bums with soccer balls."

"Bare bums?"

"I don't think so. The letter doesn't say and I

think it would if they had to strip." She paused. "I don't get it. When I interviewed Coach Buck he insisted he doesn't tolerate hazing."

"Naked Twister sounds like more fun." Phyllis downed the last bit of sausage. "Do you think they really do this stuff?"

"I don't know what to believe. Whoever's writing these letters sure thinks something's going on."

"It could be somebody with a grudge," suggested Phyllis. "Somebody who wants to make trouble for the new coach."

"Or the school," said Lucy. "This could be a really big story if the hazing is actually taking place."

"Uh-oh," said Phyllis. "Here we go. Lucy Stone, investigative reporter, tackles another challenging case." She held up a stack of papers. "But before you do, would you mind sorting these press releases for me?"

"I bet Woodward and Bernstein didn't have to sort press releases," grumbled Lucy, taking them to her desk.

That night, after supper, Lucy managed to get Sara and Zoe to agree to make doggie biscuits, so long as no raw liver was involved. She'd been assigned to produce thirty dozen of them and she needed all the help she could get.

"It's a different recipe," promised Lucy, "with cooked chicken livers."

"Eeeuw," chorused the girls.

"How about I cook the livers and you take it from there? Please?" Lucy was tired and didn't want to spend the entire evening on her feet, rolling out dog biscuits. "I'll double your allowances this week."

The girls agreed and set to work sifting flour and measuring wheat germ while Lucy browned the chicken livers. Libby was standing by her side, in hopes that a tasty tidbit would come her way.

"This is a better recipe," said Sara.

"Libby likes them," said Zoe.

"She's going to miss you girls once school starts again," said Lucy, turning the livers over.

"It's too bad dogs can't read," said Zoe. "Then she'd have something to do while we're gone."

"Are you sad summer's ending?"

Zoe nodded, stirring the dry ingredients together. Sara, breaking eggs into a bowl, shook her head. "I'll be glad when school starts. I'll see more of my friends and I won't have to work at the inn anymore."

"What about school? Are you excited about starting high school? Choosing electives? Writing term papers? Doing science experiments in a real lab?"

"Nah. School's boring. But I am excited about cheerleading. I can't wait for the first game."

"Yeah. That'll be fun," agreed Lucy, whizzing the livers in the food processor and adding the resulting goo to the dough. "Do you know any of the boys on the team?"

"Sure, Mom. I've been in school with them since kindergarten."

"Right," admitted Lucy, taking a wooden spoon to the thick dough. "Not everybody. Take Tommy Stanton, for instance. He just moved into town. What's he like?"

Lucy was hoping to pick up some information, either about her new neighbors or maybe even the hazing situation, but Sara wasn't talking.

"He's okay, I guess, but he's on the JV team. They don't count."

"That's not a nice thing to say," said Lucy, grunting as she kneaded the dough with her hands.

"It's just that the JV guys are immature," said Sara. "They're the same age as me but I'm taller than some of them."

"Give them a chance, they'll catch up," advised Lucy, who wasn't eager to see some senior take a fancy to her little freshman. "You guys can take it from here, okay? I'm going to take the garbage out and then I'm going to watch TV with Dad."

She was stuffing the black plastic bag into a trash barrel when she noticed Tommy Stanton limping down the road. He was obviously exhausted and stumbled when he got to her driveway so she called to him.

"Hey, want some Gatorade?"

He stopped, bent over with his hands on his knees, and nodded, too exhausted to speak.

She waved and went in the house to get the bottle and when she returned he was sprawled on her porch steps. His skin was white and pasty and his eyes were unfocused, making Lucy wonder if she should call the rescue squad. "You look beat," she said, handing him the bottle.

He didn't answer but took the bottle and tilted it up with shaking hands and drank.

"You don't look too good," she said. "Should I call your mom or dad to pick you up?"

Tommy's eyes widened and he put down the bottle. "Don't do that, please," he said. "I'm fine. Really."

Lucy was doubtful. "I don't think running after practicing all afternoon is a good idea."

"Coach says we have to," gasped Tommy. "Every night."

"Every night? That's too much on top of practice."

Tommy shrugged. He didn't seem in any hurry to leave so Lucy seized the opportunity to question him about the hazing. "You know, I've been hearing rumors about the team, about the upperclassmen hazing the freshmen. Do you know anything about that?"

He looked at her warily. "Nah," he said, ducking his head.

"What about your haircut?" she asked, noticing the quarter-inch stubble. "Was shaving your head voluntary or did they make you do it?"

"We all did it," he said. "Even the coach."

"But what if you didn't want to do it?"

He looked at her as if she were crazy and struggled to his feet. "I gotta go. Thanks for the drink."

"Anytime," said Lucy, watching as he limped down the driveway.

Back in the house, she'd just joined Bill on the couch in the family room when the phone rang. A minute or two later Sara brought her the cordless handset. "It's for you."

"Me?" Lucy was surprised. These days the phone always seemed to be for the girls.

But when she answered she learned there was no doubt the call was for her. "Lucy Stone? This is your neighbor, Fred Stanton."

"Hi, Fred," said Lucy. "What can I do for you?"

"I'll tell you what you can do," he shouted. "You can leave my son alone, that's what."

"I think there's a misunderstanding here," she said. "I just gave him something to drink."

"Yeah, and then you started telling him his coach doesn't know what he's doing and asking a lot of questions. Well, listen here. I won't have it. Mind your own business."

"But I didn't . . ." began Lucy, but she was cut off when Fred slammed the phone down. She looked at Bill with a puzzled expression.

"Forget it," said Bill, drawing her close. "This is the good part, where Bruce Willis sets off the explosion."

Chapter 6

Lucy was all alone in the *Pennysaver* office the next morning when the bell on the door jangled and Sue breezed in with a covered dish in her hands.

"Hi, stranger," Lucy said. "What brings you to these parts?"

"I brought the rest of my Better-than-Sex Brownies for Ted," she said, pouting. "At least he appreciates them."

"Everybody loved your brownies. I think they voted against them because they're expensive to make. Butter's three dollars a pound these days, and chocolate and nuts are expensive, too."

"I didn't get the impression that anybody was concerned about cost," said Sue, with a little sniff. "They were just sucking up to Chris. The minute she said she didn't like them they all fell right into line. She's really something. I never met anybody so intimidating."

Sometimes Lucy thought Sue was a tad intimidating, too, but she bit her tongue. "I think she's frustrated, staying at home with Pear and Apple. She used to be a big executive and now all she's got to manage is a one-year-old and a three-year-old. Sara babysits for her and she says she's got the kids' days organized down to the last minute. Sara got in trouble for giving them their healthful, one-hundred-percent organic snack ten minutes early."

"And then there's that prissy Bonnie. I mean, 'Better-than-Sex' is just a name, it's not like I'm advocating fornication or anything." Sue examined her manicure. "Though I always wonder about those goody-two-shoes types. I suspect all sorts of weird, deviant stuff goes on in their bedrooms."

"I doubt it. Her husband's quite a bit older than she is."

"That doesn't mean a thing nowadays, what with Viagra and all. He's probably got her swinging from the chandelier like a monkey."

"I don't think so," chuckled Lucy. "Sara says they've got some kind of parental control on the TV so that the only channel the girls can watch is PBS and even then the nature shows are forbidden in case the twins might see penguins mating or something."

"Listen, whose side are you on here?" demanded Sue. "I don't see why you're defending the enemy."

"Since when are they enemies? I thought we were all on the same team."

"No way. It's us versus them and you better be very clear about which side you're on," said Sue. "Otherwise, you're going to find yourself losing your old friends."

Then she was gone, leaving nothing behind except the brownies and a trace of spicy designer perfume.

"Was Sue here?" asked Ted, sniffing the air as he came in the back way.

"She left some brownies for you."

"Mercy," he exclaimed, unwrapping the plate. "Whatever did I do to deserve these?"

"She says you appreciate them—unlike the Hat and Mitten committee. They voted against the brownies the other night."

"Are they crazy?"

"Probably. It was one of those female things. One of my new neighbors, Chris Cashman, is challenging Sue's authority."

"Another alpha, hunh?" Ted had taken a big bite of brownie.

"You said it."

"Well," he continued, after swallowing. "Pam was awfully nervous that her cookies wouldn't pass that taste test you had. You women are awfully tough on each other."

"It was Chris Cashman's idea to taste-test the recipes and have everyone use the best ones, sort of like Henry Ford. She says we'll make more money this way, focusing on products with high customer appeal." Lucy sighed. "But I don't know if it's worth the hurt feelings."

Having finished his brownie, Ted was going through the mail. "Looks like another anonymous letter," he said, slitting the envelope. He shook his head, reading the letter and passing it over to Lucy. "I wish this person would sign the letters. It would make things a lot easier for us."

"I know. I'd love to talk to whoever's sending them," said Lucy. "The letters are well-written and seem quite sincere."

"It could be a very clever troublemaker," said Ted. "Somebody like your alpha neighbor."

"Her kids are babies," said Lucy. "I think the

sender has a kid on the team. How else would they know about this stuff?"

"They could be making it up," Ted reminded her.

"Blindfolding kids and making them eat strips of raw liver, telling them it's worms? Nobody could make up stuff like this except teenage boys." She thought of Tommy and how willing he was to do whatever it took to stay on the team. "I think the letter writer is telling the truth."

"You may be right. Do you think there's a story here?"

"I think there's a story but I don't know if I can get it," said Lucy. "Nobody's going to admit this stuff is happening."

"Well, I want you to try. Get over to the school and talk to the principal, okay?"

"Sure. But I can guarantee you I won't get anything from him."

"I know. But we've got to start somewhere."

High school principal Bob Berg was tall and weedy; he looked like the sort of skinny guy that cartoon bullies kicked sand at on the beach, but he didn't tolerate any challenges to his authority. He'd long ago learned to cultivate an air of absolute omniscience; even when he was wrong, he was right. Lucy could have predicted his reaction when she outlined the charges in the anonymous letters. She'd once gotten a similar reaction when she'd tried to give a cat a bath.

"That's ridiculous," he sputtered, his Adam's apple bobbing up and down. "We simply don't tolerate hazing here at Tinker's Cove High School in any form whatsoever and whoever is making these accusations is behaving irresponsibly. This is absolutely outrageous."

Something in his tone brought out the devil in Lucy. "It doesn't seem that outrageous to me," she said. "These things happen and it's entirely possible that it's happening here. I think any responsible administrator would want to investigate before making an outright denial."

"I don't need to investigate. I know there is no hazing of any kind going on at Tinker's Cove High School."

"Well, then, you won't mind if I talk to some of the players," said Lucy.

"Oh, I can't allow that. There are confidentiality issues, privacy issues. We don't allow the press access to our students."

"That's not actually true," said Lucy, as politely as possible. "Students are routinely interviewed for stories about sports and community projects. Why, just last spring I interviewed several students who were working on a Habitat house."

Faced with indisputable evidence to the contrary, the principal caved. "All right. You can talk to the players but I want to be present."

"At practice this afternoon?"

"No. Right now. As it happens, several varsity players are working out in the weight room."

"Without supervision?" asked Lucy.

"These are all honors students," said Mr. Berg. "They've earned the right to use the weight room whenever they wish."

Lucy felt a bit uncomfortable as she followed him down the long, echoing hallway. She didn't like barging in on a bunch of teenage boys when they were exercising, and she doubted she'd get much information from them with Mr. Berg listening to every word. On the other hand, this was probably the only chance she was going to get to talk to the players.

They were crossing the empty gym and had almost reached the weight room when Mr. Berg suddenly grabbed his cell phone and checked his messages. "Oh, dear, I've got to go," he said. "Let me just introduce you to our athletes."

He pulled the door open, revealing a rather scruffy, unventilated room that smelled to high heaven of sweat. This was nothing like the well-equipped gyms with Nautilus machines that Lucy saw advertised on TV. It was simply an empty storage closet with a few weight benches and a set of free weights. The three team members who were working out dropped their weights and stared at the intruders.

"Boys, this is Mrs. Stone, from the paper. She's here to interview you about the team and I want you to cooperate," said Mr. Berg. "I have to go see to a problem with the septic system."

Then he was gone and Lucy was left alone with the three boys. She gave them a little smile. "Like he said, I'm Lucy Stone. And you guys are . . . ?"

The tallest, a muscular kid with a fuzz of black hair who was well over six feet, was the first to speak. "I'm Matt Engelhardt," he said, resuming his bicep curls. The weight which he seemed to be raising and lowering so effortlessly looked enormous to Lucy. It had to be at least twenty pounds.

Following his lead, the other two players resumed their workouts, too. "I'm Justin Crane," said a shorter, stockier fellow, who was grunting with the effort of lifting an enormous dumbbell.

"And I'm Will Worthington," said the last, a tall, freckled kid. He was lying on his stomach on the bench, lifting weights with his legs.

"I guess you're all seniors?" asked Lucy, producing her notebook.

There was a round of grunts which she took to mean yes.

"Well, the reason I'm doing this story is that there have been some allegations of hazing on the football team. In particular, the rumor goes, the varsity players have been humiliating the JV players and physically abusing them."

There was an uncomfortable silence in the small room, as the boys continued to work out.

"Do you have anything to say, Will?" asked Lucy, sensing he might be the weak link.

He wasn't. "No," he said, glaring at her.

"Does hazing take place, Justin?"

"Not that I know of."

"What about you, Matt? Have you seen any hazing? Say, making the new players line up and throwing soccer balls at them?"

"We're *football* players," said Matt, getting a laugh from the other guys.

Lucy, who was standing next to the water cooler, was obliged to get out of his way as he strode over to get a drink. She found herself boxed in a corner, between the cooler and the wall, while he stood in front of her, downing one cupful after another.

Lucy tried to ignore her discomfort and continued with her questions. "I understand you guys all go away to summer training camp for a week or so. Did any hazing take place at the camp? Like playing Twister?"

Justin had joined Matt at the cooler, increasing Lucy's sense of confinement. She was beginning to think the boys were not simply inconsiderate but were purposely harassing her.

"Twister? That's a game for kids," said Justin.

"Not the way you guys play it, at least that's what I've heard," said Lucy, trying to make a joke.

It didn't go over well. Now Will had joined the others at the cooler. They seemed to be moving closer, pressing her against the wall.

"Uh, fellas," she said, protesting. "This is a pretty small room but I don't think we all need to stand so close."

"What, don't you know about huddles?" Matt punched Justin in the arm, and he lurched towards her, knocking the pad from her hand.

Lucy felt herself growing angry. She was in a ridiculous situation and she couldn't see a way out of it. Her instinct was to tell them off, to assert her authority as an adult, but she sensed they would just laugh at her. Physically, she was much smaller than they were and she had a feeling that this was a situation in which size mattered. "Come on, guys," she said, keeping her tone light. "This is enough. You say there's no hazing, there's no hazing. Now I've got other things to do."

She might as well have been talking to the wall. Justin had now raised one hand in a defensive posture and was pummeling Matt with the other. Will was jumping up and down, encouraging him. Lucy was shrinking back into her corner, trying to avoid their fists. She was so absorbed in trying to protect herself that she didn't notice the door had opened until the boys stopped boxing and moved away from her.

"What's going on here?" demanded Coach Buck.

"Uh, nothing, sir," said Matt.

"It didn't look like nothing to me," said the coach, turning to Lucy. "Are you all right?"

"Fine," said Lucy, simultaneously relieved to be rescued and embarrassed that it was necessary. "The boys were just horsing around."

"Well, I think they owe you an apology," he said, glaring at them.

"Sorry," muttered Matt, followed by the others.

"No problem," said Lucy, taking a deep breath and stepping away from the wall.

"He gave the boys a warning glance and ushered her out into the gym. "What was that all about?"

"I was interviewing them for a story and when Mr. Berg was called away, they got a little rowdy. That's all."

His eyes met hers. "What sort of story?"

"The hazing rumors. They all denied it, but their behavior in there makes me wonder," said Lucy, as they walked together toward the exit.

"Why didn't you come to me?" asked Coach, an edge to his voice. "Why did you go behind my back?"

Lucy didn't like being put on the defensive. "I already asked you about it and I didn't get anywhere. Meanwhile, we're still getting letters at the paper about naked Twister, forced alcohol, beatings with soccer balls."

Coach Buck's expression was a mixture of shock and incredulity. "That's ridiculous. Where do people get these ideas? Believe me, I would not tolerate anything like that. No way." He paused and shrugged. "Boys will be boys, I guess. I'm sorry they behaved so rudely. You can be sure they'll be doing some extra wind sprints today."

"Well, I'm glad to hear it," said Lucy.

They were standing by the front door, and Coach Buck extended his hand. Lucy took it, finding his grasp warm and strong. He smiled and Lucy found herself gazing into his eyes, eyes that convinced her he had nothing to hide. Reassured that the players were in good hands, she said good-bye and headed for her car. It wasn't until she was back at the paper and got a call from Willie Westwood that her doubts began to grow again.

"Lucy, I just thought I ought to let you know that Sara seemed edgy today when I picked her up to take her to practice. In fact, I had to stop the car so she could throw up."

"Maybe it's the flu," said Lucy. "Did you take her home?"

"I tried, but she insisted on going to practice. I'm sorry to bother you at work but I thought you should know."

"Not at all. Thanks for calling."

After the call Lucy tried to concentrate on the task at hand, the list of mortgage rates offered by local banks that ran every week, but found her mind drifting back to the uncomfortable few minutes she'd spent in the weight room. She was beginning to wish that Sara had gone out for girls' soccer or volleyball instead of cheerleading.

Chapter 7

Concerned about Willie's warning, Lucy watched Sara closely all week for signs that something was troubling her but, if there was, Sara was adept at concealing it. And when she drove her to the school on Saturday morning for the traditional preseason game against the Northport Fish Hawks, there was no indication she was anything but excited. Perhaps too excited, fretted Lucy. This year the game was in Northport and the cheerleaders would be riding the bus with the varsity team. After the anonymous letters and her experience in the weight room she wasn't all that happy about her freshman daughter riding with the varsity players, mostly juniors and seniors, but the younger JV team had no cheerleaders.

Despite her concerns, Lucy had to admit Sara looked adorable in her outfit, a short skirt and tank top in the team colors of red and white. She'd tied her hair up in a perky pony tail and was practically bouncing in her seat when Lucy pulled into the Westwoods' driveway. As usual, several cats were sunning and grooming themselves in various spots on the warm asphalt, and the dog, an aged golden retriever, ran out to greet them. There was no sign of the controversial pot-bellied pig; Lucy supposed it was kept in a pen of some sort. Or perhaps it was an indoor pet. She figured she'd make its acquaintance one of these days.

Sassie was excited, too, and as soon as she jumped in the car the girls began practicing their cheers. Lucy would have liked to ask them about the boys on the team, and warn them to sit together on the bus, but she couldn't get a word in edgewise. There wasn't even time to say good-bye when she pulled up at the high school; the girls were out of the car the second it stopped.

As she watched them run to the bus, their shiny white saddle shoes gleaming in the sunlight, she figured something was definitely up. Her highly sophisticated maternal radar could detect when the anti-parental defense shield was in operation, but her shield-piercing missile was unfortunately still in development. She hoped to have it operational by the time Zoe was in high school.

Lucy's mind was miles away, trying to think of a tactic that would get Sara to open up, when she arrived at the outlet mall with three hundred and sixty individually-wrapped gourmet dog biscuits. The sale was scheduled to start at nine, when the mall opened but now, at a few minutes past eight, Chris was already setting up tables.

"Hi, Lucy," she said, greeting Lucy with a big smile. "I see you're another early bird."

"I had to drop my daughter off at the high school. The big Northport game is today and she's a cheerleader."

"They grow up fast, don't they?" said Chris. "I'm trying to decide if public school will be challenging enough for Pear and Apple or whether I should start researching private schools."

"The public school's the only game in town, unless you're considering the Christian academy run by the Revelation Congregation."

"Christian academy?" Chris was laying colorful sheets over the tables. "I guess that would be okay. We're Episcopalian."

"They don't believe in evolution," explained Lucy. "They teach something called intelligent design."

Chris's eyebrows shot up. "That would hardly prepare Apple and Pear for Harvard or Duke," she said.

"Hardly," agreed Lucy. "Where do you want the dog biscuits?"

"At the far end," said Chris. "There are some signs in my car—would you mind getting them?"

Lucy followed Chris's instructions and found a stack of professional-looking signs in the back of her SUV. She was carrying them back when she met Frankie, who was toting a big basket of madeleines.

"Oh, Lucy, I'm glad to see you. I can really use some help. My house was the collection point for Prudence Path so my car is full of baked goods." She rolled her eyes. "I don't like to think how many calories are in there."

"It's a pity the car can't run on them, considering the price of gas," joked Lucy, placing the signs on the table and heading back to the parking lot. She was carrying several baskets of granola bars when she noticed Sue speeding into the parking lot in her enormous Suburban. She'd stuck a sign in the back window that said: "Yummy Treats. Follow me to the bake sale."

"Am I late?" she called, leaning out the window.

"No. We're just setting up."

"Great. I've got Rachel and Pam's cookies, too. They're on the afternoon shift."

"That's right," said Chris, consulting her clipboard. "Along with Willie and Bonnie. There are only four in the afternoon because I figured it would be slower." She was checking off names. "Everybody's here except Mimi." She looked at Frankie. "Do you have her Yummy Pumpkin Kisses?"

Frankie shook her head. "No. She was the only one who didn't bring her cookies over."

"Did you call her?" demanded Chris.

"No. I figured she'd bring them herself since she was on the morning shift."

Chris's tone was accusatory and the sinews in her neck were showing. "Well, she's not here and the sale is due to start in five minutes."

People were already starting to gather at the sale tables, attracted no doubt by the aroma of freshly-brewed coffee. Chris had borrowed a huge pot used for the coffee hour that followed Sunday morning services at her church and it was proving a big draw.

"Well, we have to open up without her," said Frankie, with a shrug. "These people aren't going to wait forever and we don't want to lose them to the food court."

"We need Mimi," insisted Chris, a note of panic in her voice. "There are too many people. We're not going to be able to manage without her."

"Calm down," said Lucy. "It's a bake sale. People will understand."

Chris was checking her watch. "I know. We've got a few minutes before we officially open. Lucy, will you go and see what's keeping Mimi—and her Yummy Pumpkin Kisses?"

"Me?" Lucy was reluctant; she was hardly on the best of terms with Mimi.

"I think it would be best," snapped Chris. "After all, Sue doesn't know where she lives and her car is a good advertisement for the sale. Frankie's already pouring coffee and I need to stay and make sure everything runs smoothly."

"Okay," said Lucy, overwhelmed by her argument. "When you put it that way . . ."

"We don't have time for this," snapped Chris, losing patience. "Just go and get back as fast as you can. We need all the help we can get."

It was true. The people in the line were definitely getting restless. One man had even commented, quite loudly, that the service was better at Dunkin' Donuts.

"I'll be as fast as I can," she promised, running to her car.

Her heart was pounding and she was out of breath when she started the engine and spun out of the parking lot. It was the squeal of the tires that brought her to her senses. She'd never left rubber in her life and she wasn't about to start now, not for a bake sale. Chris was a tad overwrought, she thought, slowing to a sedate and legal thirty miles per hour. Just because she was a frustrated housewife who missed her high-powered executive job didn't mean everybody had to go along for the ride as she turned a simple bake sale into an emotional roller coaster. You'd think she was on some TV reality show or something but as far as Lucy knew Donald Trump wasn't coming to Tinker's Cove to point his finger and announce "You're fired!" if the bake sale didn't meet its goal.

She was tempted, in fact, to turn right around and go back to the bake sale. She didn't like being Chris's messenger girl and she didn't like checking up on Mimi. The woman worked in the town hall, after all; she'd probably been called in to work an extra shift because somebody was sick or something. Or maybe she had a family emergency. Or maybe she'd decided to go and see Tommy play his first JV game. Whatever it was it wasn't any of Lucy's business and she felt uncomfortable playing truant officer.

She hesitated for a minute when she pulled into the Stantons' driveway, worrying that she might encounter Fred instead of Mimi, then decided she was being silly. If anyone should be embarrassed it was him, for making nasty phone calls. It was too late to leave anyway; by now somebody would surely have noticed her car. She might as well see if Mimi was home and, if she was, politely remind her of the bake sale. She'd make it clear that Chris sent her, that she was in a sense following orders, and was in no way a busybody. Having decided on her approach, Lucy reluctantly got out of the car and immediately noticed the scent of burned sugar.

That explained it, she thought, walking up the drive. Poor Mimi had burned her cookies and was probably frantically mixing up a new batch. Though that would be a big problem for Mimi because making cookies from scratch wasn't something you could rush. The butter and sugar had to be creamed, the batter had to be thoroughly mixed and you could only fit a couple of pans in the oven at one time. Poor Mimi, thought Lucy, as the scent grew stronger. This batch definitely seemed to be burning, too.

Her eyes were already stinging and she could hear the smoke alarm ringing when she got to the kitchen door. She opened it cautiously and was forced back by a noxious cloud of smoke. She was beginning to think she should go back to the car and call the fire department when the smoke began to thin, thanks to the open door, and she noticed Mimi slumped over the faux-granite island. Minutes, no seconds, counted in a fire and Lucy knew she couldn't delay. She had to get Mimi out of there, into the fresh air, so she pulled her stretchy jersey T-shirt up over her nose and ran into the smoky room. She immediately began sputtering and coughing but, reassured by the fact she wasn't hit by a blast of heat, she staggered onward until she reached the island. She bent over Mimi, intending to hook her arms under her armpits to drag her towards the door, when she felt something hard hit her chest. Taking a closer look she noticed Mimi's eyes, half-open and sightless, and identified the object that had banged her chest. It was the wooden hilt of a large chef's knife that was protruding from Mimi's back.

Her mind simply didn't take it in. Her body did, however, and instinct took over. She found herself outside, on the farmer's porch, shaking and moaning. She'd wrapped her arms around herself and was rocking back and forth, fighting waves of nausea until, once again, her body took over and she threw up into a brightly colored Mexican pot of geraniums. Feeling marginally better, she sat down on the steps and called 9-1-1.

She knew Chris would expect her to call, she even had her cell phone number on the bake sale instruction sheet that was in the car, but she didn't move. She sat, shaking and completely drained, concentrating on holding herself together until help arrived. In reality it was only minutes, but it seemed hours before she heard the screech of sirens and the deep honk of the town's brand new hook and ladder truck. Soon Prudence Path was filled with fire trucks, police cars, and an ambulance.

There was very little for any of the helpers to do. EMTs rushed to Mimi's aid, but there was no help to be given. She was obviously dead and they were not allowed to move the body of a crime victim. All the firefighters could do was turn off the oven and set up fans to clear the smoke.

There was no question Mimi had been murdered. As one EMT said, "She sure didn't do that to herself."

The rescuers all knew Mimi, who had been a colleague, after all, and a few were obviously struggling with their emotions. One female firefighter, dwarfed by her helmet, coat and boots, was in tears and several cops were stone-faced, staring straight ahead at nothing. Everybody kept a respectful distance, almost as if keeping vigil over her body. Outside, a couple of officers were stringing yellow crime scene tape from the bushes, but there was no crowd to keep back. Nobody was home on Prudence Path this Saturday morning.

Lucy, who had been instructed to wait for the arrival of the state police investigative team, had moved out of the way and was sitting on the deacon's bench that Mimi had placed on the farmer's

porch just a few weeks earlier. Still feeling somewhat shaky, she was wondering who had done this
terrible thing to Mimi. The first person who came
to mind was Mimi's husband. After all, everybody
said Fred Stanton had a terrible temper. She remembered the conversation at the Hat and Mitten
Fund meeting, when the Prudence Path neighbors
had spoken about the way he used to abuse Mimi.
Lucy had received some of his abuse herself when
he called up and yelled at her to mind her own
business that evening when she'd given Tommy
that bottle of Gatorade.

"You're looking very thoughtful. Have you decided who did it?"

Lucy looked up and saw the familiar face of
State Police Detective Lieutenant Horowitz. Summer was almost over, but Horowitz wasn't sporting
a tan. He was pale as ever, dressed in rumpled shirt-
sleeves and wrinkled gray pants. His thin brown
hair was receding and he was wearing wire-rimmed
bifocals.

"When did you start wearing glasses?" asked
Lucy.

"When they said I'd have to have one contact
lens for distance and one for reading. I couldn't
get the hang of switching from one eye to the
other." He sat beside her. "So tell me what happened."

Lucy told him about Mimi's absence from the
bake sale and how she'd been sent to get her, only
to find her with a knife in her back. "It must have
been the husband, don't you think?"

"I think it could have been anybody, including
you," said Horowitz.

"You're joking, right?"

"Yeah. You're a pain in the butt but I never knew you to actually commit murder." He stood up. "Now I know this is a big news story and all, and I know you're going to write about it, but I don't want you starting some cockeyed investigation of your own, okay? Leave the investigating to the professionals."

"But . . ." began Lucy.

"No buts. I don't want to see you with a knife in your back. When you get that urge to stick your nose in where it doesn't belong, just remember how that lady looked, okay?"

Lucy felt a tingling right between her shoulder blades. "Okay," she said.

He turned to go back in the house, then paused, looking down the cul-de-sac. "Is it always this quiet around here?" he asked. "Where is everybody?"

Lucy considered. "Some of the women are at a bake sale, that's where I'm supposed to be." She sniffed. "Mimi, too." She looked at the houses, neat as pins, each set in the middle of a square of lawn. "He's a vet, he's probably at his office and she teaches riding, Saturday morning's a popular time for lessons," she said, pointing to the Westwoods'. "Frankie LaChance is a single mom, she's at the bake sale and her daughter's at the football game. The Burkharts, they're across from Frankie, well, he's the football coach and I don't know where she is. Maybe shopping for back-to-school clothes for the twins. As for the Cashmans, Chris is at the sale and her husband is probably chauffeuring their kids to computer class or something." She paused, thinking. "Mimi's youngest son is on the football team. Fred, that's her husband, is probably there. His brother, too."

"What about your family?" he asked, looking towards Lucy's house.

Lucy's face paled. "Bill's at work, Sara's at the football game, and Zoe slept over at a friend's house last night."

"Your son?" asked Horowitz.

"He doesn't live with us anymore—he's on his own now—and Elizabeth's back at college in Boston."

"We'll need their addresses," he said, going back inside. A few minutes later, an officer sat down on the bench beside her and took her statement, including the addresses, then told her she was free to go. She was sitting in her car, starting the engine, when she saw the men from the medical examiner's office wheeling out Mimi's body, encased in black vinyl, on a wheeled stretcher. She sat, silent, watching as they lifted the stretcher over the porch steps and rolled it down the driveway. There was a pause and a jolt as they collapsed first the front legs and then the rear and slid it into the van. Then they got in and drove off. Lucy waited until they were gone before starting the engine.

It was later than she thought, she realized, too late to go back to the bake sale. She had ignored Chris's calls to her cell phone and they'd finally stopped. There was no way she could tell her what had happened to Mimi—word would have spread like wildfire and impeded the police investigation— and she hadn't had the energy to think up a plausible lie. Now it was almost one and time for her to head over to the high school to pick up Sara and Sassie.

From the honking procession of cars, with screaming teens leaning out the windows waving streamers in the school colors, and the boisterous attitude of the players and cheerleaders who tumbled out of the two yellow school buses when they arrived in the parking lot, it was obvious the Tinker's Cove Warriors had carried the day.

She found herself smiling as Sara and Sassie skipped across the asphalt, shaking their pom-poms.

"I guess the Warriors won," she said, as they slid into the backseat.

"Even the JV team," announced Sara.

"Wow." Lucy was amazed. Wins were few and far between for the Warriors and she couldn't remember when the JV team had won a game. Their losing record had assumed legendary proportions.

"You had a good time?" asked Lucy, starting the car.

"It was awesome, Mom. Awesome."

Sara's enthusiasm was almost enough to make Lucy forget the terrible scene she'd witnessed at the Stanton house—until she spied Tommy Stanton, standing quite alone on the sidewalk, obviously looking for his ride. A ride she doubted would be coming.

"Who picks up Tommy?" she asked the girls.

"His mom. Sometimes his dad."

Lucy knew that Mimi wouldn't be coming, for sure, and she suspected that Fred was otherwise occupied. She'd have to give the kid a lift, it was only decent. She drove over and stopped in front of him, leaning out the window. "We're headed your way—want a ride?"

Tommy looked around at the rapidly emptying parking lot. "Sure." He ducked into the front seat. "Thanks."

"I hear your team had a big win," said Lucy. In the backseat the girls giggled.

"Yeah." Tommy nodded proudly. "I made a forty-yard run."

"All that running's paying off," said Lucy, her heart aching for him.

"Yeah." He couldn't stop smiling. "Did you see Mikey Meehan's touchdown?" he asked, turning around to face the girls.

"Sorry. We didn't watch the JV game," said Sassie. "You guys never win."

"We did today," he said, practically singing.

"Maybe we'll watch next time," said Sara, erupting into giggles.

Lucy was tempted to delay the return to Prudence Path. "You guys want to stop for some ice cream or something?" she asked.

"Thanks, but I've got to get changed and get to my job," said Tommy. "I'm a bagger at Marzetti's."

"Good for you," said Lucy, finding it hard to swallow because of the lump in her throat. In truth, a giant lump seemed to be forming around her heart and it was pressing against her stomach, growing heavier with every mile that brought them closer to Red Top Hill. As they began the climb she came to a decision—she couldn't take Tommy home without telling him what had happened.

"Girls, I'm going to drop you at our house. You can walk home from there, Sassie."

Something in her tone brooked no protest and the girls got out meekly when she stopped at the end of the driveway. She turned to Tommy.

"There's something I have to tell you," she said. "I have some bad news. Very bad news."

Tommy looked puzzled. What did this woman, practically a stranger, know about him?

"I went to your house today, to get your mother for the bake sale."

He nodded. He knew all about the bake sale.

"When I got there she was . . ." Lucy's voice failed her. "Not well," she finally said.

"She said she thought she was coming down with a cold," he said, looking concerned.

"It was worse than that." Lucy put her hand on his. "She was dead."

"Dead?" Tommy repeated the word, as if he didn't know its meaning.

"I'm afraid so." Lucy waited for his reaction, not knowing what to expect. Tears? Hysterics? Angry accusations? But nothing came. Tommy sat, hunched over, staring at his knee. "I'm sorry to be the one to tell you," she said, wondering if she'd made a big mistake. Maybe it would have been better for him to hear it from his father. But she didn't know if his father was home, if anybody was home. She didn't know what he was going to walk into and she wanted him to be prepared. Maybe the cops were still there, or a gaggle of relatives. "I just thought it would be better if you knew."

"It's okay," he said, pulling his hand out from under hers. "I better get home."

"I'll drive you," said Lucy. "It's just around the corner."

He didn't protest so she made the short trip to Prudence Path, stopping in front of his house at the end of the cul-de-sac. "Uh, thanks for the ride," he said, climbing out of the car.

Lucy waved, unable to speak. She was blinking back tears, determined not to break down in front of him. Eyes glistening, she gave him a sad little smile and watched as he began the climb up his driveway. As he approached the porch she couldn't hold the sobs in any longer and she let herself cry, holding on to the steering wheel with two hands and letting her head fall. She sat there, shaking with sobs, until she was all cried out. Then she lifted her head, wiped her face with the back of her hands, and slid the gear shift into drive. She looked around, checking that the way was clear, and noticed Fred Stanton standing at the kitchen door. She hesitated, wondering if she should go to him, but something in his expression warned her off. He was looking at her, she thought, as if he wanted to kill her.

Chapter 8

Sunday morning dawned bright and sunny. The cloudless blue sky, always a rare treat in New England, promised a perfect day on this holiday weekend marking the end of the summer season. On such a day Prudence Path would normally be a hive of activity as faithful residents drove off to church and the unfaithful mowed their lawns, hooked up boat trailers to their SUVs, or revved up the gas grill for a barbecue. But this morning an eerie silence hung heavily over the little cul-de-sac, broken only by the muted voices of churchgoers, careful not to slam their car doors.

The only exception was Preston's Harley, which roared to life around ten-thirty as he departed on some errand. At least, that's what Lucy presumed, giving him the benefit of the doubt. He could hardly be joyriding the morning after his mother's death, could he? No, he must be fetching groceries and newspapers, or tending to the myriad details that accompanied a death. There were funeral arrangements to be made, food and flowers to be ordered, clothing to be delivered to the funeral home, and then there were the ordinary necessities of life to be gotten because life went on. Prescriptions to be picked up, gas tanks to be filled, trips to the ATM to get cash, on and on it went.

Apart from Preston's trip, there was no sign of life at the Stanton house. By mid-afternoon all of the neighbors had taken the short walk to the end of the cul-de-sac to deliver covered dishes and express their condolences, but no one was admitted. The door opened, the dish was passed inside, and the door closed. Fred Stanton remained alone with his sons; there was no gathering of friends and family to share the grief and the memories. Even Mimi's colleagues from town hall were turned away.

Labor Day was usually one of Lucy's favorite holidays. Unlike Memorial Day and the Fourth of July, which brought hordes of summer people and vacationers to Tinker's Cove, Labor Day was more subdued. Summer people were closing up their houses and heading home early to avoid the traffic, families with kids had already taken their vacations and were replaced by older couples taking advantage of the last warm days of summer, dubbed the "shoulder season" by the Chamber of Commerce. The big rocks bordering Blueberry Pond, the popular freshwater swimming hole, would be empty save for a few late-season sun worshippers. So would the town beach on the ocean, which had been so crowded just last weekend that you couldn't find a single empty place in the parking lot. Instead of the shrieks of children, the only sound would be the occasional call of a herring gull; there would only be the fresh smell of the sea—and a faint, lingering whiff of fried clams—now that the snack bar had closed because the college-age staffers had all gone back to school.

But instead of packing up her sunglasses and towel and joining the family for one last lazy afternoon on the beach, Lucy found herself staying in the house, unable to give up her vantage point on the scene of the crime. She didn't know what she expected to see, but she kept peering out the windows overlooking Prudence Path, checking on the activity there. The fact that there wasn't much activity at all didn't discourage her. It was a compulsion, like a scab you had to pick even though you knew it would bleed. When the phone rang she leaped on it, beating Sara and Zoe.

"I couldn't believe it when Ted told me," said Pam. "Poor Mimi."

"You can say that again," said Lucy. "She was stabbed with a big old kitchen knife. It was horrible."

"That's right. You found the body. That must have been awful."

"It was." Lucy didn't want to go into it. "I'm trying not to think about it."

"Of course." Pam sounded a little disappointed. "Well, I do have some good news. The bake sale raised over twelve hundred dollars."

"You're kidding."

"No. Honest. Isn't that amazing?"

"Just from our cookies and stuff?"

"Well, I suspect a lot of it came from the coffee and cold drinks. Chris is going to do an analysis."

"I don't doubt it," said Lucy.

"She was pretty frantic when you didn't come back and she couldn't get you on your cell phone. She ended up calling me around ten and I went in to help."

"There wasn't anything I could do. I had to stay and wait for the police. I couldn't call and tell what had happened because I knew the police wouldn't want the news spreading all over town before they started investigating." Lucy paused. "You must've been short-handed, though."

"We were busy, that's for sure. In fact, we closed early because we ran out of cold drinks. We still have some leftover baked goods—they're in my freezer. I was thinking of giving them to the football team, after their next game."

"I wouldn't do anything without checking with Chris," warned Lucy.

"Oh, right." She giggled. "I don't want to end up like Mimi."

"No," said Lucy. "Chris wouldn't have killed her before she finished baking those Yummy Pumpkin Kisses."

They fell silent. "I'm sorry I said that," said Lucy.

"Me, too," said Pam. "This isn't something to joke about."

"No, it sure isn't. I don't know why we're so cocky. Maybe there's some knife-wielding serial killer running around. Maybe we're next."

"I hadn't thought of that," said Pam. "I'm going to go lock my doors."

Lucy hung up and considered locking her doors, but quickly gave up the idea as impractical. The kitchen door might as well have been a revolving door, considering how often they all came and went. The dog alone was in and out several times a day and she couldn't use a key, though she could nose the screen door open.

While Lucy was amusing herself with the idea of stringing a key around the dog's neck the phone rang and this time it was Chris. Speak of the devil.

"I just got the word from Pam that the sale made

twelve hundred dollars," crowed Chris. "More than ever before."

"I think you can take credit . . ." began Lucy.

"Oh, no. It's really due to everyone's hard work. Including you, Lucy. It was a team effort and we all played a part. You really came through with those dog biscuits and you deserve a big thank you."

"I was glad to do it," said Lucy. "I hope you understand about yesterday, why I couldn't let you know what was going on."

"Of course," said Chris. "And how absolutely terrible for you. I feel guilty about sending you."

"You couldn't have known," said Lucy.

"No. But I should've guessed something was seriously wrong. Mimi was such a stickler for doing everything right." A note of resentment was creeping into Chris's voice. "I mean, if she said she was going to do something, she did it."

"That's for sure," said Lucy, thinking of her lilacs. Had they gotten a reprieve or had Mimi already set the wheels in motion for their execution?

"If you ask me," continued Chris, "I think she must've pushed somebody too far."

Lucy was surprised. "I heard her husband was abusive . . ."

"He's no peach, that's for sure, but he wasn't home that much. They seemed to go their separate ways a lot." She paused, then continued in a whisper. "I used to see him over at Frankie's place a lot, especially on the nights Mimi worked. He'd park in his own driveway and hotfoot it through my back yard."

"Oh." Lucy was thoughtful. "Maybe Mimi found out and they had a big fight and he lost his temper and stabbed her."

"She didn't mind a fight, that's for sure. You know she reported me to the town for running a home business?"

"You have a home business?"

"Not really. I have a handful of clients from my days as an investment banker, mostly widows who felt they were in good hands with me and didn't trust anyone else to handle their stocks and bonds. It's really more of a favor than anything else, I don't make much money from it, I just felt bad for the old dears. I'd be in big trouble with the bank, though, if they thought I was stealing customers."

"How did she find out about it? It isn't like you've got a line of old ladies on your front lawn."

"The postman accidentally delivered my outgoing mail to her box," said Chris. "She saw my business name on the return address and questioned me when she brought the letters over. Like a fool I told her all about it when I should've told her to mind her own business. I finally got so ticked at her I told her about Fred and Frankie and you know what she told me? She said he was repairing her closet doors." Chris snorted. "Like anybody would believe that! I've called, we've all called about one thing or another not working and he doesn't do a thing to help. These houses could fall down and I swear he'd walk right by, insisting it wasn't his responsibility."

"What did the zoning board do?" asked Lucy. "About the home business."

"I don't know. The meeting is next week," said Chris.

"I hope it goes well," said Lucy.

"Me, too," said Chris.

* * *

Lucy was fidgety on the ride over to Sue's house; she hadn't exactly been looking forward to the annual Labor Day cookout that had been a shared tradition for the two families ever since she and Sue were young mothers. In those days, it was a potluck affair, and Lucy would bring a big bowl of potato salad along with hot dogs and hamburgers to be cooked on the grill. But now that Sue and her husband Sid were empty-nesters—their only child Sidra was a producer on the "Norah! Show"— Sue liked to do all the cooking herself and experimented with recipes from *Gourmet* and *Bon Appetit* magazine.

With nothing to hold in her lap, Lucy found herself nervously kneading her hands together. She tried to tell herself there was nothing to be anxious about, but she knew Sue too well to think that she wouldn't be getting back at her for supporting Chris's ideas for the bake sale. She also hoped Sue hadn't forgotten that Zoe and Sara were coming and hadn't gone too overboard with the gourmet stuff. The girls, especially Zoe, weren't adventurous eaters and would turn up their noses at anything unfamiliar. Last year's gorgonzola hamburgers—and the girls' reaction—was something Lucy would prefer to forget. The one bright spot, she reminded herself, was the fact that Sue had invited Toby and Molly. Now that the couple had moved in together Lucy didn't see much of her only son and she was looking forward to catching up with him—and Molly, too, of course.

The young couple was already seated on the Finches' back deck when Bill and Lucy arrived with the girls. Toby jumped up and gave her a big hug and Lucy marveled all over again that her little seven-pound baby had grown into this handsome six-footer. Even more amazing, thought Lucy as she embraced Molly, was the fact that he'd managed to snag such a genuinely lovely girl. Toby was working on a frosty Sam Adams and Molly was sipping at a Green Apple Martini. Lucy hoped she knew how much alcohol the drink contained and wouldn't give in to pressure from Sid to have another and another and another. He was justifiably proud of his bartending skills, but tended to forget that not everyone had Sue's ability to handle booze. Though, from the look of things, Sue had started drinking in advance of the party.

"Well, you're here at last," she said, making it sound more like an accusation than a welcome.

"Oh, you know us. We're never on time," said Lucy. "Bill tries but it's hard to get three females out of the house. There's always somebody who needs a last peek at the mirror."

"I can see you went all out," said Sue, checking out Lucy's white pedal pushers and striped top. "You wore lipstick."

As usual, Sue was dressed to the nines in a flowing caftan and heeled sandals. Her glossy black hair was combed into a perfect pageboy, she was dramatically made-up with plenty of mascara and dark red lipstick and her manicure was flawless. Lucy didn't have a clue how she managed to wear all that makeup and still look human; she felt like a clown whenever she experimented with eyeliner or blush.

"As always, you look lovely," she said, hoping to charm her with flattery.

Sue smiled. "Sid, Lucy and Bill need drinks," she called, sounding as if she were addressing a hired waiter. She turned to Sara and Zoe. "Girls, there's soda and snacks in the TV room, and I got the new Hilary Duff video for you."

Zoe, Lucy was happy to see, made a polite display of enthusiasm but Sara looked disgruntled as she clumped into the house. "She's at an awkward age," she told Sue, by way of apology.

"Too old for Hilary Duff?"

"She certainly thinks she is," said Lucy, taking a sip of the cocktail that had miraculously appeared in her hand. "She thinks R ratings are ridiculously unfair."

"Talk about ridiculously unfair—I can't believe you managed to get out of working at the bake sale."

"I found Mimi's body," Lucy reminded her. "It wasn't exactly a picnic."

"Oh, right, I forgot," said Sue, drifting into the kitchen.

Put off by Sue's callous attitude, Lucy didn't follow her but took a chair on the deck, next to Toby. "So what are you guys up to?" she asked, setting her drink down on a little white plastic table. It was too sweet for her taste.

"We started house hunting," said Molly, tucking her long blond hair behind one ear. "Toby's had a really good summer fishing and we've saved enough for a down payment."

"That's great," said Lucy, hoping that assuming a mortgage together might be the spur the couple needed to get married. "Where are you looking?"

"Anywhere and everywhere," said Toby. "Trouble is, prices are rising faster than we can save."

"It's true," nodded Molly. "Even with what we've got we're worried we won't qualify for a mortgage. It's the monthly payments—plus Toby's income falls in the winter."

"I ought to do a story on this for the paper," said Lucy. "How rising prices are locking young people out of the housing market."

"It isn't just prices," said Sid. "It's all these regulations. Young folks can't just buy an old fixer-upper like we did and take their time renovating it. Now you can't even get a mortgage on a house unless its septic system is up to code—that adds a good five or ten thousand to the cost."

Lucy thought of the years she'd struggled with a failing cesspool, carefully timing baths and flushes and pumping the washing machine water out a hose running through a window into the back yard. She'd never get away with that now, especially with a nosy neighbor like Mimi. Then she remembered that Mimi was gone, murdered, and finished off her drink.

"Let me get you another," said Sid, hopping to his feet as Sue appeared with a tray of hors d'oeuvres.

"Be sure to try the mini spanikopita," said Sue. "They're yummy."

The little spinach pies were delicious, and so were the cheese and olive swirls and the bruschetta and the crab and artichoke dip. Lucy was feeling full, and a little bit woozy from the second apple martini, which went down a lot quicker than the first, when Sue announced dinner. They all gathered around the big round table under a market umbrella that Sue had set with Provence-style linens and pottery and Sue started passing the mustard-seed crusted burgers on home-made rolls. Then came the horse-radish slaw, warm mushroom and stilton salad, pea tendrils with lemon dressing, cauliflower-leek kugel, and Southern-fried chicken. "That's for anyone who doesn't like fancy burgers," said Sue, with a nod to the girls.

Lucy knew she shouldn't, in fact, she kept saying so, but she was unable to pass on any of it, declaring she'd have "just a taste."

"That's what French women do," said Sue. "That's why they never get fat."

"And what's your secret?" asked Lucy, wondering how Sue could cook the way she did and still stay rail thin.

"She doesn't eat during the week," said Sid, earning a sharp glance from his wife.

"That's not exactly true, I just try to balance it out. If I have a big dinner, I just have coffee for breakfast."

So when the lemon curd mousse cake and strawberries with mint sugar and lavender syrup came, Lucy tried to pass. "I couldn't eat another bite," she said, rubbing her taut tummy.

"Oh, Lucy, you have to try it. I worked for hours," coaxed Sue.

"It's true," said Sid. "It's what she does now. She cooks all day long."

"I wish Lucy would cook like this," said Bill, diving into his cake. "Lately all she's been cooking is dog biscuits."

Lucy gave him a dirty look and shook her head. "No, no. None for me. Everything is delicious but I'm too stuffed."

"Oh, just a bite . . ."

"Okay," said Lucy, "a bite."

Sue handed her a plate with an enormous slice of cake topped with heaps of glistening berries. It was too much for Lucy who could hardly bear to look at it; she was beginning to feel sick to her stomach from all the rich food.

"Well, aren't you going to taste it?" demanded Sue.

"I really don't think I can," protested Lucy. "Could you wrap it up for me so I can take it home?"

"I can't believe this, Lucy Stone," snapped Sue, her dark eyes flashing angrily. "You know perfectly well you eat everything you're served when you're the guest."

"Be reasonable, Sue. This was an awful lot of food. Absolutely delicious . . ."

There were nods all around.

". . . but a body can only manage so much."

"I don't think you like my cooking. You didn't eat my Better-Than-Sex Brownies, either."

"I would have but Ted ate them all before I got a chance," joked Lucy, feeling rather green about the gills.

"You've been listening to that Chris Cashman, that's what it is. All that nonsense about cholesterol and calories and nuts are the new broccoli."

"Sue, this is ridiculous," said Lucy, standing up. She knew if she continued to sit there she'd throw up on the table. "I'm just not feeling well. It has nothing to do with Chris or you or your cooking. It's probably the flu. Now, if you don't mind, I have to go home."

"Well, I do mind," said Sue. "You're ruining my barbecue."

"I'm sorry," said Lucy. Hoping to convince her that her distress was real, she added, "Maybe it's a delayed reaction from finding Mimi yesterday."

"Well, if you're going to investigate, I know where you can start. You should have heard what your good buddy Chris had to say about Mimi yesterday at the bake sale. She was really ticked that Mimi reported her home business to the planning board."

"I know," chuckled Lucy, immediately realizing she'd made a mistake. Sue's radar would zero in on this little blip.

"You've already talked to her?" snapped Sue.

"She called to tell me how much the sale made," said Lucy, rising to the bait.

"And how much was that?"

"Twelve hundred dollars."

"Well, we could have made more if she'd only let me bring my brownies." Sue's eyes gleamed mischievously. "In fact, I wouldn't be surprised if Chris was the murderer."

"Oh, don't be ridiculous," said Lucy, heartily sick of Sue. She wanted to get home and out of her tight pedal pushers. She turned to Sid. "Thanks for having us. Everything was wonderful."

Sue pointedly ignored her, busying herself cutting another piece of cake for Toby.

In the car, with the windows open and a cool breeze blowing on her face, Lucy felt better. "I don't know what's gotten into Sue," said Bill. "She was really on your case."

"She's jealous of Chris Cashman," said Lucy.

"I didn't know you were good friends with her," said Bill.

"I'm not. It's completely irrational," replied Lucy.

She shrugged. "Maybe she's worried about Sid's job. He works for Fred Stanton, doesn't he?"

"I asked him about that," said Bill. "He says the work schedule hasn't changed. Fred's going full-speed ahead."

Lucy sat quietly, digesting this bit of information along with her huge meal as they followed the winding road that ran along the shore, high above the rocks and seething water below.

"Mom, look, there's Tommy," said Zoe.

He was walking along the side of the road with his head down, shoulders hunched and hands in pockets. He didn't seem to have any sense of purpose but was just shuffling along, giving the occasional pebble a half-hearted kick.

"Can we give you a ride?" asked Bill, yelling out the window as he slowed the car.

Startled, Tommy looked up, then shook his head. His face was red and puffy, as if he'd been crying.

"Are you sure?"

Tommy nodded and there was nothing they could do but drive on. "I feel awful for him," said Lucy, turning to watch his sad little figure straggling aimlessly along the empty road.

"Me, too," said Bill.

Chapter 9

Weeks with Monday holidays were always hell at the *Pennysaver* and this week was worse than usual because of Mimi's murder. Ted was already working the phone trying to track down Lieutenant Horowitz when Lucy got to work on Tuesday morning.

"You won't get anything from him, anyway," said Lucy, when he slammed down the receiver in frustration.

"Then I can write 'no comment' which is a lot better than 'was unavailable for comment.'"

"What exactly is the difference?" inquired Phyllis, who was entering some last-minute classified ads into the computer.

"'No comment' means you at least got to talk to the guy; 'unavailable for comment' means he won't even bother to speak to you. It's a bigger put down," said Lucy, who was flipping through her mail. There were lots of press releases but no anonymous letter; maybe the writer was busy over the holiday weekend. Or maybe, she realized with a start, Mimi was the writer. And if Fred had discovered the letters, it might have precipitated a fight that ended with her death.

"Thanks for that insight, Lucy," said Ted, interrupting her train of thought. "Just for that you get to write Mimi Stanton's obit."

"That's not fair," protested Lucy, but Ted was already out the door.

"I guess he showed you," said Phyllis. "He's unavailable for comment."

"Maybe Fred will be, too," said Lucy, punching in the Stantons's number. She hated interviewing bereaved family members; it was the hardest part of a reporter's job and it was always worse when the deceased died suddenly, like in a car crash. The absolute worst, of course, was when the deceased was a victim of violence, like Mimi, and you suspected her husband of being the murderer.

"Hello." The voice was male, but Lucy wasn't sure if it was Fred or Preston or some other family member.

"This is Lucy Stone, at the *Pennysaver*. Could I speak to Fred Stanton, please?"

"Speaking."

"I'm sorry. I didn't recognize your voice," began Lucy. "Let me begin by telling you how sorry I am for your loss. We'll all miss Mimi."

"Right." Fred's tone was curt. Maybe he was limiting himself to one-word answers because he was afraid of breaking down or maybe he wasn't going to be missing Mimi much at all. Lucy couldn't tell.

"I mostly need basic facts for the obituary," said Lucy, keeping her voice gentle and soothing. "Let's begin with her maiden name."

"Mary Catherine O'Toole."

After she went over the spelling, apologizing profusely for being such a stickler, she asked for information about Mimi's parents and place of birth.

"Boston."

"She was born in Boston," repeated Lucy, giving him a chance to correct her if necessary, "and her parents?"

"Don't know," he said, cutting her off.

"You don't know who your wife's parents were?" persisted Lucy.

"Never met 'em." Fred sounded defensive.

"Sisters? Brothers?"

"No," he answered, raising his voice.

"So you and the two boys are the only survivors?"

"Why do you want to know?" Fred's tone was becoming hostile.

"It's just a formality. It's always included in an obituary."

"How long is this going to take?" he asked abruptly.

"I have quite a list of questions. It's a summation of her whole life, you know."

"I don't have time for this."

"But don't you want people to know about her life? What she did, what was important to her?"

"No." He paused. "And don't go bothering my boys either."

"Oh, I wouldn't . . ." began Lucy, but the line had gone dead.

The usual trick in that case was to call back immediately and say the line must have been disconnected but Lucy didn't think it would work. Fred wasn't going to talk to her. Luckily, there were plenty of other people who knew Mimi, like her colleagues at town hall, but it would take forever to track them down.

Lucy had to finish up the obituary on Wednesday which, in addition to being deadline day, was the first day of school. The school year wasn't getting off to a great start, at least not in the Stone household. Sara and Zoe were running late, and the fact that the school bus now stopped over at Prudence Path instead of at the end of their driveway meant they couldn't count on the driver honking and waiting for them as she had in the past.

"Girls! You've got to get over to the bus stop NOW!" yelled Lucy, who was nervously keeping an eye on the Regulator clock in the kitchen.

A desultory series of thumps announced Zoe's arrival at the foot of the back stairs. She was wearing her brand new back-to-school outfit, a pink track suit just like the ones Britney and Jessica wore.

"Do you have a T-shirt on underneath?" asked Lucy, who knew it was going to be another hot day. "You'll roast if you can't take off that hoodie."

"I'm not going to take it off."

"Okay," said Lucy, who had learned to pick her battles. "Whatever. Have you got your lunch? And where's your sister?"

"She's in the bathroom."

Lucy pounded up the stairs and found Sara leaning over the bathroom sink, applying mascara with leisurely strokes punctuated with long pauses to examine the effect she was creating.

"You're going to miss the bus—you'll have to finish that at school."

"The school bathrooms smell."

"I don't care. You have got to go. Now."

"You could drive us," said Sara, slowly screwing the top of the mascara tube.

"In your dreams. GO!"

She gave Sara a shove towards the stairs but she detoured into her bedroom.

"What now?"

"I need my book bag."

Peering into the bedroom the girls shared, Lucy saw no sign of a book bag.

"Where is it?"

"I don't know. I can't remember where I put it."

"When exactly was this?" inquired Lucy.

"Last June."

"There's no time. We'll look for it later. You have to go."

"I'll get in trouble."

"Maybe you should have thought of that yesterday," said Lucy, reaching for her final card. "I will not drive you. If you miss the bus you will be late or absent. Is that how you want to start your high school career?"

"Okay, I'm going, Mom."

Sara managed the stairs with the speed of a death row prisoner taking the last mile, but eventually she made it down to the kitchen and out the door with her sister. Lucy stood for a moment, savoring the view of the two departing girls, then turned back to the counter to pour herself a celebratory cup of coffee. That's when she noticed Sara's lunch still sitting on the counter. Grabbing it, she ran after them, catching up just as they joined the group of parents and children waiting for the bus. All the Prudence Path moms were there, except for Chris, whose kids were still too young for school.

Sara wasn't all that pleased to see her. "Mom, I don't want it," she hissed, reluctantly taking the bright red insulated bag Lucy had bought for her. "The cheerleaders all buy lunch."

"We didn't discuss this . . ." began Lucy, but thought better of continuing in front of the entire neighborhood. She suspected the cheerleaders didn't eat lunch at all, probably subsisting on diet soda from the controversial machine that some parents were trying to have removed from the cafeteria, but this wasn't the time to go into that. She pulled a couple of crumpled dollar bills from her pocket and gave them to Sara just as the big yellow bus came into view. There was a flurry of hugs and kisses and waves and then the kids were all aboard, the door closed, and they were on their way.

The women stood about awkwardly, occasionally casting glances towards the Stanton house at the end of the cul-de-sac. Mimi's murder was on everybody's mind but nobody wanted to be the first to bring it up.

"It's been a long summer," said Willie, speaking to nobody in particular.

"You can say that again," agreed Frankie, determined to be friendly.

Willie pointedly ignored her, practically turning her back on her in a way that excluded her from the circle. "Summer vacation is too long. The kids get bored after the first few weeks."

"I can't believe my girls are in kindergarten,"

said Bonnie, dabbing at her eyes with a tissue. "They're still babies."

"School is the best thing that ever happened to mothers," said Frankie. "Trust me."

"She's right," added Lucy. "Lydia Volpe, the kindergarten teacher, is an old friend of mine. Your girls will love her."

"I'm going to miss them," wailed Bonnie.

"You'll be surprised how fast the time goes. They'll be home before you know it," said Lucy.

"Anyone for coffee?" asked Frankie. "I just made a fresh pot. I thought Bonnie might need a little coffee and sympathy."

Willie recoiled, as if Frankie had suggested something improper, but Bonnie accepted the invitation eagerly. Lucy reluctantly declined. She'd love to hear what the women thought of Mimi's murder but she didn't have time. It was deadline day and she had to finish that darned obituary.

"That was a nice tribute you wrote about Mimi," said Officer Barney Culpepper, easing his big frame next to Lucy in the pew. They, and a couple hundred other people, were attending Mimi's funeral mass on Thursday morning in Our Lady of Hope church.

"Thanks, Barney. I did my best. You were a big help," said Lucy, looking around the packed church. "Funny, I didn't think she knew that many people."

"It's 'cause o' the way she died," said Barney. "They all come out of the woodwork for a murder." He sighed. "She was a nice lady. Everybody at the station liked her. Felt sorry for her, you know, 'cause of her husband. Now I'm not sayin' he hit her or anything but some men don't have to, if you know what I mean. They get their wives scared and keep 'em scared, always afraid he'll lose his temper." Barney shifted in the pew, which groaned under his weight. "But lately, things seemed to be looking up for her. She seemed happier, more relaxed. The boys were older and more independent, they had that nice new house and, well, Fred's business was doin' better. I don't care what people say, 'bout money not mattering, believe me, it matters. I've seen a lot of tragic situations that coulda been avoided if people coulda got a night out, gone on a vacation, fixed the car. You know?"

Lucy nodded. She knew.

"And now, jus' when she was starting to enjoy life a little, she goes and gets herself killed." He shook his head mournfully and his jowls quivered. "T'rr'ble."

The organ music stopped and everyone stood as Fred Stanton and his sons entered through a side door and took their seats in the front pew. All three were wearing somber expressions, new suits, and fresh haircuts; Mimi would have been proud. The congregation began singing a hymn and, as she struggled to follow the unfamiliar tune, Lucy's mind wandered. She wondered if Mimi had ever seen the men in her family all dressed up, all at the same time. She wondered why Fred and the boys seemed to be the only family Mimi had. Was she an only child? What happened to her parents? What was her marriage to Fred really like? Did he really not know anything about her life before she met him, or was he hiding something? What was he really feeling? she wondered, as the music stopped and he followed the priest's instructions to kneel in prayer, only feet away from his wife's body.

Thunderous organ chords announcing the final hymn broke into Lucy's reverie and she stood with the rest of the congregation. When the hymn ended, the priest blessed the congregation, then the pallbearers from the funeral home hoisted the coffin onto their shoulders and carried it down the aisle, accompanied by somber chords from the organ. Fred and the boys followed the coffin while everyone waited to be released by the ushers, pew by pew. It was a slow process and, since Lucy and Barney were sitting in the back of the church, they were among the last to leave the church and join the throng gathered on the sidewalk.

"Are you going to the cemetery?" asked Barney, smoothing his graying brush cut with his hand before replacing his cap.

"I don't think so," said Lucy, who hated standing by that gaping hole in the ground and watching as the coffin was lowered and the ritual handfuls of earth were thrown in. It was an all-too-graphic reminder that death was inescapable.

Barney doffed his hat and headed for his police car, which would lead the procession with lights flashing. Lucy joined Willie and Bonnie, who were chatting together on the church lawn.

"It was a lovely service," Lucy said.

"If you like that sort of thing," snorted Willie. "I sure don't want a lot of people crying over me. I told Scratch to cremate me when I go and toss my ashes on the compost heap where they'll do some good."

"You know, there's a company that can take people's ashes and turn them into diamonds," said Frankie, joining the group. "I think that's what I'd like. Turn me into a sparkling gem."

"Who would wear such a thing?" asked Willie, a shocked expression on her face.

"My daughter, my sisters."

"Yuck. That's disgusting," insisted Bonnie. "I think a traditional funeral is best: music, flowers, sobbing mourners."

"Not too many sobbing mourners here today," observed Lucy. "It seems that most people came out of curiosity rather than grief."

"I think a lot of people wanted to get a look at that husband of hers," said Willie.

"Do you really think he did it?" asked Lucy.

"Yes!" chorused Bonnie and Willie. Frankie didn't join the chorus and Lucy wondered if the rumors about her and Fred were true.

"The husband is always the most likely suspect," said Lucy, hoping to get the gossip flowing by priming the pump, "but we all know that Mimi could be awfully bitchy. She made a lot of enemies."

"I liked her fine until she reported me to the health department for keeping a farm animal in my living room," muttered Willie. "As if Lily were some sort of hog or something. Why she's cleaner than most people I know."

"She got me in trouble, too," confessed Frankie. "Renee had a few friends over after school and she called the cops saying it was an unsupervised party. They sent a social worker to question me and decide if I'm a fit mother."

"That seems a bit extreme," observed Lucy.

"Tell me about it. I was furious, but I couldn't

let on because they could take Renee from me and put her in foster care. It was terrifying."

"I know exactly what you mean," said Bonnie. Her tone was so intense that they all turned to look at her, expecting a real horror story, but that was all she said.

"Don't tell me she left you alone," said Frankie, raising an eyebrow.

"Not at all," stammered Bonnie. "But it wasn't a big deal. She just came over and told us we had to register our cars in Maine. We had Massachusetts plates, you see. And of course, we knew that but, well, you know how it is when you're busy." She blushed. "It was a helpful reminder, really."

"I'd call it being a busybody," said Lucy. "So do you think there's going to be some sort of collation at the house?"

"If there is I'm not going," said Frankie. "I've got to show a house."

Willie sniffed, as if showing a house was somehow unseemly. "I've got a new riding student coming in half an hour. I've got to get changed and get over to the stable."

"I'd go," said Bonnie, "but I don't think they've planned anything. The minister, I mean priest, didn't mention it and they usually do, don't they?"

"They do," agreed Lucy, whose eye was caught by an extremely unkempt man hovering around the edge of the thinning crowd. He was obviously out of place, with his long hair, shaggy beard, and ragged green Army jacket and people were beginning to notice him. Lucy watched as one older man, dressed in a gray suit, registered his presence. He reacted by taking his wife's hand—she was a trim woman with white hair dressed in a blue linen dress—and leading her to the car. As others did the same thing, the stranger was left standing all alone, beneath the white statue of the Virgin Mary that stood in front of Our Lady of Hope church.

The symbolism wasn't lost on Lucy and she approached him, intending to offer help. As she drew closer she saw that he was in a genuinely sorry state. Bits of leaves and twigs clung to his hair and beard, the sleeves of his jacket were frayed at the cuff and there were holes in both elbows, and his hands and face were filthy. She could tell because the tears running down his face left tracks in the grime.

"Is there something I can do for you?" she asked, fumbling in her purse for her wallet. "Do you need money?"

The man stood staring at her for a moment, then shook his head.

"Are you looking for someone here in town?"

He didn't say anything but began to shake so violently that Lucy thought he must be having an attack of some kind.

"I'll call for help," she said, pulling out her cell phone. She flipped it open and dialed 9-1-1, but when the dispatcher answered, the man was already running along the front of the church.

"There's a man in some sort of distress at Our Lady of Hope," said Lucy, flipping the phone shut and following him. When she got to the corner of the building, however, there was no sign of him. He must have disappeared into the woods behind the church. Lucy considered following him there, but decided against it. For one thing, she didn't know him and he might be irrational, even violent. A lot of homeless people were and that's what this man seemed to be. But, in truth, Lucy wasn't afraid of him; she was sorry for him. Whoever he was, he seemed to be the most sincerely grief-stricken of all the mourners at Mimi's funeral.

She was walking back to her car when the cruiser arrived and she pointed out the path the man had taken. "We've had some other calls," the cop told her, after she described the man. "So far he hasn't broken any laws so there isn't much we can do."

"What about protective custody?"

"He'd have to be a danger to himself or others," said the cop.

"Right," said Lucy, watching as he drove off. She had a feeling that whoever this guy was, he was connected to Mimi, which meant he was either dangerous or in danger himself.

Chapter 10

Phyllis took one look at Lucy's face when she got back to the office after the funeral and handed her the box of tissues. "That's why I hate funerals," she said, looking up from the stack of press releases she was filing in chronological order. "They're just so damn depressing."

"And she was so young. Only thirty-nine," added Ted, who was paying bills.

"I was thinking," sniffled Lucy, dabbing at her eyes, "how proud Mimi would be of her boys in their suits and haircuts and she probably never saw them like that." Lucy was really crying now and Phyllis got up and enveloped her in a big Jean Nate-scented hug. "She never got to see them graduate from high school or get married or have kids of their own."

"I know. I know," said Phyllis, patting her on the back.

"And it isn't like she had cancer or something that wasn't anybody's fault," continued Lucy. "Somebody killed her. Stabbed her. Who could do something like that? Why would they do it?"

"From what I've heard, everybody thinks it was

her husband," said Ted, looking very somber. "In fact, that's what I'm writing my editorial about this week. The nationwide increase in domestic violence and how we're not immune from it even here in Tinker's Cove."

Lucy wiped her face and blew her nose, pulling herself together, and went over to her desk. "I don't know why I'm acting like this," she said. "I didn't even like her and she sure wasn't popular with her neighbors on Prudence Path. But I saw this man, he looked like he's been living in the woods, and he looked really sad. Much sadder even than Fred and the boys. He was crying." Lucy shrugged. "Maybe grief is catching. Maybe I caught it from him."

"You know, I think I saw that guy yesterday," said Phyllis. "He's got long hair and a beard and wears one of those olive green Army jackets?"

"That's the one," said Lucy. "He looks like a homeless person."

"Could be. I saw him hanging around the back of the IGA, near the Dumpsters."

"Probably looking for food," said Lucy, shuddering at the thought.

"I always expect to see homeless people when I go to Boston or some other big city, but not in Tinker's Cove," said Ted. "Here we take care of each other."

By and large he was right, thought Lucy. Foreclosures and evictions were a thing of the past since several churches and social service agencies had gotten together and formed a committee that provided financial assistance to people who needed occasional help with rent or mortgage payments. They'd discovered it made a lot more sense, and was a lot more economical, to help people stay in their homes instead of helping them find scarce affordable housing after they'd been evicted.

"He must have some connection to Mimi," said Phyllis. "Otherwise why would he go to her funeral?"

"That's what I can't figure out," said Lucy. "Fred said Mimi had no family except for him and the boys."

"Even if he is some long-lost relation, how would he have heard?" asked Phyllis. "It's not like he's a subscriber to the *Pennysaver*."

"There was a brief in the *Sunday Globe*," said Ted, referring to the Boston paper. "Homeless people use discarded newspapers for bedding, for padding their clothes when it's cold, for stopping holes in their shoes—he could've seen it."

"So how'd he get here?" asked Lucy. "Hitchhike? I wouldn't pick him up."

"Some trucker might've been glad for some company on a long overnight haul. Or maybe he took the bus. He could have got the fare panhandling."

"I wish I could have talked to him," said Lucy. "Maybe I could have helped him. He seemed really upset."

"You better be careful, Lucy. He might be crazy," said Phyllis. "Forgot to take his meds and found himself at a fu . . ."

Phyllis was talking but nobody could hear a word she said thanks to the fire truck that was screaming down the street, horn honking and siren blaring. It was followed by an ambulance and a couple of police cars. As soon as they'd passed, Ted raised the volume on the scanner and as the wail of the siren receded they heard the dispatcher announce the Stantons' home address.

"I'll go," said Lucy, grabbing her purse.

Ted was so absorbed in his editorial that he didn't object. "Let me know what's happening," he said.

"I will, just as soon as I know," promised Lucy.

When she got to Prudence Path, the little cul-de-sac was filled with emergency vehicles. The sound of their throbbing diesel engines and rhythmic flash of their roof lights triggered Lucy's emotions; these accompaniments to disaster never failed to fill her with dread and she found her pace slowing as she approached the Stanton house on foot. An officer had been stationed at the end of the road and was turning everyone away, so Lucy had parked in her own driveway and taken the path through the lilac bushes that separated her property from the Prudence Path development.

As was usual on a weekday, the street was deserted. Only Bonnie and Chris, along with Pear and Apple, were standing at the edge of the Stantons' driveway and Lucy approached them. "What's going on?" she asked.

"Tommy Stanton tried to kill himself," whispered Bonnie.

Lucy wasn't surprised, she realized, which meant that on some level she'd been expecting Tommy to do something like this.

"When they got back from the funeral I went over to see if there was anything I could do for them. I was there when Preston went in his room and found him."

"How awful," breathed Lucy.

"He was barely alive," replied Bonnie. "They're still working on him, trying to resuscitate him."

"What did he take?" asked Chris, who had Apple on her hip and was pushing Pear back and forth in her stroller.

"Nothing. He hung himself."

Lucy was sick with horror—and guilt. She'd sensed Tommy's desperation and unhappiness, but she hadn't actually given it much thought. She was like a person who hears a gunshot and thinks it's a car backfiring.

Chris gave Apple a squeeze and buried her nose in her soft, blond hair. "The funeral must have been too much for him."

Lucy remembered the night she'd given him Gatorade and how grateful he'd been for such a small kindness. She wished they'd insisted he get in the car when they passed him on the road after Sue's cookout and she couldn't put the image of his skinny, hunched body out of her mind. He'd looked so fragile and alone then. Maybe if they'd reached out to him it would have been enough to tip the balance and he wouldn't have felt so desperate.

"I hope he makes it," she said.

"It's in God's hands," said Bonnie.

"God and the rescue squad," said Chris. It seemed a long time before the porch door opened and a couple of EMTs emerged pushing and pulling a stretcher. Tommy's prone figure was hooked up to an IV and his face was uncovered.

"He's alive at least," said Bonnie, echoing Lucy's thoughts.

She knew those were good signs and she hoped Tommy was out of the woods. At the same time, she feared he might have suffered irreversible brain damage. They continued to watch as the stretcher containing his motionless body was loaded into the ambulance and Lucy's mind flashed back to a similar scene the day his mother died.

"The rescue squad is here too often," she said.

"It's always the Stantons," said Bonnie, a hint of resentment in her voice.

"They sure are unlucky," said Chris.

Lucy didn't contradict her, but she doubted that bad luck had anything to do with it. Something was seriously wrong in the Stanton household and Lucy was determined to find out what it was before it grew out of control and engulfed the whole neighborhood.

"Tell me about Tommy, if you can," said Lucy, remembering her job and pulling out her notebook.

"Well," began Bonnie, "Buck says he's a bit of a loner . . ."

The words sent a chill up her spine. How often had she heard them used to describe a killer, some sociopath who'd gone on a murder spree? Was Tommy like that? Had he killed his mother as the result of some stupid argument and then been so filled with remorse that he killed himself?

Lucy couldn't shake that thought as she re-traced her steps down Prudence Path and along the winding path through the lilacs to home. Teen-agers were so emotional and so unpredictable, and movies and video games were so permeated with violence that it was no wonder they reached for a knife or gun when frustrated. Lucy had heard of instances where teens killed parents for refusing to allow them to attend a rock concert, or for making them go to church. And then there were the school shootings that seemed to occur with sickening regularity ever since Columbine. She was convinced that all this youthful anger was a symptom that something was wrong, but she wasn't sure exactly what. Maybe teenage boys should be sent off to live in a hut with tribal elders until they were deemed fit to marry and assume their place in society, as was the custom with some primitive tribes. There were certainly times when she'd wished she could hand her own son, Toby, off to some wise shaman who would teach him the secrets of manhood. Bill had certainly tried, but like most kids, Toby had found it hard to take advice from his father when his father was the very same person he was trying to separate himself from in order to establish his own identity.

There had to be a better way than the present system of intense peer pressure in high school combined with the stress of academics and college admission, she thought, as she climbed the porch steps and went into the kitchen. A minute or two later Willie's car turned into the drive and Sara climbed out. "What's going on?" Sara asked, bursting into the kitchen. "There's a police car at Tommy's house."

Lucy took a deep breath. "Tommy tried to kill himself."

Sara was stunned. Her mouth dropped and she sat staring straight ahead, speechless. Lucy felt like kicking herself for not taking a gentler approach.

"I shouldn't have sprung it on you like that," she said, squeezing her daughter's shoulders. "I'm sorry."

Sara's eyes widened. "Is he dead?"

"No. His brother found him in time, at least that's what I heard. He was alive when they took him away in the ambulance."

"So he'll be okay, right?"

"I hope so. There could be brain damage and he could have broken his neck."

"Broken his neck?"

"He tried to hang himself."

Sara's face went white and her knees began to buckle. Lucy quickly pulled out a kitchen chair for her to sit on and shoved her head between her knees. In a minute or two she sat up but her color hadn't improved. "That's sick. I can't believe he'd do that."

"I noticed he seemed pretty unhappy even before his mother died," said Lucy, dragging another chair out from under the table and sitting next to Sara. "I've been hearing rumors that the JV football players are getting bullied and hazed a lot. I wouldn't be surprised if his mother's death was the straw that broke the camel's back and he just couldn't go on anymore."

Sara was silent and Lucy knew she had to find a way to get her to open up.

"If there is hazing and you know about it, you have to speak up. What if some other kid decides to kill himself? How would you feel then?"

"C'mon, Mom. Tommy was screwed up, right?"

"So it's his fault he tried to hang himself?"

"Well, nobody did it to him, did they?"

"I think we all bear some responsibility, everybody who knew him."

"How could they know he'd do something like this?" she demanded, her face flushed with anger.

Aha, thought Lucy. She'd finally hit a nerve. "Who couldn't have known?" she asked.

"The varsity guys."

"All of them?"

"Pretty much," admitted Sara. "It's what guys do. No big deal." Sara shrugged, and then, to Lucy's amazement, began sobbing.

"Oh, honey," she cooed, wrapping her arms around her but Sara shrugged out of her hug, wiping her eyes.

"I'm being stupid. I don't know what came over me."

"You have a right to your feelings," said Lucy. "If you can't trust yourself, who can you trust?"

Sara sighed and paused, as if weighing her options. Finally she spoke. "Some of the players got a little obnoxious today after practice, that's all."

"What do you mean?" asked Lucy. It was gradually dawning on her that Sara was upset about more than Tommy's attempted suicide. "Did they do something to you?"

Sara looked at the ceiling. "They kind of cornered a few of us, me and Sassie and Renee, and well, Renee's really busty and they wanted to know if her boobs were real so they made me squeeze them and say if they were."

Lucy was appalled. "You did that?"

"Renee said it was okay."

"And where was the coach during all this?"

Sara shrugged. "I don't know."

"Does this sort of thing happen a lot?"

"No, Mom." She was on her feet. "I don't want to talk about it anymore." Then she flounced out of the room and pounded up the back stairs to her bedroom.

Lucy's emotions were in turmoil and she dashed after her, catching her in the upstairs hallway. "I think we have to talk about it," she said, grabbing her by the shoulder and spinning her around. "This is serious."

Sara was so shocked by her mother's unusual behavior that she simply stood in the tiny hallway as if waiting for her to regain her senses. Lucy was too upset for that, though. She was out of control.

"You're going to quit cheerleading, that's what you're going to do," she said, waggling a finger at her daughter.

Sara shook her head. "No, I'm not and you can't make me."

"Oh, yes I can," insisted Lucy. "Just you see."

Then she whirled around and marched down the stairs, determined to give Coach Burkhart a piece of her mind. She didn't like the way the football team was run and she was going to let him know exactly what she thought. The players had no business harassing cheerleaders and the coaches had a responsibility to protect the girls from that sort of behavior. It was insulting, it was demeaning. It was unsportsmanlike, that's what it was. She was panting and red-faced when she crossed the tiny square of emerald green lawn punctuated by a dwarf Japanese maple and knocked on the Burkharts' door.

Luckily for her, she thought, and unluckily for him, the coach answered the door.

"I just want to let you know," she began, spitting out the words faster than she could think, "that I am absolutely disgusted by the behavior of the football players towards my daughter and the other cheerleaders and I happen to have good reason to think this sort of thing is not only tolerated but encouraged and you ought to know better!"

The coach folded the newspaper he had been reading and tucked it under his arm. "Why don't you come in?" he suggested. "We can talk inside."

"You just want to get me inside to shut me up and I'm not going to shut up," proclaimed Lucy. "I want everybody to hear."

Coach Buck nodded. Over the years he'd developed a few tactics for dealing with angry parents and had learned that direct confrontation was to be avoided at all costs. "Fine, fine. We can talk here. Now what exactly is the problem?"

"You know exactly what I'm talking about. All this pretending that hazing doesn't exist when you know it does. I know Tommy was having a rough time . . ."

Coach Buck nodded his head sympathetically. "We're all upset about Tommy, but it wasn't hazing. It was his family that was the problem and there's only so much the school can do in a situation like this."

Lucy realized she'd let her emotions carry her away but she was too angry to yield the ground entirely so she backtracked. "What about what happened today? To the cheerleaders? Did you know that some of the older players cornered them and wanted to know if their breasts were real?" she demanded, challenging him.

"That is certainly deplorable behavior and I certainly don't condone it," he said, giving Lucy encouragement. He paused, apparently deep in thought, then asked, "Did one of the players actually touch the girls' breasts?"

"Well, no," admitted Lucy, a bit deflated. "They made one of the girls do it."

"Well, then, it was one of the girls who actually harassed the others, wasn't it?"

Lucy couldn't believe it. This was the classic tactic of blaming the victim. "Where were you? If you'd been doing your job there'd be no opportunity for this kind of thing, would there?"

"I can assure you that I make every effort to supervise the players and I'm going to take immediate action and get to the bottom of this. If what you say is true, I can assure you that the offenders will be punished."

Lucy knew how these things worked. First thing tomorrow he would call the girls to his office to question them. They'd be embarrassed and humiliated and in the end it would be their fault, not the players.

"I don't think that will be necessary," she said. "But thank you for the offer."

The coach's expression oozed concern. "Are you certain?"

Lucy knew she'd lost the battle. "Absolutely. And I'm sorry for bothering you."

"That's perfectly all right," he said. "That's what I'm here for. Now, have a nice day."

Lucy's anger had subsided into a simmering resentment when she left Coach Burkhart's house and she paused for a moment before turning onto Prudence Path to look at the Stantons' house. Its situation at the end of the cul-de-sac made it a

focal point for the entire development and, building for himself, Fred Stanton had lavished extra
care on its construction. The house was larger and
grander than the others with a two-car garage and
a large, landscaped lawn enclosed by a fence. She
was starting down the road when a movement
caught her eye; someone was running along the
fence.

Curious, she turned in the opposite direction and
walked towards the Stantons's house but, when
she got to the end of the cul-de-sac, the fleeing figure had vanished. Who was it? she wondered. Certainly not Fred or Preston, they would be at the
hospital with Tommy. She stood, searching for a
trace of the trespasser, when she spotted a figure
standing at the edge of the woods. It was the homeless man, or at least she thought it was, from the
brief glimpse she got before he disappeared into
the shadows.

Chapter 11

Lucy's spirits were low as she made her way home on the path that wound through the lilac bushes. So much had happened in such a short period of time that she felt completely overwhelmed. Mimi's murder and the funeral had been depressing and frightening, but Tommy's suicide attempt had totally unnerved her because she felt she bore some responsibility for it. She'd known he was troubled but she hadn't really tried to help him.

But what could she have done? Tears sprang to her eyes and she leaned against a tall pine tree, pounding her fist against its rough bark in frustration. This was one situation where she could see the problem but was unable to act. It was like being in a maze—she was constantly finding herself at dead ends.

She knew that Tommy was unhappy on the football team, but when she spoke to his father he wouldn't hear of it. She knew hazing was taking place, but when she complained to Coach Buck he had shifted the blame right back onto Sara and the other cheerleaders. If was quite clear to her that if she pursued the story, it would be the victims who suffered and not the perpetrators. And, finally, there was the elusive figure of the homeless man. She was certain he was connected to Mimi and suspected he might hold the key to her murder, but he remained just out of reach. If only she could talk to him!

Lucy sighed in frustration and rested her back against the tree. She had never felt so powerless. It was like watching some awful disaster approach and being unable to do anything to stop it. Feeling something crawling on her hand, she shook it, sending a large black ant into space. It landed on the ground near the foot of the tree and promptly righted itself and headed straight back to the tree. Lucy watched, fascinated, as the little half-inch creature made its way along the fissures in the bark, apparently determined to climb the tree.

"Okay, ant," she said, straightening her shoulders, "I get the point. You can't give up when you meet an obstacle, you have to pick yourself up and try again."

She was starting back along the path when a chickadee landed on a pine bough quite close to her, making its characteristic "dee-dee" sound. She smiled at the tiny creature's boldness, amazed that a wild creature would come so close to a much larger animal. But the chickadee wasn't at all interested in her, she realized. It was fixing its beady black eye on the ant, which was stubbornly climbing into pecking distance.

"Shoo!" exclaimed Lucy, waving her hand at the chickadee, which took flight. "Don't bother to thank me, ant," she said, hoping that whatever guiding hand was running the universe would be watching out for her well-being, too.

* * *

Another anonymous letter was waiting for Lucy when she got to work on Friday morning, detailing the same incident that had upset Sara. Not only was the letter proof positive that the writer was telling the truth, it also demolished her theory that Mimi was the writer. It was just her bad luck, she thought, that now she knew beyond doubt that the writer was telling the truth that she would have to give up following the story. Ted would never let her continue now that Sara was involved.

"You're too close, too involved," he would say, and that's exactly what he did say when Lucy told him how the players had harassed Sara and the other freshman cheerleaders.

"But we have to follow this story," she argued. "The letter writer's account is virtually the same as Sara's."

"That's just one incident," said Ted. "We have no verification that the rest—the naked Twister, the soccer balls—happened. We only have the anonymous writer's word for those."

"C'mon, Ted. How many times have you told me that where there's smoke there's fire? Something is definitely going on and I have a hunch it was part of the reason Tommy Stanton tried to kill himself." Lucy paused. "I know everybody thinks he was upset because of his mother and that's true, I'm sure, but he was pretty messed up even before that. I saw him one night after a required run and he was awfully strung out."

Ted was scratching his chin. "I could write the story," he said slowly, "but I'd have to interview Sara."

"Do you have to use her name?"

"I might," said Ted.

Lucy bit her lip. It was a dilemma she'd faced before. How could she insist on preserving her family's privacy when she asked people to tell their stories for publication every day? It would be hypocritical to insist on keeping Sara's name out of the paper when she wrote about other people's personal problems all the time. Why, the paper even printed an annual list of real estate tax delinquents in a blatant effort to embarrass them into paying up, and the court report listed everyone who got into trouble, from housewives who accidentally wrote a bad check at the grocery store to upright citizens who insisted on finishing that expensive bottle of wine at the Queen Vic and then attempted to drive home.

Her instinct was to protect Sara, of course, but she understood that refusing to go public about the hazing would be more dangerous in the long run because it would continue. The only way to stop it was for victims to come forward, and she knew that when one person came forward it often encouraged others to tell their stories, too.

"I'll understand if you don't want to do this," said Ted.

"I do want to get it out in the open, believe me, but I don't think Sara will go along with it and I don't blame her. She has to face those kids every day."

"Now that the Warriors have won a few games, most people in town think the coach walks on water and the team are his disciples," said Phyllis. "Even Elfrida was raving about what a terrific quarterback Matt Engelhardt is and until now the only sport she had any interest in was curling." Seeing

Ted and Lucy's puzzled expressions she continued. "Her husband's a curling fanatic."

"You're right. People are already talking about how they might take the Moose Bowl this year," said Ted.

"There has to be a way of approaching this that makes the administration the focus, not the kids. We need to go right to the top."

"Well," said Phyllis, who was typing the school calendar into the events listings, "it says here that the superintendent's monthly administrative meeting is in fifteen minutes."

"And who goes to that?" asked Ted.

Phyllis consulted the calendar. "All the principals, the guidance director, the student services director, the curriculum specialist . . . and the athletic director."

"Then let's go," he said, turning to Lucy.

As Lucy grabbed her bag and followed Ted out the back door to the parking lot, she kept one very large doubt to herself. She had a feeling the administrative meeting wasn't covered by the state's open meeting law and therefore not open to the press except by invitation.

And in fact, when they arrived at the Superintendent's office, the first words out of his secretary's mouth were, "Administrative meetings are private."

"This state has an open meeting law," said Ted.

"I have a copy of the law right here," she said, handing him several sheets of paper that had been stapled together. "I believe the relevant portion is section four paragraph five."

"I believe we can attend if we're invited," said Lucy, while Ted pored over the fine print.

"You're not invited," said the secretary.

"I'm quite sure the superintendent will want to hear what we have to say in light of the fact that some serious allegations have been raised concerning the sports program. Perhaps you could check with the superintendent?"

She picked up the phone and, a minute or two later, Superintendent Bob Sabin popped out of his office. "What can I do for you?" he asked, smiling genially.

With his reddish hair and round cheeks, Lucy always thought the superintendent looked a bit like a chipmunk. His slightly protruding front teeth added to the image, but nobody dared mention the resemblance. Sabin was a former Marine officer who turned to education when he retired after putting in his twenty years and he maintained a rigorous fitness routine that included running twenty laps around the track every morning.

The smile wasn't genuine. It was a defense he employed whenever trouble loomed. He was on alert, balancing on the balls of his feet, ready to leap into action to protect his little fiefdom, the Tinker's Cove Public Schools, from any threat, whether it be a bomb scare, bathroom graffiti, angry parents, or the teachers' union.

"It's about the football program," began Ted, planning to ease into such an uncomfortable subject.

"Allegations of hazing," said Lucy, eager to get to the point and earning an evil look from Ted for interrupting him.

"Absolutely absurd," said Sabin. "Hazing is not tolerated in the Tinker's Cove Public Schools. The student handbook is very clear on that point."

Lucy wasn't about to wait for Ted to get around to a follow-up question. "It's happening, nevertheless."

"Do you have something specific in mind?"

"Yesterday my daughter and two other cheerleaders were harassed by a group of varsity players."

Sabin seemed relieved. "One incident, while unfortunate, is hardly worthy of a *Pennysaver* story. If you will make an appointment with the assistant principal, I'm sure he will take care of it." He had shifted his weight in the direction of his office. "Thank you for bringing this to my attention and now, if you'll excuse me, I must get back to my meeting."

"It's more than one incident," said Lucy. "It appears to be a ritualized process that new players are subjected to as part of their preseason training."

"That's absurd," insisted Sabin. "On what basis are you making these accusations?"

"We've had a series of letters," said Ted.

"And one of your players attempted to kill himself," said Lucy.

"If you're referring to Tommy Stanton, I believe his situation is rather complicated . . . though, of course, I do not make a habit of discussing students' personal lives, it is no secret that his mother was murdered and that was most likely the precipitating factor."

"How can you be sure?" asked Lucy. "Tommy was obviously in serious distress long before his mother's death."

"Well, as I say, I can't discuss students' confidential records."

"I know you want to deny that this is happening but it's too late," said Lucy. "The dam is broken and pretty soon you're going to have a flood of controversy on your hands."

"She's right," said Ted. "Believe me, I've seen it happen plenty of times."

Sabin felt a definite tectonic shift and stepped quickly to regain his balance. "Over the years I've learned it's best to tackle issues like these head on, before the rumor mill gets going. I think the best approach is to hold a parent meeting to announce an investigation of these allegations, an investigation I feel sure will show them to be completely unfounded." He turned to the secretary. "Judy, check the calendar and set a date for a parent meeting."

"How soon?"

"As soon as possible."

"Next Thursday?"

"Fine." He turned to Ted and Lucy. "I trust you'll publicize this in the *Pennysaver* so we'll have a good turnout?"

"You can depend on it," said Ted, shaking his hand.

"What do you think about that?" asked Lucy as they crossed the lobby.

"Sabin's no dope. He knows he has to nip this thing in the bud or it will eat him alive."

They were standing in the shade on the school steps, looking out over the black asphalt parking area where the shiny metal cars were shimmering from heat waves.

"This isn't like Tinker's Cove," continued Ted.

"I know, it's unseasonably warm, isn't it? And I can't remember the last time it rained."

"Maybe that's it," mused Ted, shrugging and starting down the steps. "Maybe it's the heat driving everybody crazy, but it seems to me the whole town is changing for the worse. Here we've got an unsolved murder, the football team is running amok, we've got a teen suicide attempt and even a homeless guy." He shook his head. "Somehow we've lost the community spirit that made this town such a special place. I mean, look at the trouble Pam had with the Hat and Mitten Fund bake sale."

"In the end we raised more money than ever," said Lucy, following him. "We just had to use different tactics."

"That's what bothers me," said Ted, turning to face her. "Instead of depending on the people in the community, you had to go outside, to the tourists at the outlet mall. In the past, the fund got all the support it needed from local folks, but not anymore."

"I sense an editorial coming on," said Lucy, climbing into the passenger seat of his car.

"You betcha," said Ted. "And I also want you to put your investigative reporting skills to work to get this homeless guy's story."

"Righto," said Lucy, adding a little salute for emphasis.

Lucy wasn't sure her so-called investigative reporting skills were up to the task she'd been assigned, but she was determined to do her best. It was almost time to pick up Sassie and Sara when she finally cleared her desk, but she wanted to get a start on the story. She decided to begin her search where she'd last seen the homeless man, in the woods behind Prudence Path, after a quick stop at Jake's for a coffee to go and a bag of doughnuts. It worked for the Salvation Army, maybe it would work for her.

There was no sign of life when she parked her car at the end of the cul-de-sac and got out. There were no cars parked in the driveways, no kids riding around on Big Wheels or swinging on the expensive backyard play sets, no housewives gossiping as they hung the laundry out to dry. What was she thinking? she wondered. She was getting as bad as Ted. Nobody hung out laundry anymore, they all had dryers. And these days kids weren't allowed to play outside without supervision, either.

Since nobody was around to mind her trespassing, Lucy headed straight for the woods, carrying the coffee and doughnuts and cutting boldly through several backyards to the spot where she remembered seeing the homeless man. There was no sign of him today, but she did notice a faint path, probably a deer track, and she decided to follow it. The path meandered about in no particular direction but Lucy was pretty sure it would eventually lead to Blueberry Pond. She wasn't worried about getting lost, this was familiar territory to her, besides, she was in sight of the Prudence Path houses.

There wasn't a breath of wind in the woods, the birds were quiet, and the only sound was the late summer hum of cicadas. Lucy trudged along the path getting sweatier and itchier with every step and considering whether she dared take a cooling plunge in the pond when she stumbled on a rock. Looking down, she realized it was part of a fire ring and she immediately squatted down to see if the ashes were still warm. Perhaps the homeless man had been camping there within the last few hours.

The fire was cold, but she continued to squat, imagining herself in his place. The campsite was not in a clearing, in fact she would never have noticed it if she hadn't stubbed her toe on the rock, but as she looked around she eventually made out a pile of brush. Upon closer investigation she realized it was a crude shelter for sleeping. Encouraged, she searched the site for a cache of food or other personal belongings but there was no sign of either. If this was indeed the homeless man's campsite he had been very careful to make it as unobtrusive as possible. There was no sign of any empty cans or trash of any sort. Of course, she had no way of knowing if he would return or if he had moved on. She decided to leave the food and coffee, just in case. She'd come back tomorrow in hopes of catching him and she could pick up any litter then.

In the meantime, she decided the best course of action would be to question people in town. She knew he'd been spotted Dumpster-diving behind the IGA and some of the workers there might have noticed him. Or he might have been hanging around the harbor, hoping for a handout or just making conversation.

She was on her way back to the car when her cell phone rang; it was Sara.

"Mom! Where are you?"

Guilt-stricken, Lucy checked her watch. "Ohmigosh, I had no idea it was so late. I'm so sorry. I'll be right there."

"Can you hurry up? Sassie and I have been waiting for hours."

"I'll be as fast as I can," she promised, hurrying through the woods.

She was quite surprised then when she arrived

at the high school just in time to see the girls piling into Willie's big Wagoneer with numerous animal stickers plastered on the rear bumper. "You didn't need to come," she said, pulling around and coming up beside the SUV. "I was working on a story and got distracted, but I came straight over as soon as Sara called."

"This seems to happen quite a lot," said Willie, waspishly. "I understand you have a busy schedule and it's no trouble for me, really."

"My schedule is unpredictable," said Lucy, her face reddening. "But I'm never very far away. All the girls have to do is call and I can be here in a few minutes. There's no need for you to put yourself out."

"I'd rather do it myself than worry that the girls will be left hanging around."

"It was only for a few minutes," protested Lucy.

"I know you don't think you're irresponsible, Lucy, but sometimes it seems to me you're awfully casual when it comes to fulfilling your commitments."

Lucy felt as if she'd been slapped. "I don't think I'm irresponsible," she said, "but I'll certainly make sure I'm on time from now on."

"It's so important to set a good example," continued Willie. "If we want our children to be prompt we can't very well keep them waiting ourselves, can we?"

"You're absolutely right," said Lucy, who was heartily sick of the whole issue. "So to make up for today, I'll pick them up Monday."

Willie nodded in agreement but didn't look convinced as she drove off with Sara in the back seat.

Lucy followed, trying to decide if she really was irresponsible. She did have a somewhat loose approach to time, she admitted to herself. It came from years of juggling her job, a demanding one that involved deadlines, with the needs of her family. Perhaps she'd taken advantage of her family, expecting them to be flexible because deadlines weren't.

She was mulling this over as she proceeded down Main Street, following Willie's rather stately pace and fighting the urge to zoom off down a side street because that would probably be proof positive that she was irresponsible, when her cell phone rang again. This time it was Pam.

"Am I irresponsible?" asked Lucy.

"No. Why do you ask?"

"Never mind, it's not important," said Lucy. "What's up?"

"Well, Ted told me about the parent meeting and I was wondering if we ought to set up a table and sell the leftover baked goods. What do you think?"

"Sounds like a good idea."

"So you'll help?"

Lucy looked for an out. "If I don't have to cover the meeting."

"Ted said he'll do it."

Lucy was trapped and she knew it. "Okay, then," she said. "You can count on me."

Chapter 12

Prudence Path seemed to return to normal when the weekend rolled around. Coach Burkhart was mowing his lawn and keeping on eye on the twins, who were riding their bicycles up and down the street. Chris Cashman's husband, Brad, could be seen in his driveway, changing the oil in the family SUV. Snatches of pop music could be heard coming from the LaChances' deck where Renee was sunbathing. Willie was on her knees, weeding the flower bed and casting disapproving glances in Renee's direction. Only the Stanton house remained closed and silent, except for one brief excursion Sunday morning when Fred left and returned a half hour later with Tommy. After that, its inhabitants remained closeted inside.

As Lucy came and went, going about her weekend errands, she wondered what was going on behind that impressive front door. The whole town had pretty much decided that Fred was guilty, it was all anyone was talking about. The boys must have heard the rumors. What was it like for them, cooped up with him? Did they suspect him as well, or had they closed ranks against outsiders, convinced of his innocence? And when, everyone wondered, would the police get around to arresting him?

The answer came on Monday morning, when the moms and children had gathered to wait for the bus. Lucy had accompanied the girls, hoping to pick up some neighborhood gossip, and had no sooner joined the group when the entire Tinker's Cove police force of three cruisers, lights flashing but without sirens, swooped onto Prudence Path and halted in front of the Stanton house. The women fell silent, watching as four officers took up positions behind their cruisers, weapons at the ready, and two others marched up to the Stantons' front door and knocked. The door opened, there was a brief conversation and then Fred Stanton stepped out, was handcuffed and escorted without incident to one of the waiting cruisers. Then, as quickly as they had arrived, the police were gone.

"I can't say I'm surprised," said Frankie.

"I suspected him all along," said Willie. "He has such a temper."

"More than a temper," said Bonnie. "I'd call him abusive. I bet poor Mimi tried to leave and that's when he killed her."

Lucy had heard the scenario before. The cycle of abuse, the increasing tension, the explosion into violence. The abusive partner's obsessive need to control and dominate the other even to the point of murder if the victim tried to escape. Somehow it didn't quite fit.

"Mimi had friends on the police force," said Lucy. "She knew about the resources for battered women and she had plenty of support from her coworkers, she doesn't sound like an abused wife to me."

"It doesn't matter," said Bonnie, sounding uncharacteristically sure of herself. "Abuse crosses all socioeconomic lines; anyone can be a victim."

"You seem to know a lot about it," said Frankie, challenging her.

"I used to be a social worker. I've seen this sort of thing more times than I can say."

"What about Tommy? What'll happen to him?" asked Lucy.

"Now that he's out of the hospital his older brother will probably get temporary custody," answered Bonnie.

"But Preston's just a kid," said Lucy. "How can he be expected to care for a mentally unstable person?"

"He's eighteen, that makes him legally an adult."

"Besides," said Frankie. "Did you see Tommy? They've got him so drugged he could barely walk."

"I can't believe this," said Lucy. She couldn't imagine what sort of system would give an eighteen-year-old motorcycle maniac the responsibility of caring for an extremely fragile suicidal sibling. Leaving the others she walked down the street to the Stanton house and knocked on the door. Preston answered, opening the door only a few inches. He looked, she thought, meeting his dark eyes, like an animal that hadn't decided whether to defend his den or flee.

"I just wanted you to know that if you need anything, anything at all, we're right here. Just give me a call."

"We're fine."

"Well, you never know what might come up," said Lucy. "If you have any trouble I'll be more than happy to help."

"You're that reporter, right?"

"I'm here as a neighbor, that's all," said Lucy. "A concerned neighbor."

"A big nosy-body, you mean," he said. "Well you can just mind your own business and leave us alone."

"Okay," said Lucy, backing away. "I was only trying to help."

She didn't know why she bothered to say it, she was talking to a closed door. She started down the street towards home, aware that it was getting late and she really ought to get to work. But first, she decided, since she was so close to the woods she might as well take a quick look and see if the homeless man had returned to his camp. Unwilling to trespass on the Stantons' property she cut through the Cashmans' yard. Nobody was out. Chris was probably giving Pear and Apple their one hundred percent organic breakfast or prepping them for one of the day's activities.

She had no trouble finding the path and hurried along keeping her eyes out for the ring of stones she'd discovered yesterday. She soon found it but there was no sign of a recent fire. Some animal, probably a raccoon, had spilled the coffee and eaten the doughnuts, leaving the ripped paper bag stuck in a bush. Discouraged, she picked up the trash and retraced her steps, heading for home. Somehow the morning hadn't gone the way she had planned. Instead of a restorative half-hour with a cup of coffee and her own thoughts, she'd witnessed Fred Stanton's arrest. If that wasn't upsetting enough, she'd also discovered that Tommy and Preston were left to their own devices and would have to manage as best they could without either mother or father. She knew there was nothing she could do about it, but that didn't mean she had to like it.

When Lucy arrived at work an hour late, Ted was simultaneously talking on the phone, holding the receiver against his shoulder by crooking his neck, picking away at his keyboard with one hand, and waving a handful of papers at Phyllis with the other. Phyllis was also multi-tasking, talking on the phone while applying a fresh coat of Tropical Melon to her nails.

"About time you got here," he muttered to Lucy, throwing the papers down on his desk.

"The cops arrested Fred Stanton," she said. "I saw the whole thing."

"That's great," he said, covering the mouthpiece. "You can write a first person account. Then I want you to cover . . ." He held up his hand, signaling that she should wait for him to continue, and spoke into the phone. "So when do you expect we will know the tax rate?" he asked. "What do you mean, not until October? The fiscal year began July 1, didn't it?" He slapped his hand over the mouthpiece and turned to her, picking up where he had left off, ". . . the police press conference. It's at ten. When you're there you can ask them about the homeless guy—some of the fishermen found his body floating in the harbor early this morning."

Lucy sat down hard in her chair. "I can't believe it."

"If you ask me, he was an accident waiting to

happen," said Phyllis. "Wandering around town half-drunk."

"Did he drink?"

"All homeless people do, don't they? That's the reason they're homeless."

"I think that might be an oversimplification," said Lucy, recalling the extremely neat campsite she had discovered in the woods. There hadn't been a single liquor bottle.

"I guess some of them do drugs," conceded Phyllis.

"Ah, ladies, I hate to interrupt this discussion but it's almost ten."

"I'm on my way," said Lucy, grabbing her bag and rushing out the door. The bell tinkled behind her as Ted resumed his conversation with the town assessor. "So you don't actually inspect the properties to set their value but you use some sort of mathematical formula?"

Like most reporters, Lucy detested police press conferences. They always seemed to feature the same self-congratulatory parade of pompous officers reciting identical litanies of praise for each other's organizations: "We could never have brought this case to a successful conclusion without the help of Chief Zero Tolerance and his entire department . . ." and "I want to acknowledge the selfless dedication of Assistant District Attorney Got Hisman . . ." and the inevitable "Teamwork is what made the difference." These productions were as tightly scripted as the annual Oscar awards show, without even the mild suspense offered by the wait for the winners to be announced. And, like those so-called town meetings held by the president, questioning was only allowed by those who had displayed unswerving fidelity to the police community. Any reporter who included the merest hint in a news story that something wasn't quite kosher about an arrest or an investigation soon became invisible when it was time for questions.

Lucy figured today's conference would be worse than usual. It was the first since Chief Crowley's retirement and the new chief, Frank Kirwan, would be eager to strut his stuff. Nevertheless, attendance was necessary, if only to pick up the official press release, and Lucy wasn't surprised to find a crowd in the basement bomb shelter-turned-crisis management center at the police station. The Boston and Portland media, from TV to radio to newspapers, were well represented. Chief Kirwan would be pleased.

Lucy found a seat in the front and waited impatiently for the dog and pony show to begin, promising herself that she'd get out of there as soon as the press releases were distributed. She hoped that Audrey, the department secretary, had fired up the Xerox machine and was printing them out at this very moment.

But when the procession of officials began filing into the room, led by Chief Kirwan, the secretary and her pile of fresh-from-the-copier press releases were conspicuously absent. There was a collective sigh of resignation from the assembled journalists as they opened their notebooks and switched on the cameras and recorders.

It wasn't until the official square dance of thankyous and acknowledgements and hymns to cooperation had ended and the DA was answering questions that the evidence against Fred Stanton was even mentioned, and Lucy found it less than compelling. The fact that Fred's fingerprints were on the murder weapon was hardly surprising; after all it was his knife, from his house, and he might have used it to cut a ham sandwich. More interesting to Lucy was the mention that a witness reported seeing him leave the house in what the DA described as "an agitated state" on the day of the murder. Lucy had doubts about the value of that information, too. It seemed to her she left the house in an agitated state most mornings due to the fact she was often running late, or the girls were dawdling or the dog had gotten into the trash. There was always something. She raised her hand.

"Yes, there, you in the back," said the DA, pointing to her.

"I was wondering if you have any information about the body that was found in the harbor this morning? Has the man been identified and was there any foul play?"

There was a flurry of interest from the reporters, but the DA wasn't giving anything away. "No, we have not made an identification and no, there were no signs that his death was anything but an accidental drowning, but as you know it's up to the medical examiner to determine the exact cause of death."

"And when do you expect that report?" asked someone in the front row.

"That also is up to the medical examiner," said the DA. "Now, I'll take one more question before closing."

Lucy was hurrying out of the police station, finally clutching the not-very-informative official press release, when she ran into Barney Culpepper.

"Hi, Barney. How's Marge coming with the triathlon? And how's Eddie doing over there in Iraq?"

"Eddie's counting the days 'til he comes home— and so are we," he said, looking grim.

"We all are," said Lucy, who could imagine how worried they must be.

"Marge says I need to get my mind off the war. She wants me to start training with her," he said, glumly, hitching up his pants. He fastened his belt underneath his sizable belly and it tended to slip. "She's threatening to get rid of my La-Z-Boy."

"Oh, no." Lucy knew how much Barney enjoyed reclining in his favorite chair, watching football and baseball games, even golf if nothing else was on.

"She hid the remote. Said it's good for me to get up and change the channels on the TV."

"Well, maybe she has a point," said Lucy.

"Have you ever tried to switch from channel five to channel sixty-three by pushing that little up button one channel at a time?"

"Can't say I have," said Lucy, spotting an opportunity. "Listen, you can watch TV at my house if you do me one itsy bitty little favor."

"Oh, no. I can't. The new chief wouldn't like it."

"How do you know he won't like it? I haven't even told you what it is."

"C'mon, Lucy. If the chief won't mind why don't you ask him, hunh?"

"Because you're right, he'll probably mind. But I really want to know if the medical examiner has got a cause of death on that guy they pulled out of the harbor this morning."

Barney gave his jowls a thoughtful scratch. "It just happens I know somebody who works over there. Luke Martin, remember him? Good little shortstop, maybe a year or two younger than Eddie and Toby."

"He's working in the ME's office?"

"Yeah, flunked out of pre-med." Barney was already dialing the phone and, after a brief discussion of the Red Sox prospects for the Series, learned that preliminary toxicology tests had revealed a blood alcohol level of 0.19.

"So he was drunk?" asked Lucy.

"Drunk as a skunk," said Barney.

"Thanks. I owe you big time," said Lucy, blowing him a kiss and dashing for the door. She was already writing the story in her head as she hurried along the sidewalk to the *Pennysaver* office, but soon realized that apart from the *when* and *where* she didn't have the least idea as to the *who, why,* and even the *what.* The tests seemed to indicate death by misadventure due to drunkenness but Lucy had her doubts. There'd been no sign of booze at the homeless man's camp, in fact, he was extraordinarily neat and tidy for a drunken bum.

Chapter 13

When Lucy got back from the press conference, Ted had left the office and Phyllis was
stuffing subscription renewal notices into envelopes.

"How was the press conference?" she asked.

"About usual. Not very informative."

Phyllis went on folding and filling the envelopes;
she could do it in her sleep. "Have they got much
of a case against Fred?"

"Not unless they've got more evidence than they
gave at the conference," said Lucy, looking at her
with interest. "Why'd you ask?"

"Oh, I don't know," she replied with a shrug. "It
doesn't make sense to me. If your wife works for
the town and has friends in the police department
you'd have to be crazy to kill her, and I don't think
Fred is crazy. He's very shrewd. And self-interested.
He doesn't do anything unless it benefits him."

"How come you know so much about him?"

"Last year I collected donations for the Eastern
Star's benefit auction."

"Did he donate something?"

"Yeah. A closet system. But he insisted that we
feature it in our ads for the event, he specified

what size print we used for his name, and he insisted on a receipt so he could get a tax deduction."

"Doesn't everybody?"

"Well, yeah. All the donors got a receipt as a matter of course. But he demanded his right up front. He couldn't wait for the treasurer to get around to it, if you know what I mean. He hounded the poor woman to distraction over it when her husband was in the hospital for a quadruple bypass."

"I guess you'd say he's a stickler for details?"

"Oh, yeah."

"Not somebody who'd impulsively stick a kitchen knife in his wife's back?"

"No. Definitely not." Phyllis considered. "He might hire a contract killer—but he'd want a receipt for his taxes!"

Lucy chuckled. "Maybe you could be a character witness for him."

"Not likely." She gathered the envelopes together and gave them a sharp smack against her desk, creating a neat pile. "Did they say anything about the homeless guy? I keep wondering what brought him to Tinker's Cove, anyway? I mean, it's not like there's a food kitchen or a shelter, is there?"

"He was at the funeral. That's where I first saw him, anyway. I guess he must have some connection to Mimi." Lucy shrugged. "Fred said she didn't have family so maybe he was an old boyfriend or something."

"Maybe he was just a crazy guy who liked funerals." Phyllis was applying polish topcoat with all the care of Michelangelo painting the ceiling of the Sistine Chapel.

"Nobody goes to funerals for fun," said Lucy,

coming to a decision. "I'm going to call Fred's lawyer and see if Fred's ready for a visitor."

"He wouldn't talk to you before," said Phyllis, waving her hand back and forth as if conducting the Boston Symphony.

"That was before he went to jail," said Lucy. "Maybe he's lonesome."

Phyllis wasn't convinced and neither was Fred's lawyer. "The last thing I want him to do is talk to the press," said Will Esterhaus, speaking from his Portland office.

"But this is different," said Lucy. "I'm from the local paper, and there's a lot of sympathy for him here in Tinker's Cove."

"I think not," said Esterhaus. "He is charged with killing his wife, after all. I doubt there's a great deal of sympathy for him."

"Small towns have big hearts," said Lucy.

Across the room, Phyllis rolled her eyes as she unscrewed the top of a bottle of correction fluid.

Now it was Lucy's turn to roll her eyes as she thanked the attorney for his time which, she thought sourly, was all she got from him.

"You could start the listings," said Phyllis, dabbing the white fluid onto her checkbook register.

Lucy was too restless to start that job, just the thought of spending the afternoon at the computer made her legs twitch. "Not today," she said, grabbing her bag. "If the mountain won't come to Mohammed, Mohammed will have to go to the mountain."

"What's that supposed to mean?" yelled Phyllis, raising her voice to be heard over the jangling bell on the front door.

* * *

Not quite sure where to begin, Lucy drifted down Main Street toward the harbor. She intended to ask anyone she might see there if they had observed the homeless man but at eleven o'clock on Monday morning the sidewalk was practically deserted. The summer people had all gone home, the kids were back in school, and the only people peering into the shop windows seemed to be shoulder-season tourists.

She intended to talk to the fishermen at the harbor who had discovered the body but as soon as she turned the corner onto Sea Street and saw the smooth blue water of the cove, flat as a pancake, she realized her mistake. The entire fleet would be out today, taking advantage of the calm weather. Discouraged, she decided on Plan B and went back to the *Pennysaver* to get her car. There was no harm in seeing if Preston and Tommy had changed their minds and were ready to talk to a friendly neighbor.

"I already told you," said Preston, pausing to let the lawnmower idle while he mopped his sweaty forehead with the back of his hand, "we don't want to talk to nobody."

"How's Tommy doing?" asked Lucy, undeterred.

"He's fine. Okay? So just leave us alone."

"I've been wondering about that homeless guy," continued Lucy, squinting in the bright sun. "Do you have any idea why he attended your mother's funeral?"

"I don't know what you're talking about," said Preston, losing patience. "And if you don't stop bothering me, I'm going to call the cops."

"I was only trying to help," said Lucy, beating a hasty retreat.

"Busybody," muttered Preston, giving the mower a push.

Lucy was climbing back into her car, intending to go home and make herself some lunch, when she spotted Frankie coming down the drive towards her mailbox. Frankie, she remembered, was rumored to have been having an affair with Fred Stanton. At least that's what Chris seemed to think. Lucy gave her a wave and hurried down the street to meet her at the box, which had been embellished with paint and a carved wooden head and tail to look like a mermaid.

"I've been meaning to ask you," began Lucy, seizing on the unusual mailbox as a pretext for a conversation. "This is so adorable. Where did you get it?"

"It is cute, isn't it?" said Frankie, giving her a big smile as she extracted a pile of letters and a Delia's catalog. "But I don't know where it came from. It was a housewarming gift from an old friend. I can ask her where she got it, if you want."

"Would you? That would be great," said Lucy enthusiastically. "I wouldn't want to copy you but maybe they have other styles. Like whales. Or maybe I could get one like my dog. Labs are pretty popular and they put them on a lot of stuff."

"You know, ever since Mimi was, well, you know, I've been thinking of getting a dog."

"You have?"

"Yeah. For security. But I never had a dog," said Frankie. "Say, have you had lunch?"

"Uh, no," said Lucy.

"Well, I was just going to make myself a salad. Why don't you join me and tell me all about Labs."

"Okay," said Lucy. "I'd love lunch, but I don't think you want a Lab for protection. They love everybody."

"That's the trick, isn't it," said Frankie, as they walked up the drive. "I want a dog that's a good pet, but one that will let me know if an intruder's coming. One that barks at the right time, if you know what I mean."

"We all want that dog," said Lucy, following her through the door and into her kitchen. "Tell me if you find it."

Lucy hadn't really given the matter much thought, but she hadn't expected Frankie's house to look the way it did. Since Frankie was a single mom with a teenage daughter, she was prepared for a somewhat casual, messy approach to home décor, probably featuring cheerleading pom-poms and a generous scattering of shoes and other teen detritus. Something like her own house, where antiques and flea market finds were haphazardly mixed with family hand-me-downs and a few upholstered pieces purchased from a discount furniture store.

Frankie's kitchen couldn't be more different from Lucy's if it were on the moon. Pristine white enamel cabinets gleamed beneath an uncluttered granite countertop which featured a colorful porcelain rooster. A round white table stood on the terra cotta tile floor and, instead of a week's worth of mail and newspapers, the only thing it held was a Quimper tureen. The matching chairs were also bare of anything except charming yellow and blue Provençal print cushions.

"This is really nice," said Lucy. "It looks like a house in a magazine."

"Thanks," said Frankie. "I guess because I'm in real estate I know the importance of interior decoration."

"I could certainly learn a thing or two from you," said Lucy, studying the great room that extended beyond the kitchen island. There a couple of over-stuffed white love seats with colorful flowered accent pillows were set at right angles around a low coffee table holding a neat stack of magazines and a fresh flower arrangement. A coordinating entertainment center probably held the TV and DVD player, but its louvered doors were discreetly closed. Lucy sighed, thinking of her family room, where the huge TV held center stage because Bill didn't want to have to fuss with a lot of doors and things when he collapsed into his battered corduroy recliner to watch Monday night football.

"Are you planning to redecorate?" asked Frankie, who was busy slicing and chopping an assortment of vegetables and arranging them on two plates.

"Not anytime soon," said Lucy. "We've got one daughter in college and two more coming."

"Maybe you should consider taking a real estate course," said Frankie. "I'm sure you'd do quite well, certainly better than at the paper."

"Most anything would pay more than the paper," admitted Lucy. "But I love it. I couldn't give it up."

"Good for you," said Frankie, setting the table with blue woven placemats, crystal goblets, and cheery napkins that matched the seat cushions. "How about we celebrate our good fortune with a glass of wine? I've got a nice buttery chardonnay."

"Oh, why not," said Lucy, throwing caution to

the wind. She didn't usually—make that never—drink wine with lunch but then she usually had peanut butter and jelly. This was a grown-up lunch and she might as well have a grown-up drink.

Frankie took a large bottle out of the refrigerator and filled the goblets right up to the brim before setting the bottle in a marble cooler. Then she brought the plates of salad to the table and gestured for Lucy to sit down. "Bon appetit!"

"This is really lovely," said Lucy, spearing a piece of goat cheese. "Do you eat like this every day?"

"I try to." Frankie shrugged. "I'm French, at least my family is, and this is the way I was brought up. Food, mealtimes, were always important to us."

"No fast food?"

"My mother didn't know the meaning of the phrase." Frankie was lifting her glass. "She was all about slow food. Cassoulet that took days to prepare, pork pies, homemade sausage, fruit tarts . . ." She waved her hand. "I could go on and on."

"My mother was more the 'dump a can of Campbell's cream soup into it and call it a casserole' kind of cook," said Lucy.

"The important thing is that she was there for you," said Frankie, waving her fork for emphasis. "That's why I went into real estate—so I could be home for Renee. At first I only worked during school hours and, now that I've built up my clientele, I pretty much work from home. I'm here when she needs me."

"I have flexible hours, too," said Lucy. "For me the problem is getting Sara to tell me what's on her mind." Before she quite realized what she was doing, Lucy was pouring out her worries about Sara and the way the football players were harassing the cheerleaders. "The only way we're going to stop this is if somebody goes public, but I can't get Sara to tell me what's really happening and she flat-out refused to let Ted, he's my editor, interview her for the *Pennysaver*."

"You can't blame her," said Frankie. "No one wants to be a whistle-blower, especially at her age. She wants to be popular." She nodded knowingly. "These girls will do anything to be popular."

"Has Renee talked to you about this?"

"Renee is old for her years." Frankie took a sip of wine and held it in her mouth, savoring it, before she swallowed. "She spent six weeks in France this summer, with her cousins. She came back very sophisticated." Frankie grinned. "She thinks American attitudes to sex are silly. At least that's what she says. I suspect it's not quite that simple for her."

"There's going to be a meeting Thursday night, about rumors of hazing on the team. Will you go?"

"Of course."

Lucy put her fork down and sat back in her chair. Wine with lunch was a terrific idea. She felt relaxed and completely at peace. "It's so quiet here," she said. "You don't even get road noise from Red Top Road. And Prudence Path seems deserted."

"It seems like that but it isn't really." There was a little gleam in her eye. "There's a lot of coming and going."

Lucy swallowed the last of her wine. It seemed as if Frankie had something she wanted to tell her. "I noticed you didn't join the chorus at the bus stop yesterday when Fred was arrested. Do you think somebody else did it?"

"I don't think Fred did it, that's for sure." She

paused, refilling her glass. "Those other women, they don't really know Fred. He's a good guy."

Lucy swallowed hard. She had to ask. "I've heard rumors that you know him extremely well."

Frankie nodded. "I do. He asked me to sell those new condos he's building on the other side of town and we've been working together on a marketing plan."

So much for the grapevine, thought Lucy. "Is he the sort of guy who'd abuse his wife, like they say?"

"He yells and screams, sure, but that's just his style. He's loud. My father was like that. A lot of bark but no bite." She smiled at the memory, then raised an eyebrow. "I can tell you, I would rather have a man who gets it all out than some sneaky-Pete who goes around knocking at the neighbor's back doors when I'm not looking."

Lucy grinned mischievously. "And who does that?"

"Willie's husband. What's his name? Scratch. She maybe loves her horses a little too much because Scratch is definitely looking for love in lots of places."

Lucy thought Scratch, who was a skinny string bean of a man with thinning hair, wire-rimmed glasses, and a stoop was an unlikely Lothario. "Really?"

Frankie was well on her way through her second glass of wine. "He came knocking on my door but I sent him on his way." She made a little moue with her mouth. "He's not my type. Too English. No fire."

"He must have a few smoldering embers," observed Lucy.

Frankie laughed. "Well, I think Mimi found a way to fan his flames, if you know what I mean."

"Mimi?"

Frankie nodded.

"Do you think he killed Mimi?"

Frankie shook her head. "No. He wouldn't hurt a flea. He's a vet, you know. He loves all the fuzzy little creatures."

Lucy thought she was right. But what about his wife? "Does Willie know about this?"

"Sure. Why do you think she hates me so much? She knows Scratch would hop into bed with me if I gave him the least encouragement."

"Did she know about Mimi?" asked Lucy, wondering if Willie might have been jealous enough to kill Mimi. If she had, it might explain her recent odd behavior.

"I think she must have. It's a pretty small street, after all." Frankie got up and removed the empty plates. "I have a bit of crème brulee left over from last night. Would you like some? And coffee?"

"Sure," said Lucy, "why not?" If this was how Frenchwomen stayed slim, she was all for it.

When Lucy got home she wasn't convinced the French diet really worked, not for Americans, anyway. Her pants felt tight and she could definitely use a nap. Libby seemed to sense her guilt, greeting her with a wagging tail and reproachful eyes.

"Okay, I admit it," she told the Lab. "I had wine at lunch."

The dog hung her head.

"And crème brulee."

The dog slid to the floor, front legs extended and hind legs tucked under her. She sighed and rested her chin on the floor as Lucy sat down at the table and began sorting the mail. A reminder notice that the dog was overdue for her one-year checkup gave her an idea. There was no harm in switching vets, especially since she really ought to support her neighbors. She picked up the phone and made an appointment with Dr. Westwood. She wanted to meet this Lothario and decide for herself if he qualified as a murder suspect.

Hearing her name mentioned in the conversation, Libby got up and rested her chin on Lucy's knee. She stroked the dog's silky ears and her woofily, whiskery chin. Libby responded by wagging her tail. Lucy could hardly believe a year had passed since Toby and Molly gave her the squirmy little puppy. They named her Liberty to commemorate the fact that she joined the family on the Fourth of July.

"You're a real live niece of your Uncle Sam," sang Lucy, and the dog wagged her tail enthusiastically. "Born on the Fourth of July."

Lucy got to her feet. "Well, not exactly born on the Fourth of July but you get the idea. How about a walk?"

Libby was on her feet, ready to go.

Lucy grabbed the leash, just in case they encountered a porcupine or other wild creature, and they headed across the backyard to the trail leading to Blueberry Pond. Lucy sniffed the piney air and scanned the blue sky for clouds; not a one. It hardly seemed fair that the kids had to go back to school when the weather was so fine. Libby agreed, running ahead with her tail held high as she followed scents left by various forest dwellers.

Lucy's mind wandered as she walked, thinking over her conversation with Frankie. She'd never imagined Willie's husband Scratch was less than a model husband; she'd never thought of Mimi as anything but a nuisance. It made her wonder what else was happening on Prudence Path, what passions were simmering below the surface. Or maybe not so far below the surface. Willie had certainly changed lately, becoming much crankier and nervier. Did she have a guilty conscience? She hadn't been assigned to work at the bake sale until the afternoon; she would have had time to stab Mimi before dashing off to the stable.

Suddenly, she panicked, realizing she'd lost track of Libby. Lucy began calling the dog's name, hoping she hadn't followed some deer trail into unfamiliar territory and gotten herself lost. When she caught sight of the dog trotting towards her after calling her name only a few times, Lucy was relieved—until she realized the dog had something in her mouth.

"Give it!" she ordered, fearing the worst. She knew from experience that Labs were equal-opportunity diners, and would eat anything ranging from a dead bird's wing to horse apples to rocks and sticks.

Libby squirmed away just as Lucy grabbed her collar and attached the leash. "Open!" she said, using her most authoritative voice. The dog hunkered down, clamping her teeth on the object.

Lucy put her foot on the leash and placing one hand on top of her snout and the other on the bottom attempted to pry the dog's mouth open. Libby struggled but eventually gave up and allowed Lucy to extract a soggy black wallet. From all appearances, the dog had been chewing on the wallet for quite a while and all that was left was a couple of strips of leather loosely held together at the narrow end by a few stitches. There was no money or ID. Lucy held the dog firmly and tossed the ragged fragments into the bushes, thinking no more about them as she and Libby headed for home.

Chapter 14

Thursday evening, Lucy ignored Sara and Zoe's protests that they had too much homework and were too tired besides and left them in charge of cleaning up the supper dishes while she went to the parent meeting. When she approached the high school, however, she couldn't help noticing that the people filing into the lobby hardly seemed concerned or anxious—they seemed to be in pretty high spirits.

She felt uneasy when she spotted Matt Engelhardt and Justin Crane, recalling her unpleasant experience with them in the weight room, but other people were greeting them like heroes. The two were surrounded by enthusiastic fans who slapped them on their backs and punched their arms. She even overheard Jake telling them to drop by the Donut Shack anytime for a free meal and Stan Beard, who owned a used car lot, promising them a "really good price" on a nearly new automobile.

Disgusted, she headed over to the bake sale table.

"How are sales?" she asked Pam, who was standing behind a table of baked goods along with Rachel.

"Pretty slow. I'm hoping they decide they want to pick up a snack on their way out of the meeting," said Pam. "Did you see Bonnie?"

"Uh, no," said Lucy. "Why?"

"Well, she volunteered to help but there's no sign of her," said Rachel, sounding worried.

For an awful moment Lucy's heart squeezed into a tight little ball. Not again. But then they saw her standing by the doorway, with a twin held fast in each hand.

"Over here," called Pam. Under her breath she added, "How's she going to work the table with the twins in tow?"

"Something's wrong," whispered Rachel. "The twins aren't matching."

It was true. For the first time since she'd known them, the twins weren't wearing matching ensembles. In fact, little Belle, or maybe it was Belinda, was wearing a sneaker on one foot and a sandal on the other.

"I'm sorry I'm late," said Bonnie, who was out of breath. "The sitter never showed."

"Not Sara, I hope," said Lucy.

"No. She couldn't do it. She said she had too much homework. A new girl."

"Don't worry about it," said Rachel. "We can manage. You take care of the girls."

"Are you sure?" asked Bonnie, attempting to hold on to the girls who were twisting and pulling at her arms. "They could just sit behind the table. They promised to be good."

"It's getting close to bedtime and tomorrow's a school day," said Rachel. "They'd probably be happier having their baths and listening to a story."

Bonnie's face relaxed. "If you're sure it's okay . . ."

"It's okay. Go home," said Pam.

"I'll make it up to you," promised Bonnie, heading for the door.

When she'd left, Pam turned to Lucy. "What's going on? She seemed awfully distracted, didn't she?"

Lucy shrugged. "Maybe she's nervous about the coach keeping his job. Or maybe she's thinking that moving to Prudence Path wasn't such a good idea," she said. "I was talking to Frankie today and it's quite the hotbed of intrigue."

"Oh, you two!" exclaimed Rachel. "Always looking for secrets and motives! Maybe she just had a hard time getting the twins organized. You know what it's like with kids and it must be even harder with twins."

"Twice as hard," admitted Lucy.

They had a brief flurry of business when a group of JV players arrived for the meeting. They were fresh from practice and needed to refuel. The cheerleaders, on the other hand, avoided the table like the plague. From inside the auditorium there was a sudden hush and Lucy left her friends and took a seat in the back row, next to Willie.

"I'm surprised to see you here," she sniffed, shifting in her seat.

Lucy wasn't quite sure what to say. She didn't know if Sassie had told her mother about the incident on the team bus or not. "Of course I'm interested—especially since Sara's a cheerleader," she said, hopefully opening the way for more discussion if Willie wanted it. She didn't.

"I noticed you've been spending an awful lot of time at Frankie's place," she said, glaring at Lucy.

"I was only there once," began Lucy, aware of the

absurdity of defending her social life to a neighbor. She was used to small town life, where secrets have a very short shelf life, but this was ridiculous. She turned away and turned her attention to the meeting.

There was a decent turnout, but the auditorium was hardly packed and, as she'd noticed earlier, there was a distinct lack of tension in the room. The boys on the team seemed relaxed, sitting in a group off to the side, sprawling in the seats. On the stage, the superintendent was sitting at a table along with Coach Buck, the athletic director and several assistant coaches.

"We're here today because some serious allegations have been brought to my attention concerning possible hazing on the football team, at the August training camp in particular," began Superintendent Sabin, setting off a small buzz among the audience members. He ignored it and continued, ". . . and I've asked our Athletic Director Phil Bearse to look into them and make a report."

"Thank you, Dr. Sabin," said Phil, when the microphone was passed to him. "I'm happy to report that I've conducted an extensive investigation and I have been unable to substantiate these allegations. Everyone I've spoken to, and that includes all the team members, their parents, their coaches—everyone seems to agree that the August training camp is an extremely worthwhile program that offers the players a positive experience. That is exactly what the camp is designed to do and I'd like to ask Coach Burkhart to expand on that if he would."

"Thank you, Phil," said Coach Buck, taking the microphone. He went on to outline the goals and methods used at the training camp and Lucy found herself studying the players for their reactions. Will Worthington had joined his two buddies, completing the group of players she'd interviewed in the weight room. They were sitting together, nudging each other and laughing. Nobody had taken the seats on either side of them but Lucy didn't know if this was simply a coincidence or if their teammates were avoiding them. Or maybe it was some sort of dominance thing, like who was allowed to sit with the cool kids at their table in the lunch room.

Lucy's attention was drawn back to the speakers when the superintendent announced he was opening the meeting to questions from the audience. She waited expectantly for someone to challenge the smug group assembled on the stage but no one did. Only one hand was raised, that of Tony Marzetti, owner of the IGA and president of the Tinker's Cove Chamber of Commerce.

"This sort of thing is just a shame," he said. "It's an obvious attempt to besmirch the reputation of our team at the very time we should be congratulating them. For the first time in I don't know how long, maybe ever, the Warriors stand a real chance of beating the Gilead Giants. We're off to a great start this season and I think the teams deserve a big hand. C'mon everybody, let's show our appreciation!"

And everybody did. The room erupted in cheers and applause while Lucy slipped out the back. She wasn't the only one. As she left the brightly lit lobby and crossed the dim parking lot she thought she saw Frankie moving through the parked cars, but when she called out to her there was no response. She must have been mistaken, she decided, heading for home.

*   *   *

The newscaster was announcing the Dow had dropped one hundred eighty points and was at an eighteen-month low and Lucy was worrying about the kids' college fund, which she hoped her financial adviser had invested prudently, while she pedaled steadily on her exercycle in the family room. She had recently started riding the exercycle for twenty minutes every morning as a way of warming up for her half-hour workout with Debbie, the blond and tanned exercise entrepreneur who came to her house at seven a.m. via the cable TV. "There's no need to go to a gym," Debbie said, "when you can work out with me every morning in the privacy of your own home."

And even though Lucy thought Debbie had the brain of a pea, she had to admit she felt a lot better since she'd been doing the workout. And, as Debbie never failed to remind her, it was better to exercise in the morning before getting caught up in the day's activities. "If you wait until after supper, you'll be too tired," Debbie said, and Lucy knew it was true. The most she could manage then was a short walk, or a game of ball with the dog.

"Mom!" came a cry from the kitchen. "Libby's throwing up."

Lucy dismounted from the exercycle, wondering if she'd brought this on by thinking of the dog. Did it work like that? If she'd thought of the toaster, for example, would it burst into flames? Or the cesspool. Would it overflow if she thought about it? Was it better, as Debbie advised, to think happy thoughts? Would her life be perfect then?

In the kitchen, she discovered Libby standing over a pile of soggy dog kibble, apparently trying to decide if it would go down better the second time.

"No!" ordered Lucy, opening the door and shooing her outside. Reluctantly, tail between her legs, the dog obeyed. Lucy grabbed some paper towels and started cleaning up the mess. Instead of dwelling on the loathsome dietary habits of dogs, or the possibility that something was seriously the matter with Libby, Lucy decided to take Debbie's advice and think positively. In cleaning up the mess, she told herself, she was maintaining a hygienic, healthy environment for her family. She was beautifying the house. And really, didn't the cleaner bring up the grain on the wooden floor beautifully? It looked so nice, in fact, that she gave the entire kitchen floor a wipe.

The floor was gleaming when she left the house, but she was running late. Not that she was thinking about that. No, she was only thinking bright and beautiful thoughts today, she told herself, pausing a moment to take in the clear blue sky and the clump of purple asters and yellow goldenrod blooming by the mailbox. No, she refused to think about that sham of a meeting last night, when the hazing allegations were swept under the rug. And she wasn't thinking about whether Toby and Molly would be able to buy the house they wanted, and she wasn't thinking about the upcoming quarterly tax payment, or how Sara was coping with high school and cheerleading, or if Elizabeth was safe and sound in Boston, or even about Mimi's murder and the mysterious homeless man. No, she was looking for more goldenrod which was why she didn't notice Chris Cashman's Ford Expedition shooting out of Prudence Path right into her left fender.

"Ohmigod! Are you all right?" yelled Chris, from her perch in the SUV, high above Lucy's Subaru.

To tell the truth, Lucy wasn't sure. She was definitely shaken up and thoughts of whiplash and hairline fractures were chasing away all the lovely goldenrod dreams. She took a few deep breaths, to calm herself, and decided to try getting out of the car and on her feet. Moving slowly and carefully, she unlatched the door and pushed it open about twelve inches, stopping when she heard the protesting screech of metal on metal.

"Well," she said, squeezing through the opening and surveying the damage, "I seem to be okay but my car's not."

"I'll call the police," said Chris, flourishing her tiny little cell phone.

"Good idea," said Lucy, observing that although her car seemed to have major front end damage, Chris's enormous SUV seemed unscathed.

"Oh, look at that!" exclaimed Chris, joining her and examining the front of her SUV. "My paint is scratched."

"You went through a stop sign," said Lucy, who didn't appreciate Chris's attitude.

"I know," admitted Chris, who was rather haphazardly dressed in a pair of ratty sweatpants and an ancient Wellesley T-shirt. "It was my fault. I was in a hurry because I ran out of all-natural yogurt for the girls' breakfast and I needed to get to the store and back before Brad left for work and then there was the stock market fiasco—you know the Dow is down nearly two hundred points?—and how am I going to tell my poor widows they don't have the money they thought they did and . . ."

"I understand," said Lucy. "It could happen to anybody. You do have insurance, right? Why don't we exchange information, while we wait for the cops?"

As Lucy expected, Chris was a model of efficiency and extracted a neat little folder from her glove compartment with all the necessary papers. After a bit of searching, Lucy also produced the current, crumpled registration card and an empty plastic sleeve designed to hold it that was imprinted with the name of her insurance company. That bit of business completed, the two women looked hopefully down the road for an approaching police car. Seeing none, Chris suggested moving the cars to the side of the road.

"I don't think we should, not before the cops get here, " said Lucy. "If anybody comes along they can get by."

Nobody was coming, there was no sound except the chirping of birds and the buzz of cicadas. The sun was shining, the day was warming up, and the air was filled with the scent of a few late-blooming wild roses. High in the sky, a flock of geese in a straggly V formation was headed south, encouraging each other with an occasional honk.

"What a morning," said Lucy, full of appreciation for the natural beauty that was all around her.

"You can say that again," moaned Chris. "First this, and now Brad is going to be late for his meeting and there's no way I'm going to be able to get Pear and Apple to their Gymboree class." She was tapping her foot impatiently. "At this point I'm just hoping we make it to French class."

"Aren't they a bit young for that?" asked Lucy.

"Oh, no. The younger, the better. Children's

brains absorb language easily, they have to so they can learn to talk. Think about it: they have to absorb an enormous amount of information. But as they get older they lose that ability. That's why kids who've been kept in closets or raised by wolves or whatnot," Chris shrugged and shook her head, "well, they have a very difficult time learning any language skills at all. Sometimes they remain mute."

Lucy couldn't help wondering what other interesting bits of information filled Chris's hyperactive brain, and what she might have observed from her house on Prudence Path. "You're an intelligent woman," she began. "I'm curious what you think about the murder. Do you think Fred did it? That Mimi was an abused wife?"

"Who knows? We're all so new here, and I've been so busy, I haven't really gotten to know the neighbors. If it wasn't for the bake sale, I wouldn't know anybody—but that's not enough to go on, is it? I mean, anybody can bake something, right?" She paused. "I never saw any bruises, if that's what you mean."

"You live right next door. Did you ever see any other men around, when Fred was out?"

"Mimi having an affair? Oh, please."

Mentally, Lucy put a big question mark against Frankie's assertion that Willie's husband had been carrying on an affair with Mimi.

"Did you ever see Mimi and Fred fighting?"

"No. They were pretty quiet, except for Preston and that obnoxious motorcycle of his."

"You know, I worry about those boys. Are they doing okay without their dad?"

"I invited them for supper last night but they

wouldn't come. And Brad tried to get them to join him in tossing a basketball around but they weren't interested." Chris looked at her watch. "This is ridiculous," she said, just as they heard the faint wail of an approaching siren.

"I guess we're getting the full treatment," said Lucy. "Sirens, fire trucks, ambulances, the whole works."

"No wonder property taxes are so high," fumed Chris.

The little message light on her phone was blinking when she finally got to the office. She'd walked over from Al's Body Shop where she'd been informed that it would be at least two weeks, maybe longer, before her car was drivable.

"I bet your insurance will cover a car rental," advised Phyllis, who was an expert in all matters pertaining to automobile insurance ever since her cousin Elfrida hit a moose a couple of years ago.

Picking up the phone to call her insurance agent, Lucy listened to the message. It was Bill, telling her the dog had been sick again. And again. So after she called the insurance agency, and learned she was indeed covered for a rental car, she called Scratch Westwood's office and got an appointment. Then she worked on the events listings for a couple of hours before picking up the car and getting the dog.

"When did Libby have her last bowel movement?" inquired Scratch Westwood as he palpated the Lab's abdomen. He was exactly as Frankie had described him: tall, with wire-rimmed glasses and a thinning fringe of hair. Personally, Lucy didn't think he had much sex appeal but he was a big hit with Libby, who was grinning at him in doggy adoration.

"I don't really know," admitted Lucy. "Maybe yesterday morning."

"Not last night or this morning?"

"Now that you mention it, I don't think so," said Lucy, recalling the dog had been unusually quiet the previous evening and hadn't demanded to go out as she usually did.

"I'm going to take some x-rays," said Scratch. "Has she eaten anything unusual lately? Chicken bones? Tin cans?"

Lucy chuckled. "No tin cans, but she did get hold of an old wallet."

"Ah," he said. "C'mon girl. Let's take some pictures."

Libby would have followed him anywhere, wagging her tail the entire time. Lucy sat in the waiting room, trying to think of a way to bring up Mimi's murder so she could gauge Scratch's reaction. But when she was called back to the examining room it was clear that the vet had bad news.

"I'm afraid she's going to need surgery," he said, showing Lucy the x-ray. "There's something obstructing her intestines, " he said, pointing to a bright shape, "right here where the jejunum begins."

"Is it risky?" asked Lucy, horrified.

"Well, there's always some risk with an operation, anesthesia. It's not risk free but there's really no alternative. Whatever it is, we've got to get it out." He patted her on the shoulder. "It's pretty common, especially with Labs. They'll eat anything they can swallow. Believe me, I've found some pretty weird stuff. The worst was a steak knife. Fortunately the dog swallowed it handle first. Otherwise . . ." he rolled his eyes, leaving the sentence unfinished.

"It won't pass on its own?" suggested Lucy, ever hopeful.

He shook his head. "I'm afraid not."

The house seemed oddly empty without Libby, which was ridiculous since there were four of them gathered around the table for a quick meal before they all went to the Friday night football game. Lucy wasn't really in the mood—she was worried about the dog who hadn't come out of surgery yet—but she couldn't let Sara down. This was the official season opener, the traditional game against the Gilead Giants, and Sara's debut as a cheerleader.

"Are you nervous?" asked Zoe, biting into her hot dog.

"Mostly excited," said Sara, taking tiny bites of a dill pickle slice. "We've rehearsed so much I could do these routines in my sleep." She paused. "At least I think so."

"I'm sure you could," said Lucy. "You're going to be great. And the Warriors are going to beat the Giants, too."

"In your dreams," said Bill.

Receiving a glare from Lucy he amended his statement. "I meant the Giants always win, at least

they have for as long as anybody can remember."
He smiled at Sara. "But the cheerleaders will be
great."

"Can I be excused?" asked Sara. "I need to put
on my outfit."

Lucy wished she'd actually eaten her hamburger,
instead of shredding it into small pieces on her
plate, but figured she was too nervous. "Okay," she
said, just as the phone rang.

Zoe got it, beating her sister to the draw. "It's for
you, Mom. It's the vet."

Lucy took the phone, thinking positive thoughts.
Bouncy puppies in a field. Libby leaping up to
catch a Frisbee. Apparently it worked because the
word was that the operation had been successful
and Libby was resting comfortably. "Great," sighed
Lucy, "thanks for calling." Now she could concentrate on the game. Warriors smoothly executing shot-
gun plays. Warriors completing first down. Warriors
rolling down the field like a machine. Warriors scor-
ing. Cheerleaders turning somersaults as crowd
goes wild.

Or not. At halftime the score was seven Giants
and zip Warriors. Positive thinking apparently had
its limits, thought Lucy, who was beaming with pride
in any case as Sara and the other Tinker's Cove
cheerleaders took the field.

The girls were adorable in their red and white
outfits, little tank tops and short skirts since the
weather was warm. She held her breath as Sara was
lifted to the top of a pyramid and then dove down
into the waiting arms of her teammates.

"I don't know why people pick on cheerleaders.

It's a sport in its own right—I mean, how many people can do that?" demanded Lucy.

"Not me," confessed Bill as the girls cartwheeled across the field, ending up in a neat circle. Behind them, the band and color guard were filing on the field, preparing for the big finale.

"I'm going to be a cheerleader, too," said Zoe, awestruck by her older sister's transformation into a glamorous icon of femininity.

The band started playing, the color guard started marching around waving red and white streamers on poles, and the cheerleaders were dancing, showing off some fancy footwork, when the announcement came over the loudspeaker.

"We've just received word," came the electronic voice, "that the Tinker's Cove JV Warriors have won their game versus the Gilead JV Giants. The final score: Warriors fifteen, Giants six."

The band stepped up the volume, the banner girls waved their poles frantically, and the cheerleaders went flying through the air as the crowd went wild.

"And hell's freezing over," said Bill, amazed.

Chapter 15

On Monday morning Lucy was unable to dodge the job of typing in the police and fire log. The log was extremely popular with readers, which Lucy found puzzling since it was nothing more than a chronological listing of calls to the police and fire stations for the previous week. It included items such as "Barking dog, Sycamore Lane, 10:27 p.m. Monday" and "Difficulty breathing, Shore Road, 7:12 a.m. Wednesday." All names were deleted and only the most basic details were given, so Lucy was forced to conclude that the faithful readers spent the week puzzling over the cryptic notations trying to figure out who the barking dog belonged to. Okay, that was easy, the only dog on Sycamore Lane was a pit bull belonging to Tim Rogers, a former star of the Tinker's Cove High School baseball team who didn't hold a job but nevertheless was never short of cash. The more interesting question was which of his neighbors got up the nerve to call and complain, since Tim had a hot temper. Then again, she decided, maybe the readers saw it as a challenge, just like her parents used to approach the crossword puzzle in the Sunday *New York Times*. Some weeks, it took them well into Wednesday before they finished it.

Today, however, as she worked her way through the notations she noticed numerous calls reporting a vagrant. The first call was on the day before Mimi's funeral, from someone on Parallel Street. Parallel Street ran behind Main and offered a back way into several parking areas including that of Marzetti's IGA grocery store. This was followed by a call on Wednesday morning from Church Street and another later in the day from Blueberry Pond Road.

With a growing sense of excitement Lucy unfolded the Chamber of Commerce map of Tinker's Cove and began tracing the various sightings of the vagrant, who she was now convinced was the homeless man. But when she finished she realized she hadn't actually learned that much. She'd already discovered his camp in the woods between Prudence Path and Blueberry Pond so the fact that he'd been spotted several times in that area was no surprise and neither were the numerous sightings in the supermarket parking lot, where he apparently scrounged for food in the Dumpster. He seemed to spend most of his daytime hours on the move, popping up everywhere from the harbor to construction sites around town, even occasionally in the vicinity of the high school.

Eager to learn more, she dialed the police station, intending to question the dispatcher. Such conversations were against department policy, of course, but she figured it was worth a try and she figured she was in luck when Bobbi Kirwan answered. Lucy was well acquainted with Dot, the matriarch of the Kirwan clan who worked at the IGA, and her numerous offspring who all seemed to work in either the police or fire department. The new chief, in fact, was Dot's oldest.

"Hi, Bobbi. How's the new baby?" asked Lucy, referring to Bobbi's nephew, Benjamin.

"Oh, Lucy, he's sooo cute," enthused Bobbi. "He's started to smile and he's got the whole family wrapped around his little finger. I mean, Mom and Aunt Janine were actually fighting yesterday over who was going to change Ben's poopy diaper!"

"He's lucky to have such a great family," said Lucy, remembering lonely days as a young mother newly arrived in Tinker's Cove when she didn't quite know what to do with cranky baby Toby. She would have loved to have a few relatives squabbling over diaper-changing privileges.

"Yeah, but now the pressure's on the rest of us. Mom wants to know when Jeff and I are going to get serious, as she puts it, and she keeps telling Mandy that it's risky to wait too long before starting a family."

"But you and Jeff aren't even married," said Lucy.

"At this point I don't think Mom cares. She just wants grandbabies. The more the merrier."

"So I guess little Ben is a troublemaker."

"You can say that again," laughed Bobbi. "Talking about troublemakers, I'm pretty sure you didn't call just to chat about babies."

"You found me out," said Lucy. "Actually, I was going over the log and I noticed lots of calls about that homeless guy, the one who was found dead in the harbor, and I wondered if you took any of them."

"Yeah. A lot of people called."

"Did any of them have any contact with him? Did he threaten anyone or anything like that?"

"Not that I heard," said Bobbi. "He just kind of hung around. One lady found him rooting in her garbage, another got scared when she noticed him lurking in the woods when she was hanging up her laundry. Stuff like that."

"And what happened when the officers responded?"

"As far as I know he was always gone by the time they got there. Nobody got a chance to question him."

"It seems like he was always on the move, probably trying to avoid getting arrested."

"It's too bad, because maybe we could have helped him. At least he would have had a bed for a night or two and some decent meals."

"It almost seems like he didn't want anybody to know who he was," said Lucy.

"Well, he succeeded," said Bobbi. "I've got to go, I've got calls coming in."

"Thanks for your help," said Lucy, aware that she was just being polite. Bobbi hadn't really helped at all.

After she finished entering the police log in the computer Lucy edited some copy for Ted, then took another look at her story about the homeless man. She added the little information she'd gleaned from the police log and closed the file, uncomfortably aware that while she had plenty of *what, when,* and *where* she had no *who,* and more importantly, no *why.* Glancing over the printout of the log one more time, she stuffed it in her purse and got to her feet. "I'll be back in an hour or so," she told Phyllis. "I want to do a little investigating, see if anybody talked to that homeless guy. If Ted gets nervous about the copyediting tell him I can stay late."

Phyllis's eyebrows shot up. "Are you crazy? I'll tell him you had a family emergency."

"That's true enough," said Lucy, with a wry chuckle. "My family is in a constant state of emergency."

Leaving the office, Lucy walked down Main Street to the IGA and cut through the parking lot to Parallel Street. There she decided a big old white Colonial with a gambrel roof had the best view of the Dumpster and knocked on the kitchen door. A plump woman with frizzy gray hair answered.

"Whatever it is, I don't want any," she said, before Lucy could introduce herself, "and I'm a lifelong Baptist and I'm not interested in becoming a Jehovah's Witness."

"I'm not selling anything," laughed Lucy, "and I'm certainly not a Jehovah's Witness. I'm Lucy Stone from the *Pennysaver* and I just wanted to ask you about the vagrant you reported to the police."

The woman's face softened. "Come on in," she said, opening the screen door. "I've been washing windows and I'm due for a break. Would you like some iced tea?"

"That would be great," said Lucy, taking a seat at the faux wood kitchen table. The wall behind the table was covered with framed studio photos of children and grandchildren, and the refrigerator displayed snapshots and samples of childish art work. "I thought I knew everybody in town but . . ."

"We moved here about six weeks ago," said the woman, opening the refrigerator. "I'm Millie Monroe. My husband got transferred. He's a regional manager for Northeast Bank."

Lucy knew Northeast Bank had recently bought

several smaller regional banks. A lot of local people resented the change. "He's got a tough row to hoe," said Lucy, accepting a tall glass of iced tea.

Millie shrugged. "He's due to retire soon, anyway. Sugar?"

"No, thanks. This is great." Lucy took a sip and put down her glass. "I'm working on a story about the homeless man and I wondered if you might have seen anything unusual?"

"Well, I think getting your supper out of a Dumpster is pretty unusual," said Millie. "I was horrified. It really upset me. Nobody should have to live like that. But by the time the police got here he was gone." She took a swallow of tea and turned to Lucy. "The officer told me there was nothing he could do. They said he wasn't breaking any laws and it wasn't a matter for the police." She stirred her tea. "I couldn't believe it. I told them he was obviously mentally ill and ought to be in a hospital or something but they said there was no reason to think he was crazy and if he wanted to live like that it was his choice. As if anyone would choose to eat garbage!"

"Did you see him after that?"

"Every day." She stared out the window. "I found it very upsetting."

"Did you talk to him?"

"I tried. I went out and called to him, asked him if he'd like a sandwich or a piece of pie, but he took one look at me and ran off." She sighed. "Then I heard he drowned in the harbor. The poor man. I just hate to think of him all alone like that. He must've had a family somewhere, probably missing him and worrying about him."

Lucy's eyes wandered over the photo collection.

"I keep wondering why he came to Tinker's Cove. It seems a funny sort of place for a homeless person."

"What will happen? Will they have a funeral for him?"

"Maybe your church could organize something," suggested Lucy. "Otherwise, I think the medical examiner keeps the body for a year or so and then it's buried in some sort of potter's field."

"I'll do that," said Millie. "I'll call the pastor right away."

"Well, thanks for your time—and the tea," said Lucy. "I've got to be going."

"Good luck with your story. I hope you find out who he was."

At the IGA, Dot Kirwan wasn't much help, either. "It was all we could talk about when we first noticed him," she said. "It was disgusting, seeing him rooting through the trash like that. So the deli guy, Skip, started setting stuff aside for him, things like unsold pizza slices and leftover salad bar and sandwiches, things like that. Dented cans of juice and soda, I mean, there's a lot of food here that gets thrown out anyway. Instead of tossing it in the bin, Skip would put it on a tray that he set out on a chair."

"Did the homeless man take it?"

"Yeah, at least I think he did. You better talk to Skip."

Lucy definitely planned to do that but first she wanted to ask Dot about Tommy. She remembered him saying he worked as a bagger at the store.

"Before I head back to the deli I want to ask you about Tommy Stanton."

Dot shook her head, setting the wattles under her chin aquiver. "That poor boy."

"What was he like when he worked here?"

"He was a real good worker. Had a lot of get up and go. You didn't have to tell him every little thing, like some of the other kids who work here, if you know what I mean."

"I know," said Lucy, thinking of the tactics her own kids used to avoid chores. Toby was a master of the slow-down while Elizabeth preferred a more aggressive, confrontational approach that featured shifting disagreeable tasks to her younger siblings as in "Why do I always have to do the dishes and Sara never does?"

"Did he ever talk about his family?" asked Lucy.

"No. He was real quiet. I used to try to get him to talk. I'd ask him about football and school but he'd just say things were okay. That was his favorite phrase. Everything was okay."

"But they weren't," said Lucy. Nothing in Tommy's life had been okay. Not his family, not football, nothing."

"I know," said Dot, looking grief-stricken. "I should've tried harder to get him to open up."

"Don't blame yourself. I tried, too, but he kept it all inside."

Dot glanced at the clock that hung in the front of the store. "If you're going to talk to Skip you better hustle. His shift is up in five minutes and, believe me, he doesn't stick around."

"Thanks," she said, heading for the deli counter in the rear of the store.

Lucy knew Skip; he'd sliced up many pounds of cold cuts for her through the years. He was a big, cheerful man who always had a smile for his customers.

"What can I get you today?" he asked, adjusting his white cap and snapping his rubber gloves.

"I just want some information," said Lucy, "about that homeless guy. Dot tells me you were putting food out for him."

"Just stuff that was going to go into the Dumpster anyway. I figured I'd save him the trouble of diving for it."

"Did you ever talk to him?"

Skip shook his head. "I hardly ever saw him and then it was only his back. He was like one of those feral cats. You can put food out for them and they'll eat it but if you try to pet them, off they go. He was just like that."

Lucy thought it was an apt comparison. She figured Skip was talking from experience. "That was a nice thing you did. The lady in the house behind also tried to give him food." She looked at the rows of meats and cheeses in the display case. "What a shame."

"Yeah," said Skip.

"How'd the investigating go?" asked Phyllis, when she returned to the office.

"It's just tragic," said Lucy, slumping into her chair. "So many people tried to help him. The lady in the house behind the IGA put out food for him, so did Skip. He'd take what they left but if they tried to talk to him he ran away."

"Crazy."

"Maybe," admitted Lucy. "But I still think he came here for a reason."

Phyllis slapped a stack of dummies on her desk.

"This is the fall home and garden supplement. Ted wants you to check it for typos."

"Today?"

"Yeah." Phyllis was sympathetic. "It goes to press tomorrow."

Lucy sat down at her desk and reached for the phone. She'd promised Willie that she would pick up the girls today but faced with the entire home and garden supplement there was no way she could do it.

As she expected, Willie wasn't pleased. "This is so typical," she fumed.

"Well, it was sprung on me at the last minute. I'd really appreciate it if you could get them today. I'll pick them up tomorrow and Wednesday."

"I guess that will be all right," she said, adding a big sigh.

Lucy didn't get home until almost eight, long after Bill and the girls ate dinner. But she was greeted by Libby, who was a bit unsteady on her feet but wagged her tail as enthusiastically as ever.

"What did the vet say?" she asked Bill, who was filling her bowl with water.

"She's gonna be fine. But she can only go out on the leash, no exercise, for two weeks. And we have to check her incision for swelling and redness every day."

Lucy stroked the dog's silky ears. "What did you eat, you silly girl?"

"This," said Bill, producing a bit of plastic.

Lucy took it from him and turned it over, studying it. It seemed to be a rather old Massachusetts driver's license, from the days before holograms and digital photos, when they simply laminated a cardboard license with plastic. The name was gone, but the photo was still quite clear. In fact, Lucy realized, the face on the license looked a lot like Tommy Stanton. But it couldn't be him, because his license would be a freshly minted Maine license with a black electromagnetic strip on the back. Then she remembered the wallet and felt for a moment as if Bill had slipped an ice cube down her back. The face looking up at her through the cloudy plastic was the face of the homeless man. A man who bore a very strong resemblance to Tommy Stanton.

Chapter 16

As she studied the tattered bit of plastic and cardboard Lucy's thoughts suddenly came into focus. She'd suspected all along that the homeless man was connected with Mimi and his strong resemblance to Tommy certainly seemed to confirm it. It also served to deny Fred's assertion that Mimi had no family. She did have a family, but not, perhaps, a family she wanted to acknowledge. Perhaps a very troubled family, if the homeless man was any indication. A family that both Mimi and the homeless man had left behind.

Lucy carried the card over to the kitchen sink and held it under the bright down-light there, but the name and address remained illegible. The license number, however, was faintly discernible and Lucy eagerly wrote it down. First thing tomorrow she'd call the Massachusetts Registry of Motor Vehicles and get the man's identity. She would finally fill in the *who* in her story.

* * *

"Why exactly do you want this information?" inquired the voice on the other end of the line, a voice with a strong Boston accent.

"Like I said," Lucy began, for the umpteenth time, "I'm a reporter with the *Pennysaver* newspaper in Tinker's Cove, Maine. A homeless man was recently found dead here and I'm trying to identify him from a fragment of his driver's license. All I have is the number and his photo."

"What happened to the card?" asked the voice, pronouncing card without the *r. Cahd.*

"Actually, my dog ate it."

"They're plastic. That shouldn't hurt it."

Lucy rolled her eyes and leaned her elbows on her desk. There was no point in losing patience with the clerk, not if she wanted her help. All she could do was hope to interest her in the story. "It's one of the old paper ones with a laminated coating."

"Really? That's before my time."

"The dog's teeth did some damage."

"My dog ate my wedding ring but she pooped it out." The voice paused. "I made my husband buy me a new one."

"Good thinking," said Lucy. "Actually, it made my dog sick and she had to have an operation."

"Is she okay?"

"Yeah. She's recovering nicely, but after all we've been through it would be great if you could help me identify this guy. Like I said, the license is all we have to go on."

"Sorry. I can't divulge that information."

"Why not?"

"We only give information like that to law enforcement. It's a privacy issue."

"The guy is dead."

"It's department policy. I'd get in big trouble."

Lucy didn't want Little Miss Boston to get into trouble. "Okay, just one more question. Do you actually have the information from such an old driver's license on file somewhere?"

"I dunno."

"Well, thanks for your help." Why did she keep saying this to people who didn't help her at all?

"No problem. It was nice talking to you. I hope the dog's okay."

Lucy got the last word. "Have a nice day," she said.

"That didn't sound as if you meant it," said Phyllis, whose long nails, painted magenta today with a scattering of glitter to match her harlequin reading glasses, were clicking against the keyboard.

"I didn't," grumbled Lucy. "It was classic passive-aggressive behavior. I wanted to wring her unhelpful little neck."

"So much hostility and so early in the morning, too," clucked Phyllis. "You should try to have a more positive attitude."

"That's what my exercise coach says," muttered Lucy, reaching for the phone. Seeing Phyllis's eyebrows shoot up she offered a quick explanation. *Fun and Fitness with Debbie* every morning."

Amazingly, Barney was actually at his desk in the police station. Lucy had seen it, a cluttered monument to disorganization, and understood why he tried to avoid it.

"Cruiser's in the shop," he explained. "Brake linings." He sighed a long sigh. "I'm catching up on paperwork."

"I'm sorry," said Lucy. "Would you like a diversion?"

"Not if it will get me into trouble."

"No trouble at all. I just want you to run a Massachusetts driver's license for me. I think it belongs to the homeless guy. In fact, I'll even give it to you and you can get credit for identifying him."

"So who is he?"

"That's the thing. I don't know. All that's left is his photo and the number. No name or address."

"Where'd you find it?"

"In the woods. The dog actually found it, in an old wallet. She ate most of the wallet and the license, too. She had to have surgery."

"Gee, that's quite a story. But how do you know it belonged to the homeless guy?"

"Trust me. I've got a real strong hunch."

"Okay, come on down," said Barney.

He was chatting with the dispatcher when Lucy got to the station and promptly escorted her into an interview room. "It's more private here," he said.

"And neater," observed Lucy.

"Yeah. So let me see it."

Lucy produced the license and Barney leaned over it. "He looks a lot like Tommy Stanton," Barney said.

"I know. I think they're related. I think he came to town because of Mimi."

"So you think whoever killed Mimi also killed him? That it wasn't an accident?"

"Well, I've been talking to people who saw him around town and nobody mentioned he was ever drunk, and there was no sign of liquor in his little campsite in the woods."

"You can show me where it is?"

"Sure. So how about getting his name and address?"

Barney picked up the phone and within minutes he was copying the information in his big block letters: Thomas Preston O'Toole with an address in Jamaica Plain. "The license expired in 1985," he said, sliding the paper across the table to her.

"Mimi named her sons after him," said Lucy. "Who do you think he was? A brother?"

"The age is right. He was about forty. She was a little older."

"I wonder what happened, what split them apart?"

"I can run a records check," offered Barney, just as his name was called on the station intercom. "I gotta go," he said, "I'll call you later."

Lucy felt exhilarated, and slightly frantic, as she hurried back to the *Pennysaver* office. It was exciting when a story began to gel and she found the pressure both exhilarating and scary. But it was already Tuesday. Could she pull it all together by noon tomorrow?

Google was no help at all. There were no matches for Thomas Preston O'Toole, no matches for Preston O'Toole and 4,830 matches for Thomas Preston, most of which seemed to be random notations that included the name Thomas.

"Lucy, what exactly are you doing?" demanded Ted, who had been watching her scroll through the listings for some time.

"I Googled the homeless guy, but I'm not finding anything."

"Uh, that's a surprise," he said, rolling his eyes. "He was homeless, that means he wasn't connected to society, right?"

"Well, everybody's in Google, right? Even me. And he might have been somebody important before he became homeless. Or he might have been named after a famous relative."

"I think you'd be better off with a criminal records check," said Ted.

"Barney ran one for me. It came up empty."

"Call the parish priest," advised Phyllis, oracle-like from her spot behind the reception counter.

"What?" Lucy was puzzled.

"O'Toole is an Irish name and Jamaica Plain is in Boston, that means he's most likely Boston Irish. They're usually faithful churchgoers. I bet the parish church has some information, baptism, first communion, stuff like that."

Lucy remembered Mimi's funeral service at the Catholic church, and the fact that O'Toole had attended it. "That's a good idea," she said, casting a questioning look in Ted's direction. "Just one phone call?"

"Just one," said Ted. "Then you can follow up for next week's edition. Right now, I need you to get the movie listings."

"I'm on it, Chief," said Lucy, doing a quick Google search for Catholic churches in Jamaica Plain and turning up St. Thomas Church. A call to the office, however, only yielded the information that the secretary was new to the area and hardly knew anyone and the priest was away on his annual retreat. Unfortunately, only Father Montoya could authorize the release of official church information.

"There is someone you might try," she said. "Father Keenan retired a few years ago and he was here for years."

"Where is he now?" asked Lucy.

"His health isn't good. He's at a retirement home for clergy in New Hampshire."

Lucy perked up when she heard the address; it was only about a couple of hours drive away. She could go later in the week, after deadline. "Thanks so much," she said.

"Movies," muttered Ted. "We need the movie listings."

Lucy was a little nervous going to breakfast with the girls on Thursday morning. She hadn't seen Sue since the Labor Day cookout and was worried she was angry with her. But when she approached the usual table in Jake's Donut Shop, Sue's smile was as friendly as ever.

"Hi, guys," said Lucy, taking her seat. "You won't believe what happened to me," she began, eager to tell them all about her adventures with Libby.

"You won't believe what Sue's been up to," interrupted Pam, her eyes wide with astonishment.

"Really?" Lucy felt the wind go out of her sails. "Tell me all about it."

"Well," began Sue. "To make a long story short, I'm going into business with Chris Cashman."

Lucy's chin dropped. "What?"

"I knew something like this would happen," said Rachel, nodding sagely. "It was inevitable."

"I have to admit I didn't see this coming," said Lucy. "I thought you were archenemies."

"Oh, I don't know why I got so upset about that bake sale," said Sue, with a dismissive wave of the hand. "It was just silly. And when Chris called me after the Board of Appeals meeting and said she got approval to operate her investment business from her house . . ."

"You're going to go into financial planning?"

Lucy couldn't believe it. Sue's favorite maxim was "You've got to spend money to save it."

"No, silly, I don't know anything about finances. I'm opening a day care business and Chris is going to be a silent partner."

Lucy knew that Sue had run the town's first day-care center for several years, filling a vital need for young working families who couldn't otherwise afford child care. She had since retired but the center was still flourishing.

"This is going to be different," continued Sue. "This is going to be a bit more upscale, designed for professional parents who want the very best for their kids. We'll have foreign languages, educational games, a fitness program, music appreciation—I'm pretty excited about it. We even have a name: Little Prodigies Preschool Center."

"That sounds great but do you think there are enough professional parents who can afford it?" asked Rachel. "Something like that's going to be pricey."

"Chris has done a lot of research,"

"Of course," said Lucy and Pam, simultaneously.

". . . and she says there are plenty of couples looking for top quality care for their kids. The population has really changed in the past few years. The old folks are dying off, there's been an influx of professionals who work at home, or commute to businesses that have moved out of the urban centers. There's that new industrial park in Gilead; it's full of computer and biotech outfits."

"But how did Chris know that you have a background in early childhood education?" asked Lucy.

"She was asking around for daycare options and somebody told her to call me for some referrals and one thing led to another." She looked at her watch. "Well, sorry, I've got to run. I'm meeting Chris. We're going to check out some possible properties." She stood up and picked up her purse. "Wish me luck!"

She left in a chorus of good wishes, leaving behind her amazed and befuddled friends.

"I'm floored," said Lucy. "I thought they hated each other."

"The last I heard, and I heard quite a lot, she was going on and on about what a bossy upstart Chris was," said Pam.

"It makes sense, if you think about it," said Rachel, who had majored in psychology. "Like minds attract and, let's face it, this town is too small for both of them. They either had to get together and make peace or one of them was going to have to leave."

"This is going to be good for Sue," said Lucy. "She definitely needed a new interest."

"Those two are bound to make a success of it," said Pam. "Do you think we can get in on the ground floor, before they go multinational?"

Lucy was in good spirits when she got to work, but unlike the week before, this Thursday the phones were ringing like crazy. And it wasn't because of Lucy's two-inch story about the possible identification of the homeless man based on the discovery of the driver's license, which was all Ted agreed to print without more information.

"Ted got the tax rate wrong," said Phyllis. "He printed $66.87 instead of $6.87 per thousand."

"Oops," said Lucy, uncomfortably aware that she had proofread his story on the new rate and hadn't noticed the mistake. "I think it must've been a typo at the printer's," she said hopefully.

"Uh, no. It's right here in the dummy. I don't know how we missed it." Phyllis slapped her forehead. "I looked at it, too. Never noticed."

"Oh, well, these things happen," said Lucy philosophically.

"It isn't the irate taxpayers that are so bad. It's the town treasurer. He's fit to be tied and Ted's over there now, trying to calm him down."

"I don't suppose he'll be happy with a correction?"

"No. Blood. He wants blood."

"Poor Ted."

"Poor us, you mean," said Phyllis. "I don't want to be here when Ted gets back."

"Neither do I," said Lucy, planning her escape. She was thwarted, however, by a phone call from Will Esterhaus, Fred's lawyer.

"That was some cheap trick," he said, skipping the formality of a greeting and getting right to the point.

"Well, if you think about it, the tax rate couldn't possibly be nearly seventy dollars per thousand, that would be ridiculous. If people took the time to think about it they'd realize it was a mistake. A typo. We're human after all. Mistakes happen."

"I don't mean the tax rate, though that's just typical of the sort of sloppy journalism you practice. I'm talking about the article about the homeless man. It's absolutely irresponsible to link him with the Stanton family like that."

"Well, I did find his driver's license," said Lucy.

"You have absolutely no proof of any connection between the license and the man whose body was found in the harbor."

"It was in his campsite," said Lucy, defending

her story. "And I made it quite clear that the ME will now be looking for dental records or DNA to make a positive identification."

"It was in the woods. Anybody could drop a wallet there, it may have been there for years." He paused. "The most likely case is that Mimi herself dropped it there."

Lucy was beginning to feel less sure of her discovery. Esterhaus had a good point.

"That would be some coincidence, wouldn't it? I mean, years ago, some guy who was related to Mimi Stanton was wandering around in the woods where her husband was eventually going to build a home for their family? I don't think so."

"I'm warning you. We expect a full retraction or we'll be seeing you in court."

Lucy swallowed hard. The little bell was jangling and Ted was just coming through the door. "I think you better talk to my editor," she said, putting him on hold.

"Call for you on three, Ted," she said, grabbing her bag. Sometimes there was really no option except retreat, if you wanted to live to fight another day.

Outside, Lucy paused to sniff the crisp fall air. The temperature was finally dropping and a few trees had already changed color. Fall was definitely on its way and she was looking forward to the drive to New Hampshire. Opportunities like this, when she could spend time alone on the open road with her thoughts, rarely came her way. She started the car, turned the radio to her favorite oldies rock station, cranked up the volume, and checked the gas gauge. Before she went anywhere, she was going to have to fill up the rental car.

Lucy was standing at the Quik-Mart self-serve

pump watching the numbers scroll upward and congratulating herself that she wasn't driving a Hummer, not that she'd ever seriously considered the idea, when Preston roared in on his Harley. Now *that* would get even better mileage, she thought, giving him the benefit of the doubt. Maybe he wasn't a reckless hooligan with no regard for other people's desire for peace and quiet; maybe he was a responsible steward of the planet.

"I thought it was you," he said, pulling to a stop behind her car. "Who do you think you are?"

"What do you mean?" she asked calmly, trying not to react to Preston's angry tone.

"That story. Saying the homeless guy was related to my mother."

Lucy felt her throat tighten. "I said it was likely, since your mother's maiden name was O'Toole and she came from the same Boston neighborhood. Plus the fact that he was in town at the time of her funeral. But I made it quite clear that only the medical examiner can make a positive ID."

"That could all be coincidence. I don't know this guy, I never heard of him and neither did my dad."

"That doesn't mean you're not related," said Lucy, replacing the hose on the pump. "Maybe there's some reason they drifted apart."

"Yeah, and I bet you'd like to find out all about it, wouldn't you?" Preston was jabbing his finger angrily at her.

Under the circumstances, Lucy thought it wisest not to mention her plans for the day.

"Well, listen, you," he said, snarling at her. "You leave my family alone—or else!"

Then he gunned the motorcycle and sped off, raising a cloud of dust.

Chapter 17

"Don't you threaten me!" yelled Lucy, but she knew the gesture was futile. He certainly couldn't hear her over the noise of his engine. Her words only served to vent her anger and frustration, and her fear. She didn't like being threatened, especially after two murders. He certainly didn't mean that she might be next, did he? The thought gave Lucy pause. Was Preston the murderer? Did his father go to jail to protect him?

What exactly did that "or else" mean?

Lucy started the car, but driving to New Hampshire no longer seemed like such a good idea. For one thing, Zoe would be coming home from school in an hour or so and she didn't want to leave her alone in the house, not with Preston's threat hanging over them. It would be far more sensible, she decided, to make the trip tomorrow morning when the girls were safe in school.

But even that plan seemed doomed to failure when Sara refused to eat any breakfast Friday morning, complaining she was too nauseous.

"Maybe you should stay home," suggested Lucy.

She was already rearranging her schedule and planning to work from home.

"I can't," moaned Sara. "There's a game today and I can't miss it."

"Why not rest this morning and if you feel better I can take you to school later?"

"It's an away game and there's a pep rally first thing this morning."

"They never had pep rallies before," said Lucy.

"They never had a winning team before," said Bill, his mouth full of bagel. "Face it, that second half against Gilead was incredible. Matt Engelhardt is one amazing quarterback. Let her go."

"Not if she's sick . . ."

"I feel okay, Mom, I really do."

"You can't go on an empty stomach. Not if you're going to be leading a pep rally. And where is this away game?"

"Lake Wingate."

"See!" Lucy turned to Bill. "That's at least an hour from here, maybe more. What if she gets sick on the bus?"

"I won't get sick on the bus," said Sara.

"I'm not very happy about this. Not after what happened on the bus after the last away game."

"That was just a combination of youthful high spirits and a very tired coach. You can be sure it won't happen again, not after that meeting," said Bill. "Everybody will be on their best behavior."

"Dad's right, Mom. Coach Buck really chewed out the players and told them that if anything like that happens again they're off the team, no exceptions."

Lucy was running out of arguments. "Okay," she said. "Take some nutrition bars, okay?"

"Okay," said Sara, giving her a hug.

Lucy's day was back on track. She would stop in at the *Pennysaver* office to check in with Ted and then she would head across the state to St. Bernard's Home in Salem to talk to Father Keenan. She packed lunches for Bill and Zoe, gave Sara's cheerleading outfit a quick touch up with the iron, sent everyone off with a kiss, fed the dog, tidied the kitchen, took a shower, blow-dried her hair, got dressed, and was finally ready to go. Except that when she got out to her little rental car she discovered it had four flat tires. Preston had apparently made good on his threat, she decided, as she called the rental place.

"Four flat tires? I never heard of such a thing," said the agent.

"They just don't make 'em like they used to," said Lucy, pretending ignorance. She was not about to admit any responsibility for the tires; the rental company and the insurance company would have to sort it out. "How soon can you get it fixed?"

"We'll have somebody out there right away," promised the agent.

Lucy doubted it, but she took up her position by the front window to watch for the repair truck anyway. Car trouble was a lot like a toothache, she decided, because it was hard to think of anything else. So she stood there, watching for the truck, impatiently tapping her foot.

She had a clear view of Prudence Path and watched as the school bus arrived and the kids filed aboard, followed moments later by Coach Buck's departure in his minivan. Five minutes later she heard the familiar roar of Preston's Harley when he left for school. He didn't have a passenger so

Tommy was apparently still recovering at home. With his mother dead, his father in jail accused of murder, and his younger brother to care for, it was no wonder Preston was acting out. Lucy could almost forgive him, but not quite.

Next to leave was Scratch Westwood, the vet, driving his aged Jeep. Lucy wondered if it was true that he had been having an affair with Mimi and if that explained Willie's mood swings. He was followed in short order by Chris Cashman's husband in his little Honda. The clock in the hall ticked, the road was empty, there was no sign of the repair truck. Lucy was thinking of calling again when Chris Cashman's big Expedition came into sight; Lucy wondered if today was KinderGym or French lessons or maybe AquaBabies. Thank goodness she'd raised her babies in simpler times when getting together with some other mothers and their little ones for a once-a-week playgroup was considered sufficient stimulation. A few minutes later, Willie Westwood came screeching up to the stop sign in her Wagoneer; she tapped the brakes in a token stop and was off. Golly gee, that woman sure loved her horses; she couldn't wait to get to them. Then, once again, it was quiet. Only Frankie, Bonnie, and Tommy remained on Prudence Path and soon it would likely be only Tommy, when Frankie went to work in the real estate office and Bonnie headed out to run her errands. Lucy didn't like the idea of him being there all alone but there wasn't anything she could do about it.

Finally, the repair truck chugged up the hill and turned into her driveway.

"Whoa, what happened here?" demanded the

mechanic, a slight young fellow with sun-bleached hair and grimy hands.

"I don't know," said Lucy. "This is how I found the car this morning."

"Somebody slashed these tires," he said, showing her the cuts in the black rubber. "Do you have any idea who did it?"

"Of course not. Why?"

"You better file a police report or the insurance won't pay."

"Really?" Lucy had been hoping to get on the road as soon as possible.

"Really."

It took the mechanic almost an hour to change all four tires, and then Lucy spent another half hour at the police station, filing a report that morphed into a complaint against Preston. Lucy knew it was necessary, but she didn't feel comfortable about it as she finally began the trip. The last thing she wanted was for the situation to escalate.

As she turned into the carefully landscaped grounds of St. Bernard's Home, Lucy belatedly wondered if she should have called ahead. For all she knew, Father Keenan could have one of the terrible diseases of aging like Alzheimer's, ALS, or Parkinson's. Or perhaps he was fit as a fiddle and maintained a busy schedule of golf and bridge. She'd been foolish to assume he had nothing better to do than sit and wait for her to come and ask him questions. But when she asked for him at the reception desk she was relieved to be sent out back to the garden, where she found him picking tomatoes.

"Father Keenan?"

"How can I help you?" replied a tall, lean man wearing a black cotton shirt with a backwards collar, farmer's overalls and a straw hat. His creased face was deeply tanned and he had bright blue eyes.

"I'm looking for information about a family in your parish," said Lucy. "Do you have a few minutes?"

"I surely do," said the priest, with a shrug. "And I wouldn't mind getting off my feet for a bit."

"I'm Lucy Stone, from the *Pennysaver* newspaper in Tinker's Cove, Maine," said Lucy, extending her hand.

His grip was warm and strong. "I guess you know who I am. Formerly parish priest and now gardener."

"A very fine gardener," said Lucy, eyeing the basket of ripe, red tomatoes. "Those are gorgeous. What's your secret?"

"I talk to them," said Father Keenan, a twinkle in his eye. "They say they like the carbon dioxide in your breath but I prefer to think plants enjoy a bit of company. As do I."

"I'm afraid this goes back quite a few years," began Lucy. "I'm looking for information about a family named O'Toole. They had a daughter named Mary Catherine and a son named Thomas Preston. I think they may have lived in Jamaica Plain."

She was surprised to see a spark of recognition in the old man's eyes. "I remember them well. They were adorable children. She was the older and she took great care of her little brother. I always thought what a wonderful mother she would make." He sighed. "It was a great tragedy, what happened to their father. It was in all the papers at the time, I'm sure you'll remember it."

"I didn't grow up around here," said Lucy. "I was raised near New York City."

"Even so, it made national news. It was that shocking. Their father was a police officer, one of Boston's finest. He was shot attempting to stop a bank robbery. Shot and killed. His wife, a lovely woman but very fragile, never got over it. She took her own life shortly after."

"Who raised the children?"

"They went into foster care, I believe." He shook his head. "Like I said, it was very sad."

"Were the robbers caught?"

"I believe so. There was a trial, I remember. Very sensational. It was during the last years of the Vietnam War, you see, and they had some crazy idea of robbing the bank to finance some sort of protest against the military-industrial complex. They were defended by a prominent leftist lawyer from Harvard, his name escapes me right now but it will come back to me eventually." He smiled apologetically. "Usually it does, but sometimes it takes a day or two. Funny, I can remember his long, curly hair but I can't remember his name."

"I know the feeling," said Lucy.

He smiled. "Now it's my turn to ask the questions. Why do you want to know about the family O'Toole?" A faint trace of an Irish brogue crept into his speech.

Lucy hesitated before answering. It was warm on the stone bench and the garden was peaceful and quiet. The only sound was the hum of cicadas and she could smell the peppery scent of the tomato leaves. She didn't want to bring violent death into this lovely place.

"I've heard it all before, you know," he prompted her. "I have heard things in the confessional that would curl your hair."

"I can well imagine," said Lucy. "They're both dead. Mimi, I mean Mary Catherine, was stabbed in her kitchen. Her husband has been charged with the crime. Her brother was homeless but somehow he heard about the funeral and came to Tinker's Cove but they found his body in the harbor, drowned."

Father Keenan picked up one of the tomatoes and stroked its silky skin with his callused thumb. "Did Mary Catherine have any children?"

"Yes," said Lucy, eager to give him some good news. "Two boys. Preston is eighteen and Tommy is fifteen." She saw no need to mention Tommy's suicide attempt or Preston's threats. "Nice boys."

"It must be a very difficult time for them."

"Yes." She watched as a praying mantis made its cautious way along a leafy tomato branch. Its green color was perfect camouflage. She would never have noticed it if it hadn't moved. "I've tried to help but they're very . . . private."

"I will pray for them. And for the souls of Mary Catherine and Thomas Preston." He turned to her. "Are you Catholic?"

Lucy shook her head.

"Do you pray?"

Lucy considered the question. She didn't pray regularly, but there were times when she did. "Occasionally."

"Ah," he said. "I find prayer very helpful. You should try it more often."

"Thank you for your help," she said, getting to her feet. "You've been the answer to a prayer."

His face reddened. "I try," he said, tipping his hat.

As she meandered through the hills of New Hampshire toward the Maine border and home, Lucy thought over what Father Keenan had told her about the O'Toole family. Fred had been truthful when he told her that Mimi had no family. Their parents dead, they had been raised by foster parents. Lucy wondered if they had been placed together in the same home, or if they'd been separated, as was often the case.

It seemed a cruel twist of fate that Mimi's sons were close to being in the same situation, though Preston at least was older than Mimi and her brother had been. How old were they when their father was killed? How long after that did their mother take her life? Father Keenan had said she was "fragile." Did that mean their mother suffered from mental problems even before the shooting? Lucy found that the information she'd gotten from Father Keenan was creating more questions than answers. She couldn't wait to get back to her computer and put Google to work.

She had just passed the "Welcome to Maine" sign when her cell phone rang. Normally, Lucy didn't like to talk on the cell phone when she was driving; she'd seen too many near misses by drivers who were completely oblivious to the cars around them as they engaged in a fascinating conversation. But today she practically had the road to herself and she would make it brief, tell whoever was calling that she would get back to them as soon as possible.

"Mo-o-om!" wailed Sara, when she answered

Lucy felt the car swerve a bit. "What's the matter?"

"I wanna go ho-o-me."

"Calm down and tell me what's the matter," insisted Lucy, pulling into a convenient rest stop.

"I just wanna go home."

"Are you sick?"

Sara produced a sound that could be taken as either affirmative or negative, Lucy couldn't decide which. Whatever it was, it was clear Sara was in some sort of distress and needed her.

"Where are you?"

"Lake Wah-wah-wingate."

Lucy pulled a map out of the glove compartment and discovered she was only about 25 miles away. "I can be there in about half an hour," she promised.

"Hu-u-urry," wailed Sara.

"Just take it easy," said Lucy, ending the call and peeling out of the rest area with the gas pedal pressed to the floor. This was definitely one of those times that called for prayer. "Lord," she said, raising her eyes skyward, "please let there be no state troopers for the next 25 miles."

Chapter 18

When Lucy arrived at Lake Wingate High School she didn't have to go looking for Sara; she was sitting on the front steps of the sprawling brick building waiting to be rescued. A bank of clouds was building in the west, and the wind was whipping her hair across her face. Lucy could hear crowd noises and the amplified voice of an announcer calling the plays, punctuated by the band playing a few bars of the school fight song from the football field behind the school.

"What's the matter?" asked Lucy, as her daughter got in the car. It was obvious she had been crying and equally obvious that she didn't want her mother to know it.

"I just don't feel good," said Sara, staring straight ahead.

"How don't you feel good? Tired? Nauseous? Headache? Fever?" Lucy took her foot off the brake and proceeded down the drive at a reasonable speed.

"Yeah."

"Which?" demanded Lucy, placing her hand on Sara's forehead to check for a fever.

"All of them."

"You don't have a fever," said Lucy, turning onto Main Street and heading for the highway.

"I guess I'm just tired. I should've stayed home, like you said. It's probably PMS."

Lucy wasn't buying it. Sara had always been healthy as a horse and hardly noticed her periods. "Are you sure something didn't happen on the bus? Did those players harass you again?"

Sara was quick to deny it. "No, Mom. Nothing like that happened."

Even though she was convinced her daughter was lying she also knew it was futile to keep questioning her. The more she prodded, the more tightly Sara would clam up.

"Well, just relax. We should be home soon," said Lucy, intending to have a talk with Renee and Sassie, and their mothers, too. This couldn't go on and Lucy was determined to get to the bottom of it.

Lucy switched the radio on to Sara's favorite station and soon Sara began to relax, tapping her fingers along to hits by Britney, Jessica Simpson, and Madonna. When a fast food restaurant came into view, Lucy asked if she'd like a Coke or something and Sara surprised her by asking for a whole meal. So much for being sick, thought Lucy, but she wasn't about to press the issue.

It occurred to her that Sara took a lot for granted: a pleasant home, three nutritious meals a day, a loving and supportive family, medical and dental care, stylish and appropriate clothing, a good school system, friends. These were just the basic building blocks for healthy development, but not all kids were lucky enough to have them. And even if they did have them, they could lose them, like Preston and Tommy had. It struck Lucy that the Stanton family was repeating some terrible cycle of destruction that began with the death of Mimi's father and mother. The sins of the father visited on the children? In this case it seemed more like the misfortunes of one generation being passed down to the next.

One thing was different, however. Because Preston and Tommy were older they wouldn't have to go into foster care, at least Preston wouldn't, and if he wasn't found to be a suitable guardian for Tommy, at least he'd only be in care for a few years. Lucy had heard plenty about the deficiencies of the foster care system and could cite several recent news stories about abuse and neglect. She was sure that most foster parents were decent folk who tried their best but the need was so great that a few rotten apples always seemed to slip through. Even the best-intentioned foster parents could be undone by the demands of the job. She wondered what Mimi and her brother's experience had been; she had a feeling it hadn't been good.

She was thinking along those lines when she turned into her driveway and saw Tommy and Preston standing there. Her first impulse was to lock the car doors and call 9-1-1 but Sara leaped out of the car before she could put that plan into action. She was certain the boys had come to confront her about the report she'd filed against Preston at the police station that morning.

But when she extricated herself from her seat belt she found Sara was smiling flirtatiously at Preston, swinging her hips and twirling her hair around her fingers.

"What's up?" asked Lucy, joining the group.

"I just wanted to apologize for being a jerk," said Preston. Tommy nodded in agreement.

"If you want me to drop charges, I don't think I can do it," said Lucy. "It's a rental car so it's out of my hands."

"He didn't slash your tires," said Tommy. "He was home with me all night."

Lucy looked at Preston through narrowed eyes. "Really?"

"Really," said Preston. "I understand why you thought it was me, because of the stuff I said at the gas station. But I didn't really mean that."

"He's been upset," said Tommy, "because of everything that's happened."

Preston, despite his black motorcycle leathers and long hair suddenly looked very young to Lucy, with his skinny wrists and barely-there mustache.

"You've been really nice, offering to help and all, and I want you to know that Tommy and I appreciate it."

This dramatic shift in attitude seemed a little too good to be true. "What changed your mind?" she asked.

"Dad's lawyer, Mr. Esterhaus, he got us this counselor and she's helped us sort things out."

"That's good," said Lucy, who was feeling a whole lot better about the boys' situation.

"Well, we gotta be going," said Preston.

"Just one other thing," said Tommy, making eye contact with Sara. "My dad didn't, well, he didn't do it."

"Yeah," added Preston. "That's for sure."

"Listen, guys, I found out some interesting stuff.

Why don't you come in the house so I can tell you about it."

"Okay," said Preston, with a shrug.

Inside the kitchen, Libby welcomed them by attempting her usual wiggles and jumps though she was unable to give them the full routine because of her stitches. Lucy sent Sara upstairs to take a shower and sat the boys at the kitchen table, where she passed out cold cans of soda, which they promptly drained in one gulp, setting the cans carefully on the table in front of them.

"I interviewed this priest today, Father Keenan. He's retired now but he used to work at a church in Jamaica Plain and he knew your family. Well, your mother's family."

The boys relaxed attitude suddenly changed. Lucy felt as if they were hanging on her every word.

"You don't know anything about your mother's family?" she asked.

They shook their heads. "Mom always said she didn't have any family. She was raised by a series of foster parents and the less said about them, the better," said Preston. Tommy nodded in agreement.

"Well, she did have a family. Her father was a Boston cop who was shot during a bank heist. Her mother was left with two kids, your mom and her brother, but she died soon after." Lucy decided to omit the fact that Mimi's mother had committed suicide.

"And this homeless guy who drowned? He really was her brother? Our uncle?"

Lucy nodded. "His name was Thomas Preston O'Toole. You were both named after him."

"This is really blowing my mind," said Preston. "I wonder why she never tried to contact him."

"Maybe the past was so painful she didn't want to open it up." Lucy didn't say what she thought was the more likely reason: that Mimi felt reopening the past would be dangerous. It certainly seemed that the key to her murder would be found in the past. "If you think of anything, anything at all that might help, please tell me. And remember, if you need anything, my offer's still good."

Lucy stood in the doorway as the boys left, but when Preston started his motorcycle there was no hideous roar. It turned over smoothly and quietly and purred as he rolled down the driveway.

"What happened?" asked Lucy.

"Tommy told me," chirped up Sara, who had come back downstairs, her hair still damp from her shower. "He got a new muffler. The lawyer advised him it would help community relations."

Esterhaus sounded like one smart cookie, thought Lucy, making a mental note of the name. You just never knew when you might need a good lawyer.

Lucy waited until after supper, when Sara had gone out to the movies with her friends and Zoe was upstairs getting her homework out of the way before the weekend, to tell Bill about the day's events.

"Something's going on with that football team that isn't right," insisted Lucy. "I just feel it."

"Yeah, they're winning," said Bill. "They beat Lake Wingate twenty-one to six today. Amazing."

"What are you saying? That it's okay for the boys

to haze each other and harass the cheerleaders so long as they keep winning?"

"Well, whatever's going on, you can't argue with the result."

Lucy couldn't believe her husband, Sara's doting father, was talking like this. "Are you actually telling me you'd sacrifice your daughter's well-being for a winning season?"

Bill shifted uncomfortably in his recliner, making it squeak. "No. Of course not. But maybe she just needs to develop a little tougher skin. That's what this stuff is all about and to tell the truth, if it's hazing that's producing the desire to win, well I can't say I think it's such a bad thing." He shrugged. "We all go through it one way or another. You've got to pay your dues."

"Well, the team may be winning but Sara's throwing up every morning before school. This can't go on." Lucy leaned forward. "I think she should talk to a counselor."

Bill's eyebrows shot up. "Like a psychiatrist?" He shook his head. "She's not crazy."

"But she is unhappy. I can't get her to tell me what's going on but maybe she'd open up to a professional. They know all sorts of techniques for establishing trust and getting kids to open up to them."

"Why would she trust a stranger when she won't trust her parents?"

"Apparently . . ." began Lucy, but she was interrupted by Libby's frantic barking. The dog's hair was standing straight up on her back as she paced from window to window, growling and barking.

Lucy looked at Bill. "Probably just a skunk," he

said, as the window behind his chair suddenly shattered with a crack like a gunshot. They both dove to the floor, where Lucy lay on her stomach, panting with fear. Bill began crawling, propelling himself by his elbows, and unplugged the lamp, plunging the room into semi-darkness. Then he grabbed the phone cord and pulled the instrument to him.

"What was that?" demanded Zoe, standing in the doorway.

Lucy's heart was in her throat. "Get down," she hissed. "I think somebody's out there with a gun."

Zoe began wiggling across the rug to her mother.

"Stay put. There's broken glass."

"I'm scared, Mommy."

"Everything's okay," said Bill. "The cops are coming. All we have to do is stay low."

Moments later, they heard the approaching siren of a police cruiser coming up Red Top Road. When they heard the scrunch of tires in the drive and saw the powerful lights reflected on the wall they cautiously got to their feet and Bill went to the kitchen door.

Lucy switched the overhead light on and surveyed the damage. It wasn't a shot after all that had broken the window, she discovered, but a baseball-sized rock with a piece of paper wrapped around it.

"Don't touch that," she warned Zoe, hurrying into the kitchen. There she found Bill and Officer Josh Kirwan, Dot's youngest, who looked barely old enough to vote.

"It was a rock," Lucy informed him. "With a note."

"What does the note say?"

"I didn't touch it. Don't you want to check it for fingerprints?"

"Oh, right," said Officer Kirwan, nervously fingering his notebook. "I better call this in to the station."

"I'll make some coffee," said Lucy, figuring it was going to be a long night. She gave Zoe a hug. "You go on back upstairs and start getting ready for bed."

"But tomorrow's Saturday," she protested.

"Okay. You can watch the TV in my room."

Officer Kirwan went outside to check that the rock thrower was gone and to look for evidence. Lucy and Bill sat at the kitchen table, listening to the coffee pot drip and hiss.

"I wish we could read that message on the rock," said Lucy.

"It's probably not anything you want to hear," said Bill.

"Even so. It might have something to do with Mimi's death." She sniffed the comforting smell of coffee. "Maybe the murderer threw the rock."

"Maybe you better calm down and let the police handle this."

Lucy wasn't at all encouraged when Detective Horowitz arrived, followed immediately by a white crime scene van and two technicians. They went straight into the family room, carrying an assortment of equipment cases and powerful lamps. Lucy had that odd feeling you get when your house isn't quite your own. After what seemed an eternity Horowitz emerged with the note encased in a clear plastic bag. As ever, he seemed gray and tired with his thinning hair, rumpled suit, and pale eyes.

"I'd like you to take a look at this. Do you have any idea what it's about?"

He set it on the table so Lucy and Bill could see.

It was a torn piece of yellow foolscap with blue lines. The words "You could be next" were written in large penciled block letters.

Lucy swallowed hard and looked at Bill, gauging his reaction. His eyes had hardened and every muscle was tense, but he was working hard not to show it. Rocks through the window, death threats, just a typical Friday evening in the Stone house. Lucy knew he was blaming her and there would be hell to pay later.

"I think it's a reference to Mimi's murder, and the homeless guy, too. It's from the killer," said Lucy. "Somebody slashed my tires this morning, too."

"How do you get that?" demanded Horowitz, with a rare flash of anger. "The murderer was her husband and he's in jail and the homeless guy is officially an accidental death."

"He was Mimi's brother," said Lucy.

"Yeah, and he was a homeless bum. Homeless bums die all the time."

"Yeah, but homeless bums don't come to Tinker's Cove and get themselves killed. There's a reason why he died and I think it has something to do with Mimi, with their family. It's like violence follows them. I went to talk to their parish priest today. He told me their father was a cop who was killed during a bank robbery. Their mother was so upset she killed herself. I don't know how it all comes together but somebody's out to get them and that somebody must be worried that I'm on to something." Lucy's mind was working overtime. "You know, we didn't hear a car or anything like that. I think that whoever threw this rock came on foot." She looked out the window, at the darkening night. Through the trees she could see the lighted windows of the houses on Prudence Path.

"Lucy!" exploded Bill. "This is crazy. You've got to stop. You're putting the whole family in danger and I won't have it. Enough with the investigative reporting! Why can't you write about doll makers and local artists and fundraisers like you used to?"

Lucy bit her lip and felt her face warm with embarrassment.

"Your husband has a point, Mrs. Stone. Maybe you ought to leave the investigating to the police."

"Well, I would," said Lucy, defending herself, "but the police don't seem to be doing a very good job, do they? I was the one who identified the homeless guy, and I'm going to find out who killed him and Mimi. Those boys have lost their mother but they deserve to have a father."

So there it was. Lucy hadn't realized it herself, but that was the reason she wasn't about to give up.

"It's not your responsibility," said Bill, softly.

"That's right," said Horowitz. "We have social services, foster care . . . they'll be taken care of."

Lucy rolled her eyes in disgust. "Who are you kidding? Don't you read the newspapers? The whole system's messed up."

"That's not true," insisted Horowitz. "You only read about the tragedies. Believe me, there are hundreds of success stories every day, but reporters like you only want to write about the sensational stories."

Lucy had heard it all before: it was the media's fault. Never mind the corrupt officials, the lives destroyed, bad news was always the fault of the reporter. Kill the messenger. "Oh, puh-lease," she moaned.

"I'll admit you have uncovered some interesting information," said Horowitz.

Lucy's eyebrows shot up in surprise.

"And I'm going to take another look at the case against Fred Stanton."

"That's great," said Lucy.

"But I have to warn you," he continued in his sad monotone, "that if you continue to investigate on your own, you're taking a very big risk." He shook his head mournfully. "Our resources are stretched to the breaking point. Next time you call, I can't promise we'll be able to respond."

Lucy remembered how frightened she was when the window broke, she thought of how vulnerable little Zoe was, and she was tempted to promise she would leave the investigating to the pros, but she couldn't do it.

"I'll be careful," she said.

Chapter 19

Lucy was up bright and early Saturday morning, eager to get to her computer and Google the bank robbery that resulted in Officer O'Toole's death. She didn't even bother with breakfast but poured herself a cup of coffee. The dog didn't think much of this change in schedule but after pacing around the kitchen, nails clicking on the wood floor, she finally curled up on the floor next to Lucy's computer desk with a big sigh.

The news stories she turned up took her back to the seventies, to long hair and ugly colors like mustard brown and avocado green and red-orange, to the Vietnam war, cities burning in race riots, the Black Panthers. Patty Hearst was in jail and other members of the Symbionese Liberation Army had died in a fiery shoot-out with police. Other radical antiestablishment groups had abandoned the peaceful protests of the sixties for violent action. One such group, the People's Liberation Front, had robbed several Boston area banks in order to get money to advance their cause, supposedly protecting "the people" from the "fascist establishment." Officer John Joseph O'Toole was among the offi-

cers responding to an alarm at the Boston Five
Cents Savings Bank on Washington Street. He was
the first to enter the bank and had been shot point
blank in the chest by one of the fleeing robbers.

Two of the Front members had been killed in
the ensuing shoot-out, a third had been wounded
and was later tried and sentenced to life in prison,
but the driver of the getaway car was never caught.
Numerous photos were published in hopes that
somebody would recognize him and turn him in,
but that had never happened. He still showed up
from time to time on lists of Ten Most Wanted
Criminals.

Looking at the grainy photo of the long-haired,
bearded young revolutionary, Lucy thought how
much he looked like some of the boys she went to
college with. If he was as blinded by youth and ide-
alism as they had been, he had never seriously considered the human cost of his behavior. They played
at revolution like kids today play video games,
thought Lucy, shooting anyone who got in their
way.

Lucy sat back in her chair, thinking over what
she had learned and reached for her coffee cup. It
was empty so she got up to refill it and make herself a piece of toast or something when Sara came
down the stairs.

"You're up early for a Saturday," said Lucy.

"I couldn't sleep," said Sara.

"Want some breakfast? I'll make you an egg,
French toast, whatever you want."

"I'm not hungry," said Sara, pouring herself a
glass of orange juice.

"You've never had trouble sleeping before," said

Lucy. "Was it because of what happened at Lake Wingate?"

"No, Mom. Nothing like that. I shouldn't have had that glass of Coke before I went to bed, that's all."

"Try another one," said Lucy, dismayed to catch her daughter in a lie. "It's caffeine free."

"Well, I didn't know that, did I? They say half of the effect of caffeine is in people's heads. I probably thought it might keep me awake, so it did."

"Oh, Sara," said Lucy, sliding into a chair and leaning across the table to take her daughter's hands, "give it up. Tell me what's going on and then maybe we can fix it."

"I don't think so, Mom." Sara jerked her hands away and jumped to her feet. "You'll just write a news story about it. How's that supposed to fix anything?"

"That's not fair," protested Lucy, but Sara was halfway up the stairs. Lucy heard her pound each step, cross the landing, and slam her bedroom door shut. "I only wrote about the meeting!" she yelled up the stairs.

Unable to shake the truth out of Sara, Lucy decided to see if Frankie had any idea what was going on. She certainly seemed to have an accepting approach to teen sexuality, maybe she had open lines of communication with Renee. But when Lucy emerged from the path between her house and Primrose Path she saw that Frankie's driveway was empty. Of course, weekends were prime time for real estate agents.

Lucy hesitated for a moment, studying the cloudy sky that was heavy with rain, then decided she might as well try Willie. She was well aware that Willie hadn't been all that friendly lately, but she wasn't about to go home without trying to get some answers. Besides, she had a feeling that whatever was going on might be related to Willie's attitude towards her. Maybe Sassie had told her that Sara was behaving in a way that she found upsetting, or that Willie didn't approve of. She went across the street and knocked on the door.

"Come in," yelled Willie so Lucy pulled open the door and went in, finding herself in a mudroom filled with riding boots and helmets and fishermen's waders and kids' sneakers and rain slickers. An old popcorn tin held a collection of walking sticks and umbrellas and a variety of leashes hung from a hook.

Entering the kitchen, she found Willie in front of the sink, rinsing dishes and putting them in the dishwasher. "Oh, it's you," she said with a distinct lack of enthusiasm.

"I'm sorry to bother you," began Lucy, checking out the big farmer's table, littered with newspapers and jam jars. "I don't know where else to turn."

"So I'm your last resort?" snapped Willie. She was glaring at Lucy but was distracted when the little potbellied pig ran into the kitchen, squealing, chased by the cat who was in turn being chased by eight-year-old Chip. "What do you think you're doing?" she demanded, turning on him.

"The cat ate my cereal," declared Chip. "I was watching Power Rangers."

"I suppose you left it on the floor?" Willie opened the door to let the animals out. "What do you expect?"

Lucy couldn't help laughing.

"Yeah," admitted Chip. "But she shouldn't . . ."

"Make yourself a new bowl," said Willie, rolling her eyes at Lucy. "It's a zoo around here."

"I miss those days. I can't believe Toby is all grown up."

"I'm sure I'll get all nostalgic some day but right now I'd give anything for fifteen minutes without a crisis." Willie shut the dishwasher and leaned her fanny against the kitchen counter. "So what's your problem?"

"It's Sara and this cheerleading thing. Something happened yesterday at the Lake Wingate game that upset her but she won't tell me what it was. I was wondering if Sassie might have said anything to you."

"No-o-o," said Willie, dragging out the word. "But I have been worried about her."

"She doesn't seem like herself?"

"Who knows who herself is," said Willie, shaking her head. "She certainly doesn't and I don't have a clue. But she doesn't seem very happy and she's been spending an awful lot of time moping in her room. I practically have to drag her downstairs for supper."

"Have you asked her what's going on?"

"Sure, but she won't tell me anything. She just gets upset and goes back to her room."

"It's the same with Sara." Lucy scratched her chin thoughtfully and looked out the window where she saw Frankie's car turning into her driveway. "Frankie's home. I wonder if Renee's told her something."

"Renee's probably causing all the trouble," muttered Willie. "That girl has the morals of a polecat."

* * *

Frankie was just opening her door when Lucy caught up with her. "Do you have a minute? I'm really worried about Sara and . . ."

"I'm in a terrible rush," said Frankie. "I've got a showing five minutes ago. I only came home because I forgot some important papers." She stuck her head in the door and yelled for her daughter. "Renee! Can you bring me that folder that's on my dresser?"

"Sure, Mom." Seconds later Renee bounced down the stairs, ponytail swinging, with the folder.

Frankie turned to Lucy. "I gotta run. Maybe Renee can help you." Then she was off, tottering down the path in her high heels.

Renee smiled politely at Lucy. "Is there something I can do for you, Mrs. Stone?"

Lucy looked at her. She was hardly the siren Willie had led her to expect, dressed in sweatpants and a huge T-shirt and without a smudge of make-up, not even lip gloss. Not that she needed it, not with her flawless olive skin, luminous brown eyes, and glossy black hair that fell in curls to her shoulders.

"Well," began Lucy, "it's about Sara. She seems awfully upset about something, something to do with cheerleading."

"Why don't you come in?" suggested Renee.

Lucy hesitated. As a reporter she never interviewed minors alone. She always made sure a responsible adult was present. This wasn't an interview, she wasn't working, but she still would have felt better if Frankie had stuck around. Still, Frankie was the one who suggested she talk to Renee. Lucy followed her down the hall to the kitchen.

"Coffee?" asked Renee. "Water?"

"No thanks," said Lucy, climbing onto one of the stools at the island.

Renee got a bottle of water out of the fridge and settled herself on the other stool.

"Well, like I said before, Sara's been very unhappy and upset lately and I'm sure it's something to do with cheerleading. Sara left the game yesterday, she called me to pick her up, but she hasn't told me why. I wonder if there was some teasing or something?"

"The boys on the team are always teasing us, that's just what boys do," said Renee, shrugging.

"How do they tease you?"

"Oh, you know, they think we're silly. They make fun when we touch up our makeup, stuff like that."

"I think it must be more than that," insisted Lucy. "Do they make personal remarks about your appearance? Your figures?"

"Well, you know boys. It's all about boobs to them." Renee gave a world-weary sigh. "Americans are so silly about their bodies."

"What do you mean?" asked Lucy in a small voice.

Renee took a drink of water. "I was in Europe this summer, you know . . ."

"So was my daughter Elizabeth," said Lucy.

"Really? Then you know what I'm talking about."

Lucy didn't have a clue, but then Elizabeth had only been home for a few days and there really hadn't been time for a heart-to-heart chat. Lucy was pretty sure she was going to find time now. "I didn't really get a chance to hear about her trip," she said.

"Too bad. I bet she had a great time. I sure did.

I stayed with my cousins in France, and after a while there we all went hiking in Italy, in the Cinque Terre. It's so beautiful there. Did Elizabeth go there?"

"I don't really know," said Lucy, feeling dumber by the minute.

"The point I'm trying to make is, well, people in France and Italy are a lot more comfortable about their bodies. My cousins never wore bikini tops for swimming, for example. On the beach, some do and some don't and it's perfectly okay."

Lucy swallowed hard, wondering if Elizabeth had spent half the summer prancing about topless.

"I have this funny story," said Renee, smiling and flapping her hand. "Like I said, we were hiking in the Cinque Terre. It's really rough there, the trails are steep and rocky, but gorgeous, right along the sea. You can imagine: rocky like Maine but warm and the houses have those red tile roofs. So, after hours of hiking we finally came to this place where we could swim. It was a gorgeous little cove. Beautiful blue, blue water. So my cousins and I all stripped off our clothes and jumped in and we were floating around, just relaxing and cooling off, not really noticing anything, when we heard this awful voice. This woman, this *American* woman had come along the trail after us, with her kids, and when she saw us in the water she went crazy. She was yelling at the kids to cover their eyes, not to look. We were dying with laughter, we thought it was sooo funny." Then Renee's tone changed and became more serious. "But the weird thing was, even though I knew I wasn't doing anything wrong, that woman made me feel as if I was. As if swimming without a suit was somehow dirty or something. So I decided then and there that I wasn't ever going to be ashamed of my body ever again. So that's why when this whole boob thing started . . ."

Lucy interrupted. "I don't understand. What boob thing?"

"Well, first they wanted to know if they were real . . ."

"Who wanted to know?"

"Well, Matt Engelhardt and his little sidekicks Justin and Will started it, but pretty soon the whole team was in on it. They wanted to check them out, you know, touch them. So after a while we got sick of that and told them they could touch but they had to close their eyes, you know, so they wouldn't know who they were touching."

"Sara? Sassie?"

"We all did it," said Renee. "We were hoping that would be the end of it, that they'd leave us alone, but it wasn't. Then they started wanting to see them."

"You didn't . . ." began Lucy.

"Oh, I did. I was just sick and tired of it, so I stood up and lifted my bra and flashed them. I mean, what's the big deal? If they were in Italy or France, instead of the U.S., all they'd have to do is go to the beach and they could see all the boobs they wanted."

"And where was the coach when this was going on?" demanded Lucy.

"Coach Buck usually sleeps on the bus trips," said Renee, adding a wicked smile, "or pretends to."

"You think he knows what's going on?"

"He not only knows, he encourages a lot of stuff. It's like he wants to be popular with the cool kids, at least that's what I've heard."

"From the players?"

"Not exactly. You know, I guess everybody knows that Preston and I are good friends."

Now it was Lucy's turn to smile. "I have heard something about it."

Renee rolled her eyes. "Sassie's mom gives him the evil eye every time he comes over."

"She's very protective," said Lucy.

"Whatever," said Renee, with a huge sigh. "Anyway, Preston isn't on the team but his little brother, Tommy, is on the JV team. And Preston says Tommy tells him there's all kinds of weird stuff going on, especially at that summer training camp they have." She leaned closer to Lucy. "He makes them play Twister—naked!" She giggled. "I'm going to get the game and take it to France next summer. The *cousines* will adore it. But there's other stuff, mean stuff. He says Tommy got pretty upset about it."

A little idea popped up in Lucy's brain. "Did you tell anybody about this?" she asked.

Renee shrugged. "Just my mom." She waggled a finger at Lucy. "And that's another thing that's different in France. Girls are a lot closer to their mothers there, they tell them everything, and their mothers don't give them a lot of grief like Sassie's mom. She wants to keep Sassie a baby forever. Not like my Tante Marie. She accepts that her daughters are growing up and gives them helpful advice." She paused. "And birth control pills."

Just then the door flew open and Frankie marched in. "Can you believe it? After all that, the guy was a no-show!" She stamped her foot. "I hate it when that happens."

"Well, Mom, you were late. Maybe you missed him."

Lucy wondered who was the mother and who

was the child in the LaChance household. Frankie soon set her straight.

"That's enough from you, Miss Smarty-pants," she snapped. Then her tone softened. "Were you able to help Mrs. Stone?"

"She was terrific," said Lucy. "You should be very proud of her."

"Oh, I am," said Frankie, slipping an arm around her daughter's waist and kissing her on each cheek.

Amazingly, Renee didn't push her away but returned the gesture. Lucy was so impressed by the open and affectionate atmosphere between mother and daughter that she decided to throw caution to the wind.

"Listen," she said, making eye contact with Frankie, "you don't have to tell me, and everything here stays here like it's Las Vegas, but I can't help wondering if you're the person who's been sending anonymous letters to the *Pennysaver*?"

"*Oui, c'est moi.*" Frankie grimaced and added a little shrug.

"Mom!"

"The hazing seemed so terrible and I wanted to do something to stop it." She shook her head. "I thought people would be outraged, but so far, nothing. The paper never printed my letters."

"We never print anonymous letters. If you'd signed them, we could have witheld your name."

"Oh." Frankie nodded, as if making a note for next time. "But then there was the meeting and I was hopeful but nobody would admit anything. I wanted to jump to my feet and yell at them but I knew it wouldn't do any good, so I left."

"My husband says it's because they're having a winning season."

"I guess that's why I'm divorced," said Frankie. "I never could stand that macho male attitude."

Lucy nodded agreement, but as she left the LaChance household she couldn't help thinking a macho male might be exactly what was needed right now. A tough guy who would get the coach's attention.

Chapter 20

When Lucy left Renee and Frankie, she was planning to arrange a meeting with Coach Buck, the Superintendent of Schools, and Preston. She thought Preston, as Tommy's guardian, would have credibility. But the more she thought about it, the less she thought it was a good idea. Preston also had a reputation as a troublemaker with a bad attitude. He wasn't exactly an honor student. Add that to the family's other troubles and she could just imagine Superintendent Sabin's reaction. Such a meeting would just mean more problems for Tommy and Preston, she decided, halfway down Prudence Path. Instead of continuing to the end of the cul-de-sac she turned around, intending to go home. She changed her mind when she saw Coach Buck pull into his driveway. She quickened her pace and met him at his mailbox.

"Can I talk to you for a minute?" she asked.

"Sure," he said, pulling a pile of catalogs and bills out of the box and flipping through it. "Is this in your capacity as neighbor or reporter or concerned parent?"

Lucy considered. As much as she wanted the hazing story for the *Pennysaver* she wanted Sara's happiness even more. "As a parent," she said. "This is off the record."

"Good. Do you want to come in?" he asked, tucking his mail into his briefcase.

Lucy hesitated, despite the darkening clouds overhead which threatened rain. She was well aware that the neighbors kept a close eye on each others' comings and goings. The presence of Bonnie's Caravan in the driveway, indicating she was home, reassured her. "Okay," she said.

She followed Coach Buck down the short drive to the kitchen door, which he politely held for her. She stepped into the kitchen, which was identical to Frankie's without the charming French accents. Bonnie's kitchen was purely utilitarian, with a Formica dining set and cheap discount-store cubbies for the twins' schoolbags. It had a sterile, unwelcoming atmosphere, more like a laboratory than a family kitchen. Bonnie herself was standing at the sink, wearing rubber gloves and scrubbing away at the stainless steel rim with a toothbrush.

"Oh," she said, looking up with a surprised expression. "I wasn't expecting company."

"I'm not company," said Lucy.

"Lucy has some concerns about her daughter," said Buck. "We'll go in my office."

Bonnie shrugged and started rinsing out the sink. Lucy followed Buck through the all-beige living room, which looked like a neatly arranged furniture store display, and down the hall to the tiny third bedroom which he had fitted out as a home office. This room, in contrast to the rest of the house, seemed to reflect the Coach's personality. Plaid curtains added a touch of color, there was an untidy pile of papers on the faux fruitwood assemble-it-yourself computer desk and hutch, and a matching bookcase filled with trophies and photos. Buck sat in his black vinyl desk chair and swiveled to face her, indicating she should sit in a captain's chair with the Boston University seal on the back. She sat down, realizing too late that she didn't know where to begin.

"What's the problem?" he asked. Despite the touch of gray at his temples and the crow's feet in the corners of his eyes, Coach Buck's pinkish face had an innocent, boyish look, as if his mother had just finished scrubbing behind his ears.

"I think you know what the problem is," said Lucy, suddenly angry. "It's the hazing. I know what happened on the bus to the Lake Wingate game. The players are harassing the cheerleaders, the varsity players are hazing the JV boys, and you not only tolerate it, you encourage it."

"Whoa," he said, holding up a hand. "I don't know what you're talking about. I'm not aware of any incident on the bus." He shrugged. "I must have been studying the play book."

"Napping is more like it from what I hear," snapped Lucy. "Or pretending to, while the players tease the girls. Don't tell me you weren't leering with all the rest when Renee flashed her breasts . . ."

"Like I said, I was studying the play book." He gave her a rather weak smile. "From what I hear, she's a bit loose, if you know what I mean."

"Oh, so it's her fault that she and the other cheerleaders are constantly harassed by the players. It began with talk, then it progressed to groping and now it's flashing. And I'm supposed to believe you're unaware of all this, when there have been meetings and discussions about hazing. It's intolerable and it has to stop."

"Teenagers are very sneaky, I'm sure you know that. They manage to defy our best efforts . . ."

"Don't give me that. You're not making any effort at all to stop it. There are plenty of schools that control this sort of thing. It doesn't have to happen. But for some reason you're not only tolerating it, you're encouraging it." She narrowed her eyes. "Some of the players are starting to talk."

"Are you threatening me?" he asked, just as Bonnie appeared in the doorway, still wearing the rubber gloves and holding a tray with two mugs and a Tupperware sugar and cream set.

"Coffee?" she asked, with the bright intonation of a flight attendant. "I thought you might like some."

"Isn't that thoughtful? My wife is a treasure," said Coach Buck.

His saccharine tone was just about making Lucy sick to her stomach. In fact, there was something about this whole meeting that was making her uncomfortable. She was beginning to feel trapped, like Hansel and Gretel in the witch's house. Maybe it was the small room, maybe it was the sense of falseness that was beginning to unsettle her.

"None for me, thanks. I'm probably overreacting," she said, getting to her feet. "Making a mountain out of a molehill."

Coach Buck shook his head and rolled his chair closer to her, blocking the doorway. "Not at all. You're concerned about your daughter and it's very understandable."

"Not just my daughter," said Lucy, unable to stop the flow of words. "All the cheerleaders and the players, too. They're at a very vulnerable age and this sort of thing is very damaging. It's important they develop healthy self-images, that they learn to treat others with respect." Feeling trapped, her eyes darted all around the room, looking for a way out. Spotting a photo of a bearded young man in a BU sweatshirt, she seized on it. "Is this you?" she asked, leaning over for a better look. As she'd hoped, Buck got out of his chair and joined her by the bookcase.

"It's no secret I went to BU," he said.

"My dad did, too," lied Lucy. "On the GI Bill. Class of forty-nine. What year were you?"

"Seventy-five."

"Turbulent times on college campuses," she said. "You look as if you might've been a bit rebellious yourself."

"The beard was as far as it went," he said quickly. "And it didn't last long. Too itchy. I shaved it off right after this picture was taken."

Lucy was thinking that the young man in the photo looked a lot like the fugitive getaway car driver from the bank robbery in which Mimi's father was killed, but dismissed the thought. Men with beards tended to look alike.

"I stayed clear of all that political stuff," continued the coach. "I focused on sports. Never read the paper."

"Right." Lucy smiled. "Let's work on this together," she said, trying another tack. "Maybe we can get the parents together with you and the athletic director and try to figure out a solution. Not a big public meeting but just a quiet little get-together, completely off the record. I'm sure we can come up with something if we all put our heads together."

"That's an excellent idea," he said, extending his hand.

Lucy took it, finding it surprisingly moist and

limp. "I'll be waiting to hear from you," she said, stepping into the hall.

The narrow space felt claustrophobic, with the coach following her, and she found herself hurrying for the open space of the great room. Bonnie wasn't there and Lucy assumed she was with the twins. She could hear their voices coming from another part of the house. They'd probably converted the basement into a playroom, she decided, stopping at the kitchen door.

"Thanks for everything," she said.

"No problem," said Buck, opening the door for her. "Coaching isn't a nine-to-five job."

"I appreciate that," she said, stepping outside. "I feel much better now that we have a plan."

"Me, too," he said, closing the screen door behind her.

Outside, in the fresh air, Lucy did feel better, and she was optimistic that she could round up a group of parents who would be interested in working on a committee to develop a more positive sports program. Renee would help, and she was pretty sure Willie would, too. She would call the JV players' moms, too. She was sure some of them would be willing to help. Raindrops began to plop down, dotting the ground with spots of damp and Lucy hurried along the cul-de-sac to the little path through the lilacs, hoping to get home before the rain started in earnest. Like everything else in the garden, the lilacs were definitely looking droopy and needed the rain. They were also a bit hoary with mildew and she reminded herself to put some lime on their roots as she raised her arm to push aside a leafy bough.

That's when she saw Bonnie, still wearing those yellow rubber gloves, holding her carving knife.

Chapter 21

"I tried to warn you," hissed Bonnie, her eyes glittering. Her jaw was clenched, revealing the cords in her neck, and she was gripping the knife handle so tightly that the yellow vinyl of the glove was stretched taut across her knuckles. "But you had to keep sticking your nose in."

Lucy felt suddenly cold as the rain pattered down, plastering her hair to her head and soaking her shirt. She began to shiver and wrapped her arms protectively across her chest. She couldn't believe it. Bonnie, the perfect housekeeper and mother of those adorable twins, was the last person she would suspect of murder.

Bonnie stepped closer, waving the knife dangerously. "Who do you think you are, threatening my husband?" she hissed.

"I didn't threaten him," said Lucy, taking a step backwards, feeling the ground growing slick beneath her feet and struggling to keep her voice calm and reasonable. She was beginning to regret letting the lilacs grow. If she'd cut them like Mimi had wanted, she wouldn't be in this predicament, hidden from view and at the mercy of a madwoman. She was convinced Bonnie was out of her mind. Only an insane woman would run around attacking neighbors with a kitchen knife.

"Oh, yes you did." Bonnie stepped closer to Lucy, raising the knife. Her face was a mask of certainty. She was right and Lucy was wrong. "I heard you."

"Bonnie, we were talking about the football team," said Lucy, who was rapidly putting two and two together.

"I don't believe you," she said, narrowing her eyes. "You've been out to get my husband from the day we moved in. Snooping around, just like that Mimi."

Lucy had a sudden image of Mimi, with a knife very like the one Bonnie was holding sticking out of her back. She felt herself swaying, almost blacking out and forced herself to focus. Her life depended on it.

"Bonnie, I swear I don't know what you're talking about. Now put the knife down and go home and we can forget all about this," she said. She was the voice of reason, even though she was shaking with terror; her heart was pounding so hard she thought it must be visible through her T-shirt and her mouth was so dry she could barely get the words out. "Think of your girls, Belle and Belinda. They need their mother."

"That's who I am thinking of," snapped Bonnie. "They need a mother and a father."

"Don't you think you should get back to them? It's almost lunchtime," said Lucy.

"First I have to take care of you." Bonnie raised the knife and Lucy ducked just as it came slashing past her shoulder, tearing the sleeve and missing her skin by millimeters.

Lucy jumped back and crouched, staring at Bonnie, incredulous. She couldn't believe this was happening. The woman was really attacking her with a carving knife. The blade was at least ten inches long. Lucy's first instinct was to run, but she didn't dare turn her back on Bonnie. So she began inching backwards along the path, feeling her way among the slippery rocks and roots while maintaining a defensive crouch, holding her hands in front of her face. If only she could get out of the bushes and into the open, she'd have a chance. She didn't think Bonnie would actually stab her to death in broad daylight, in front of the neighbors. That's when her foot slid out from under her and she tumbled onto her back. Bonnie was over her in a flash, pressing her knee against Lucy's middle. Lucy could see glints of sun reflecting off the blade as she brought it down.

Flat on her back, with Bonnie pressing her against the ground, Lucy's only option was to catch her wrist and try to flip her over. Bonnie had the advantage, being on top, but Lucy managed to use her leg for leverage. Bonnie rolled backwards, and Lucy rolled on top of her, still holding onto the arm with the knife. On her back, Bonnie was able to deliver a good enough kick to Lucy's diaphragm that she lost her grip. Gasping for air, Lucy tried to roll over enough to get her hands beneath her so she could push herself upright. Realizing that she had left her shoulder vulnerable, Lucy tried to scramble to her feet but lost her footing and fell face downwards, slamming her cheekbone into a rock. The pain felt like a knife driving into her face; she struggled to keep from passing out and knew she had to get back on her feet but her body just wouldn't cooperate. She felt as if she was drowning in freezing water—she knew how to swim but she couldn't make her arms and legs do what she needed them to do. She couldn't save herself, Bonnie was going to kill her. Tears sprang to her eyes.

"Bonnie, enough. Put the knife down."

It was Coach Buck.

"No. She knows. I have to kill her."

"It doesn't matter. It's over. I called the police. I'm going to turn myself in."

"You can't do that!"

"I can't not do it," he said. "I can't live like this anymore." He held out his hand. "Now, give me the knife."

Bonnie's eyes darted from Lucy to her husband and back again. "It's just you and me. Nobody knows. We can kill her and everything will be all right again."

"Bonnie, it's not all right. Because of me three people are dead. That's too many. It's over. I've been living a lie and I can't do it anymore."

From the distance Lucy heard a siren approaching, then several more. The cavalry was coming. She passed out.

Chapter 22

HOUSEWIFE CHARGED IN DOUBLE SLAYING

By Edward J. Stillings, Staff Writer

GILEAD—*Prudence Path housewife Bonnie Burkhart's days were filled with carpooling, homemaking, and baking until yesterday when the mother of six-year-old twin daughters was arraigned in Gilead District Court on two counts of first-degree murder. Prosecutors charge that Burkhart, 35, was responsible for the stabbing death of Mary Catherine (Mimi) Stanton, 39, on September 3 and the drowning death of Thomas Preston O'Toole, 41, on September 12. She was also charged with the attempted murder on September 26 of Lucy Stone, a reporter for this newspaper.*

District Attorney Frederick P. Smith told Judge Wilfred P. Lawless that Burkhart committed the murders in an attempt to protect her husband, Buck Burkhart, 55. Buck Burkhart, who coached the Tinker's Cove Warriors to an unprecedented 3-0 winning season, has admitted that he was wanted by Massachusetts police in connection with a 1976 bank robbery that resulted in the death of a Boston police officer, John Joseph O'Toole. Police killed two of the robbers, later identified as members of a radical leftist group known as the People's Liberation Front, but Burkhart, who was never identified, escaped and successfully eluded capture for nearly thirty years.

"This man," said Smith, pointing to Coach Burkhart, "whom we know as Buck Burkhart, upstanding citizen, educator, coach, and father, has been living a lie. He now admits he was the getaway driver in the robbery that took the life of Officer O'Toole."

Bonnie Burkhart, who entered a plea of not guilty, displayed no emotion during the brief arraignment proceeding, but Coach Burkhart listened with his face in his hands as Smith described the alleged murder of Mimi Stanton by his wife. "When Bonnie Burkhart realized that her new neighbor on Prudence Path was the daughter of John Joseph O'Toole, the police officer killed in the robbery for which her husband was wanted, she feared her husband would be recognized, so she took matters into her own hands. She viciously stabbed Mimi Stanton to death in her own kitchen, using the victim's own carving knife. And what was Mimi Stanton doing when she was killed? She was baking cookies for a charity bake sale."

Burkhart is also charged with murdering Stanton's brother, Thomas Preston O'Toole, by drowning. Investigators allege that Burkhart met O'Toole, a recovered alcoholic with no permanent address, in the Tinker's Cove harbor and supplied him with a bottle of bourbon. When he became drunk she tipped him into the water, holding him down with one of the life-saving poles that are kept at the docks in case someone accidentally falls into the water.

Judge Lawless refused bail for Bonnie Burkhart, who will be held in the County Correctional Institution pending trial in Gilead Superior Court. A pretrial conference

*date was set for October 20. The judge also approved ex-
tradition of Buck Burkhart to Massachusetts, where he
will finally face charges for the murder of Officer O'Toole.
Under Massachusetts's felony murder rule, anyone who
participates in a robbery resulting in a death can be
charged with first-degree murder. If found guilty, both
Burkharts could receive life sentences. Their young daughters are in the care of relatives under the supervision of
the Department of Social Services.*

*All charges have been dropped against Fred Stanton,
who had previously been charged with his wife's murder.*

*Retired Police Chief Oswald Crowley will take over Burk-
hart's job as coach of the Tinker's Cove Warriors football
team. (See related story: Crowley vows zero-tolerance for
hazing, page 19.)*

"Wow, that's quite a story," said Sue, folding her
copy of the *Pennysaver* and laying it on the table.
The Gang of Four was gathered at Jake's for their
Thursday morning breakfast together and Lucy
had brought copies of the paper for everyone to
read.

"She seemed so nice," said Rachel, shaking her
head.

"Those poor little girls," clucked Pam. "What
will happen to them?"

"That's the one bright spot. They're with the
coach's brother. He's a former priest who married
a former nun. They were too old to have children
of their own when they got married and they plan
to adopt the twins. They say this is just proof that
God works in mysterious ways," said Lucy, who had
spoken with the couple at the arraignment.

"Well, call me a heretic but I think God could have been a little tidier. Like maybe giving Coach Buck mad cow disease or something," said Sue.

"I agree," said Lucy. "Just think of all the heartbreak that could've been avoided if Coach Buck had an auto accident on the way to the robbery. Officer O'Toole would have lived, Mimi's family would have remained intact, the whole terrible chain of events would have been avoided." She took a bite of English muffin.

They all fell silent for a minute, thinking of the enormous suffering caused by a foolish college student's ill-considered adventure.

"What I don't understand," said Pam, "is how Bonnie figured out that Mimi was O'Toole's daughter."

"I wondered about that myself," said Lucy. "I don't think she ever did. I think it must have been the other way around: Mimi figured out who Coach Buck was."

"I think you're right," said Sue. "After all, she was a little troublemaker in her own way. She went right after Chris when she discovered she was operating a home business."

"She went after Miss Tilley's hedge," said Rachel. "And Lucy's lilacs."

"I think it started with the hazing. Tommy was having a hard time making the team and she might well have decided to look into Coach Buck's qualifications, something like that."

"She didn't really have to know," said Pam. "Imagine if she'd told Bonnie she didn't think much of the way the coach was running the team and was going to check him out. Bonnie would have freaked."

"Paranoia would have done the rest," said Rachel.

"You're right there," said Lucy. "She overheard me talking to the coach about the hazing situation and decided I was a threat to him. I think she'd really gone over the edge by then."

"And face it," said Sue, "emotions were running high that morning, what with the bake sale and all."

"No, no." Pam shook her head. "You can't blame the bake sale. The bake sale was a good thing. I got several matching grants from banks and businesses, plus a donation of backpacks from Country Cousins, and—ta-da!—we gave fully-stocked book bags to thirty-one kids."

"That reminds me," said Rachel, smiling at Sue, "how are things going at the other end of the economic spectrum?"

"Fantastic. That Chris is something. We have bank financing, we're going to construct our own building, we're aiming to open next September and I have no doubt everything will be on time, on target, and on budget," said Sue, positively beaming. "And we have a motto, too. 'Where every child is a wonder child.'"

They all groaned.

"I know, I know," said Sue, "it's a little over the top. But that's what parents want nowadays. Believe me, the days of 'Duck, Duck, Goose' are long gone. Now it's 'Proton, Neutron, Electron.'" Seeing their blank faces she explained, "The electron gets to run. Same game, different terms. It helps them become comfortable with scientific terminology."

"Yikes," said Rachel. "Thank goodness Richie's all grown up. I had enough trouble with all those dinosaur names."

"You did just fine," said Lucy. "He went to Harvard, after all."

They fell silent, turning their attention to their breakfasts. All except Sue, who never had anything more than coffee in the morning.

"I guess you'll be getting some new neighbors on Prudence Path," she said. "The Burkharts certainly won't be needing their house."

"Oh!" Lucy's hand flew to her mouth. "That's my big news!"

"Like this wasn't big?" said Rachel, tapping the paper.

"This is bigger," said Lucy, humming the wedding march. "Molly and Toby have set the date! And . . ." she drew out the word, "they're buying the notorious Burkhart house. Turns out, the Burkharts were only renting. And Fred is so grateful for my efforts on his behalf that he's giving the kids a real good price."

"That's terrific," said Sue, thinking ahead. "I'll be happy to help with the wedding."

"We'll have an exorcism before they move in," said Rachel.

"And I know where they can get good furniture cheap," said Pam.

"Yes to all of you," said Lucy. "Now I've got to go back to work."

"Oh, just one thing before you go," said Pam. "There was something I wanted to discuss."

Lucy sat down. "Shoot."

"Well," began Pam, "you know what a big success the bake sale was, right?"

They all nodded in agreement.

"Well, I was thinking about Columbus Day. A lot of people come to Tinker's Cove that weekend to see the foliage. Leaf-peepers. And I was thinking that since we seem to have this bake sale thing nailed, we ought to do it again and get a head start on the Christmas fund. What do you think?"

"Only if I can make my Better-Than-Sex Brownies," said Sue.

"No problem."

"I suppose I can whip up some Kitchen Sink cookies," groaned Rachel.

"And I'll make Nutty Meringues," said Pam. "What about you, Lucy? Dog biscuits?"

"Woof-woof," agreed Lucy, throwing a five-dollar bill on the table and making a fast escape.

Kitchen Sink Cookies

1 cup butter or margarine
1 cup brown sugar
1 cup granulated sugar
2 eggs
1 cup peanut butter
2 cups flour
½ teaspoon salt
2 teaspoons baking soda
1 cup rolled oats
Optional amounts of chocolate chips, raisins, or nuts

Beat butter or margarine and sugars together until light and fluffy. Add eggs, beating until well blended. Add the peanut butter, mixing well. Sift together flour, salt, and baking soda and mix in, along with oats. Stir in optional chocolate chips, raisins, or nuts. Roll into balls, place on ungreased cookie sheet, press down with a fork. Bake 12 minutes at 350 degrees.

Chris notes: *"I usually make half the batter into cookies and freeze the other half. Then, when I need more cookies I just defrost the dough, roll, and bake. Otherwise this recipe makes a huge number of cookies. The cookies do freeze well, if you prefer to bake all at once."*

Better Than Sex Brownies

1 cup unsalted butter
2 cups sugar
2 teaspoons vanilla extract

¾ cup cocoa
4 eggs
1 cup all-purpose flour
½ teaspoon baking powder
¼ teaspoon salt
1 cup chopped nuts
1 cup semi-sweet chocolate chips

Heat oven to 350 degrees. Butter 13 x 9-inch baking pan. Melt butter in large saucepan over low heat. Remove from heat and stir in sugar, vanilla, and cocoa. Add eggs, beating well after each addition. Add dry ingredients making sure everything is well mixed. Pour batter into prepared pan and bake for 30-35 minutes until brownies begin to pull away from sides of pan. Cool completely on wire rack before spreading frosting.

Creamy Brownie Frosting

6 tablespoons butter, softened
6 tablespoons cocoa
2 tablespoons light corn syrup
1 teaspoon vanilla extract
2 cups confectioners sugar
2 tablespoons milk

In a small bowl cream butter, cocoa, corn syrup, and vanilla. Add confectioners sugar and milk. Beat to spreading consistency, adding a bit more milk if needed.

Not many people in Tinker's Cove, Maine, knew Old Dan Malone. The grizzled barkeep's social circle was limited to the rough-hewn lobstermen and other assorted toughs that frequented his bar, a derelict main street dive called, appropriately, the Bilge. But when his body is found bobbing in the town's icy harbor, Lucy Stone, ace reporter for the *Pennysaver* newspaper, makes getting to know more about Old Dan a priority. And apparently, there's lots to learn.

Like the fact that local musician Dave Reilly insists Old Dan conned a winning lottery ticket worth five grand from him. And that handyman Brian Donohue claims that Old Dan stiffed him for repair work he'd done at the bar. There are even whispers about some connection to the Irish Republican Army. The confusion surrounding the death is only compounded by the arrival of actor Dylan Malone, Old Dan's brother and a prominent, if fading, attraction of the Dublin stage. Dylan has come to direct the production of *Finian's Rainbow*, the feautred event at Our Lady of Hope's annual St. Patrick's Day extravaganza. He's also come to help his brother renovate the Bilge, turning the dingy tavern into an authentic—if decidedly upscale—Irish pub.

Was Old Dan killed by someone he'd cheated, someone he'd loved, or someone who just couldn't stand the idea of losing their favorite watering hole? While Lucy can't be sure, one thing is abundantly clear—the stage is set for a murder mystery with a killer ending!

Please turn the page for an exciting sneak peek at Leslie Meier's ST. PATRICK'S DAY MURDER coming next month in hardcover!

Prologue

*T*he last customer hadn't left the bar until nearly two a.m.—well past the eleven p.m. closing time mandated by the town bylaws in Tinker's Cove, Maine—but that didn't bother Old Dan very much. He'd never been one to fuss about rules and regulations. No, he was one who took the inch and made it a mile. If they wanted him to close at eleven, well, they could jolly well send over a cop or two or ten and make him. Though he'd be willing to wager that wouldn't go down well with the clientele. He chuckled and scratched his chin, with its week's worth of grizzled whiskers. That crowd, mostly rough and ready fishermen, didn't have a high regard for the law, or for the cops who enforced it, either. No, close the Bilge before the customers were ready to call it a night, and there'd be a fine brouhaha.

And, anyway, he didn't sleep well these days, so there was no sense tossing out some poor soul before he was ready to go, because, truth be told, he didn't mind a bit of company in the wee hours. He knew that if he went home and to bed, he'd only *be twisting and turning in the sheets, unable to calm his thoughts enough to sleep.*

That's why he'd started tidying the bar at night instead of leaving it for the morning. The rhythmic tasks soothed him. Rinsing and drying the glasses, rubbing down the bar. Wiping the tables, giving the floor a bit of a sweep. That's what he was doing, shuffling along behind a push broom to clear away all the dropped cigarette butts and matches and dirt carried in on cleated winter boots. He braced himself for the blast of cold and opened the door to sweep it all out, back where it belonged. But it wasn't the cold that took his breath away. It was a bird, a big crow, and it walked right in.

"And what do you think you're doing?" he demanded, feeling a large hollowness growing inside him.

"You know quite well, don't you?" replied the crow, hopping up onto the bar with a neat flap of his wings. The bird cocked his head and looked him in the eye. "Don't tell me an Irishman like you, born and bred in the old country, has forgotten the tale of Cú Chulainn?"

He'd not forgotten. He'd heard the story often as a boy, long ago in Ireland, where his mother dished up the old stories with his morning bowl of oats. "Eat up," she'd say, "so you'll be as strong as Cú Chulainn."

He found his mind wandering and followed it down the dark paths of memory. Had it really been that long? Sixty odd years? More than half a century? It seemed like yesterday that he was tagging along behind his ma when she made the monthly trek to the post office to pay the bills. " 'Tisn't the sort of thing you can forget," he told the crow. "Es-

pecially that statue in the Dublin General Post Office. A handsome piece of work that is, illustrating how Cú Chulainn knew death was near and tied himself to a post so he could die standing upright, like the hero he was."

"Cú Chulainn was a hero indeed," admitted the crow. "And his enemies couldn't kill him until the Morrighan lit on his shoulder, stealing his strength, weakening him. . . ."

"Right you are. The Morrighan," he said. The very thought of that fearsome warrior goddess, with her crimson cloak and chariot, set his heart to pounding in his bony old chest.

"And what form did the Morrighan take, might I ask?" inquired the bird.

"A crow," he said, feeling a great trembling overtake him. "So is that it? Are you the Morrighan come for me?"

"What do you think, Daniel Malone?" replied the crow, stretching out its wings with a snap and a flap and growing larger, until its great immensity blocked out the light—first the amber glow of the neon Guinness sign, then the yellow light from the spotted ceiling fixture, the greenish light from the streetlamp outside, and finally, even the silvery light from the moon—and all was darkness.

Chapter 1

Maybe it was global warming, maybe it was simply a warmer winter than usual, but it seemed awfully early for the snow to be melting. It was only the last day of January, and in the little coastal town of Tinker's Cove, Maine, that usually meant at least two more months of ice and snow. Instead, the sidewalks and roads were clear, and the snow cover was definitely retreating, revealing the occasional clump of snowdrops and, in sheltered nooks with southern exposures, a few bright green spikes of daffodil leaves that were prematurely poking through the earth.

You could almost believe that spring was in the air, thought Lucy Stone, part-time reporter for the town's weekly newspaper, the *Pennysaver*. She wasn't sure how she felt about it. Part of her believed it was too good to be true, probably an indicator of future disasters, but right now the sun was shining and birds were chirping and it was a great day to be alive. So lovely, in fact, that she decided to walk the three or four blocks to the harbor, where she had an appointment to interview the new harbormaster, Harry Crawford.

As she walked down Main Street, she heard the steady drip of snow melting off the roofs. She felt a gentle breeze against her face, lifting the hair that escaped from her beret, and she unfastened the top button of her winter coat. Quite a few people were out and about, taking advantage of the unseasonably fine weather to run some errands, and everyone seemed eager to exchange greetings. "Nice day, innit?" and "Wonderful weather, just wonderful," they said, casting suspicious eyes at the sky. Only the letter carrier Wilf Lundgren, who she met at the corner of Sea Street, voiced what everyone was thinking. "Too good to be true," he said, with a knowing nod. "Can't last."

Well, it probably wouldn't, thought Lucy. Nothing did. But that didn't mean she couldn't enjoy it in the meantime. Her steps speeded up as she negotiated the hill leading down to the harbor, where the ice pack was beginning to break up. All the boats had been pulled from the water months ago and now rested on racks in the parking lot, shrouded with tarps or shiny white plastic shrink-wrap. The gulls were gone—they didn't hang around where there was no food—but a couple of crows were flying in circles above her head, cawing at each other.

"The quintessential New England sound," someone had called it, she remembered, but she couldn't remember who. It was true, though. There was something about their raspy cries that seemed to capture all the harsh, unyielding nature of the landscape. And the people who lived here, she thought, with a wry smile.

Harry Crawford, the new harbormaster, was an exception. He wasn't old and crusty like so many of the locals; he was young and brimming with enthusiasm for his job. He greeted Lucy warmly, holding open the door to his waterfront office, which was about the same size as a highway tollbooth. It was toasty inside, thanks to the sun streaming through the windows, which gave him a 360-degree view of the harbor and parking lot. Today he hadn't even switched on the small electric heater.

"Hi, Lucy. Make yourself comfortable," he said, pulling out the only chair for her to sit on. He leaned against the half wall, arms folded across his chest, staring out at the water. It was something people here did, she thought. They followed the water like a sunflower follows the sun, keeping a watchful eye out for signs that the placid, sleeping giant that lay on the doorstep might be waking and brewing up a storm.

"Thanks, Harry," she said, sitting down and pulling off her gloves. She dug around in her bag and fished out a notebook and pen. "So tell me about the Waterways Committee's plans for the harbor."

"Here, here," he said, leaning over her shoulder to unroll the plan and spread it out on the desk. "They're going to add thirty more slips, and at over three thousand dollars a season, it adds up to nearly a hundred thousand dollars for the town."

"If you can rent them," said Lucy.

"Oh, we can. We've got a waiting list." He shaded his eyes with his hand and looked past her, out toward the water. "And that's another good thing. A lot of folks have been on that list for years, and there's been a lot of bad feeling about it. You know, people are not really using their slips, but hanging on to them for their kids, stuff like that. But now we ought to be able to satisfy everyone."

Lucy nodded. She knew there was a lot of resentment toward those who had slips from those who didn't. It was a nuisance to have to ferry yourself and your stuff and your crew out to a mooring in a dinghy. With a slip, you could just walk along the dock to the boat, untie it, and sail off. "So you think this will make everybody happy?" she asked. "What about environmental issues? I understand there will be some dredging."

He didn't answer. His gaze was riveted on something outside that had caught his attention. "Sorry, Lucy. There's something I gotta check on," he said, taking his jacket off a hook.

Lucy turned and looked outside, where a flock of gulls and crows had congregated at the end of the pier. "What's going on?" she asked.

"The ice is breaking up. Something's probably come to the surface."

From the excited cries of the gulls, who were now arriving from all directions, she knew it must be something they considered a meal. A feast, in fact.

"Like a pilot whale?"

"Could be. Maybe a sea turtle, a dolphin even. Could be anything."

"I'd better come," she said, with a groan, reluctantly pulling a camera out of her bag.

"I wouldn't if I were you," he said, shaking his head. "Whatever it is, it's not going to be pretty, not this time of year. It could've been dead for months."

"Oh, I'm used to it," sighed Lucy, who had tasted plenty of bile photographing everything from slimy, half-rotted giant squid tentacles caught in fishing nets to bloated whale carcasses that washed up on the beach.

"Trust me. The stench alone . . ."

She was already beginning to feel queasy. "You've convinced me," she said, guiltily replacing her camera. Any photo she took would probably be too disgusting to print, she rationalized, and she could call him later in the day and find out what it was. Meanwhile, her interest had been caught by a handful of people gathered outside the Bilge, on the landward side of the parking lot. Tucked in the basement beneath a block of stores that fronted Main Street, the Bilge was a Tinker's Cove landmark—and a steady source of news. It was the very opposite of Hemingway's "clean, well-lighted place," but that didn't bother the fishermen who packed the place. It may have been a dark and dingy dive, but the beer was cheap, and Old Dan never turned a paying customer away, not even if he was straight off the boat and stank of lobster bait.

Lucy checked her watch as she crossed the parking lot and discovered it was only a little past ten o'clock. *Kind of early to start drinking,* she thought, but the three men standing in front of the Bilge apparently thought otherwise.

"It's never been closed like this before," said one. He was about fifty, stout, with white hair combed straight back from a ruddy face.

"Old Dan's like clockwork. You could set your watch by it. The Bilge opens at ten o'clock. No earlier. No later," said another, a thin man with wire-rimmed glasses.

"He closed once for a couple of weeks, maybe five or six years ago," said the third, a young guy with long hair caught in a ponytail, who Lucy knew played guitar with a local rock band, the Claws. "He went to Ireland that time, for a visit. But he left a sign."

"What's up? Is the Bilge closed?" she asked.

They all turned and stared at her. Women usually avoided the Bilge, where they weren't exactly welcome. A lot of fishermen still clung to the old-fashioned notion that women were bad luck on a boat—and in general.

"I'm Lucy Stone, from the *Pennysaver*," she said. "If the Bilge has really closed, that's big news."

"It's been shut tight for three days now," said the guy with the ponytail.

"Do you mind telling me your name?" she asked, opening her notebook. "It's Dave, right? You're with the Claws?"

"Dave Reilly," he said, giving her a dazzling, dimpled smile.

Ah, to be on the fair side of thirty once more, she thought, admiring Dave's fair hair, bronzed skin, full lips, and white teeth. *He must be quite a hit with the girls*, she decided, reminding herself that she had a job to do. "Has anybody seen Old Dan around town?" she asked.

"Come to think of it, no," said the guy with glasses.

"And your name is?" she replied.

"Brian Donahue."

"Do you think something happened to him?" she asked the stout guy, who was cupping his hands around his eyes and trying to see through the small window set in the door.

"Whaddya see, Frank?" inquired Dave. He turned to Lucy. "That's Frank Cahill. You'd never know it, but he plays the organ at the church."

"Is he inside? Did he have a heart attack or something?" asked Brian.

Frank shook his head. "Can't see nothing wrong. It looks the same as always."

"Same as always, except we're not inside," said Brian.

"Hey, maybe we're in some sort of alternate universe. You know what I mean. We're really in the Bilge in the real world, having our morning pick-me-up just like usual, but we're also in this parallel world, where we're in the parking lot," said Dave.

The other two looked at each other. "You better stick to beer, boy," said Frank, with a shake of his head. "Them drugs do a job on your brain."

"What am I supposed to do?" replied the rocker. "It's not my fault if Old Dan is closed, is it? A guy's gotta have something. Know what I mean?"

"You could try staying sober," said Lucy.

All three looked at her as if she were crazy.

"Or find another bar," she added.

"The others don't open 'til noon," said Brian. "Town bylaw."

"Old Dan has a special dispensation?" she asked.

The others laughed. "You could say that," said Dave, with a bit of an edge in his voice. "He sure doesn't play by the same rules as the rest of us."

"Special permission. That's good," said Brian.

"Yeah, like from the pope," said Frank, slapping his thigh. "I'll have to tell that one to Father Ed." He checked his watch. "Come to think of it, I wonder where he is? He usually stops in around now."

My goodness, thought Lucy, echoing her great-grandmother who had been a staunch member of the Woman's Christian Temperance Union. She knew there was a lot of drinking in Tinker's Cove, especially in the winter, when the boats sat idle.

Some joker had even printed up bumper stickers proclaiming: "Tinker's Cove: A quaint little drinking village with a fishing problem," when government regulators had started placing tight restrictions on what kind of fish and how much of it they could catch and when they could catch it. She'd laughed when she first saw the sticker on a battered old pickup truck. After all, she wasn't above pouring herself a glass of wine to sip while she cooked supper. She certainly wasn't a teetotaler, but her Puritan soul certainly didn't approve of drinking in the morning.

The laughter stopped, however, when they heard a siren blast, and the birds at the end of the pier rose in a cloud, then settled back down.

"Something washed up," said Lucy, by way of explanation. "Probably a pilot whale."

The others nodded, listening as the siren grew louder and a police car sped into the parking lot, screeching to a halt at the end of the pier. The birds rose again, and this time they flapped off, settling on the roof of the fish-packing shed.

"I've got a bad feeling about this," said Dave. "Real bad."

He took off, running across the parking lot, followed by Brian and Frank. Lucy stood for a minute, watching them and considering the facts. First, Old Dan was missing, and second, a carcass had turned up in the harbor. She hurried after them but was stopped with the others at the dock by Harry, who wasn't allowing anyone to pass. At the end of the pier, she could see her friend Officer Barney Culpepper peering down into the icy water.

"I know Barney," she told Harry as she pulled her camera out of her bag. "He won't mind."

"He said I shouldn't let anybody by," insisted Harry, tilting his head in Barney's direction.

Lucy raised the camera and looked through the viewfinder, snapping a photo of Barney staring down into the water. From the official way he was standing, she knew this was no marine creature that had washed up. "I guess it's not a pilot whale?" she asked, checking the image in the little screen.

Harry shook his head.

"It's a person, right?" said Dave. "It's Old Dan, isn't it?"

Lucy's fingers tightened on the camera. There was a big difference between jumping to a conclusion and learning it was true, a big difference between an unidentified body and one with a name you knew.

"I'm not supposed to say," said Harry.

"You don't have to," said Brian. "It's pretty obvious. The Bilge has been closed for days, and there's been no sign of him. He must've fallen in or something."

"Took a long walk off a short pier," said Dave, with a wry grin. "Can't say I'm surprised."

"He was known to enjoy a tipple," said Frank. He eyed the Bilge. "He'll be missed."

"What a horrible way to go," said Lucy, shivering and fingering her camera. "In the cold and dark and all alone."

"Maybe he wasn't alone," said Dave, raising an eyebrow.

"What do you mean?" asked Lucy. "Do you think somebody pushed him in?"

"Might have," said Frank. "He made a few enemies in his time."

Dave nodded. "You had to watch him. He wasn't

above taking advantage, especially if you'd had a few and weren't thinking too hard."

Something in his tone made Lucy wonder if he was speaking from personal experience.

"And he wasn't exactly quick to pay his bills," said Brian, sounding resentful.

Another siren could be heard in the distance.

"So I guess he won't be missed," said Lucy.

"No, I won't miss the old bastard," said Frank. "But I'm sure gonna miss the Bilge."

The others nodded in agreement as a state police cruiser peeled into the parking lot, followed by the white medical examiner's van.

"The place didn't look like much," said Brian.

"But the beer was the cheapest around," said Dave.

"Where else could you get a beer for a buck twenty-five?" asked Frank.

The three shook their heads mournfully, united in grief.

PLAINFIELD PUBLIC LIBRARY
15025 S. Illinois Street
Plainfield, IL 60544